The Petunia-Coloured Coat and Other Stories

THE PETUNIA-COLOURED COAT AND OTHER STORIES

Elaine Crowley

CENTURY

LONDON SYDNEY AUCKLAND JOHANNESBURG

A Summer's Day was first published in *A Baker's Dozen*, Poolbeg Press, Dublin

The right of Elaine Crowley to be identified as the author of this work has been
asserted by her in accordance with the Copyright, Designs and Patents Act 1988.

First published in Great Britain in 1991 by
Random Century Group
20 Vauxhall Bridge Road, London, SW1V 2SA

Century Hutchinson South Africa (Pty) Ltd
PO Box 337, Bergvlei 2012, South Africa

Random Century New Zealand Ltd
PO Box 40–086, Glenfield, Auckland 10, New Zealand

The catalogue data for this book is available from the British Library

ISBN 0 7126 4544 6

Typeset by Deltatype Ltd, Ellesmere Port
Printed and bound in Great Britain by
Mackays of Chatham PLC, Chatham, Kent

For
Ulla, Ellen, Bridie, Jenny and Cis

Contents

The Petunia-Coloured Coat

The coat was the colour of a pink petunia and its soft woollen cloth as smooth as the flower's petal. I knew because I had tried it on. Going to the shop with someone who was buying clothes and pretending I was also interested in buying something. As soon as I saw the coat I fell in love with it and asked the price. My enquiry, although I was only fourteen, was not considered unusual nor my shabbiness an indication that I couldn't afford a coat costing forty-nine and eleven. Most of the shop's customers were girls from the factory where recently I had started to work. They bought on credit – on dockets supplied by the shop to a woman in the factory who earned commission on the dockets, sold to the girls who repaid her weekly.

'Will you take it?' asked the shop assistant.

'I'll have to ask my mother first,' I said, taking off the beautiful coat and handing it back.

'You won't want to leave it too long. There's not many of that colour in stock. Petunia is all the rage.'

'Oh, I won't. I'll find out tonight,' I promised.

'It's gorgeous, Mammy. You want to see the colour – like one of them petunias, the pink ones. And it's only forty-nine and eleven, and Rosie'll let me have a docket at half a crown a week, that's all. Please, Mammy. Everyone has a new coat sometimes.'

'I couldn't afford a shilling a week, never mind half a crown.'

'That's not fair. I'm earning. Every one of the girls in work has a new coat except me.'

'Everyone in work hasn't a sick father. The coat you have will have to do. It's a fine warm coat with plenty of letting down. I'm telling you, put it out of your mind.'

'I can't. I want it.'

'Well, you're not having it.'

But I'd made up my mind I was. And every night when I came home from work I raised the subject of the coat. Pleading. Crying. Accusing my mother of not loving me, of not caring how I looked. How ashamed I felt, how awful I looked in the old dark brown coat. How I hated its colour, which reminded me of a habit, and its rough cloth which in cold weather chafed my neck. 'It isn't fair!' I cried. 'I'm working – why can't I have a new coat?'

But nothing moved her. And so I prayed for the coat. Saying three Hail Marys at bedtime and countless Aspirations during the day. 'Sacred Heart of Jesus help me to get the coat. Blessed Mary ever Virgin grant my intention. Holy Mary, Mother of God, the woman in the shop said they haven't many in stock, help me Blessed Mother.'

I was obsessed by my want, by my fear that the coat would be sold. By the transformation I knew it would work on me. I would be beautiful. My straight, lank hair would come to life, have a gloss on it, lie how I wanted it to lie. My skin would be pink and soft, the pimples which grew on my forehead and chin disappear. Everyone would see the change in me, remark on it. I'd be noticed when I went to work, when I got on a bus. Even a boy might notice and think how nice I looked.

One night as I continued to plead and rail by turns for the coat my mother said, 'You should be ashamed of yourself. *Ashamed of yourself*,' she repeated, 'asking for a new coat and your father lying dying in the Hospice. You haven't a grain of conscience or feeling in your whole body.'

I was deaf to her criticisms. Not interested in her explanation that half a crown a week for the coat would cripple her with debt. How she managed her money wasn't my concern.

'And if I hear one more word out of you about the coat I'll tell your father, so I will. That's what you'll drive me to – worrying a man at death's door.'

I thought of my father propped on his pillows coughing his little dry cough. I loved him more than anything in the world. More than the coat. But I had him. And of course he wouldn't die! How could he die? Other people's mothers and fathers died, but not him. He wouldn't die. My mother was only saying that. I loved him and I loved the coat. I had him but I didn't have that and have it I must before the end of the week.

It was springtime. There were blossoms on the trees and flowers in the gardens. I saw them in parks and gardens from the top of the bus as I went to work. Everything in the world seemed bright and new. I craved for the petunia-coloured coat that was bright and new and would make me beautiful.

Thursday came and still God hadn't answered my prayers. Long ago I had noticed that often He didn't answer my prayers. He didn't let me win the prize for Catechism at the Feis even though I was the best in the class at Catechism. On the day of the Feis all the answers flew out of my head.

And when my father got sick I prayed that he had pleurisy and not consumption. God didn't answer that prayer, either. So now that it was Thursday and the coat maybe sold by the end of the week I decided that I had to help myself.

After I had eaten my sandwiches at lunchtime I ran all the way to the shop to ask if the coat was still in stock. My heart was in my mouth with the fear of it having been sold. But there it was in the window on a wax model and more beautiful than I remembered it. A slight flare to its skirt, two side pockets, nice revers and a tie belt round the mannequin's narrow waist. I was having it. Tomorrow I was buying it. I took a big breath and went into the shop and told the assistant.

'When?' she asked.

'Tomorrow night after work. Will you keep it for me?'

'All right,' she agreed, 'but only till tomorrow night.'

We were paid on Friday afternoon. The beautiful, aloof secretary came into the workroom, an office junior pushing a small trolley beside her. On the trolley our wage packets were laid in rows with our names and clock numbers on them. The trolley stopped by each machine, the secretary handed over the envelopes, we identified them and then signed for them. I waited until the trolley had moved away and then with shaking fingers tore open the packet and took out the ten shilling note. Thoughts flew through my mind. Never before had I opened my wages. How would I explain to my mother the opened envelope and the nine shillings instead of eleven and six? And where would I hide the coat until the right moment to produce it? When would *be* the right moment . . .

I was frightened now, wishing I hadn't done it. Wishing the packet was intact. And yet at the same time determined to have the coat. And in any case, I told myself, I'd reefed the envelope – it couldn't be stuck down now.

The factory manager was roaring. He roared more on Fridays because we stopped sewing while the wages trolley came round. What did we think we were being paid for? The order was days behind. We were a useless lot. I left the opened packet on my lap and raced a pair of sleeve linings through the machine and another pair and another pair, all the while my mind working on the concoction of a story to satisfy my mother when she noticed that my wages had been broken into. I'd tell her a girl's wages had been stolen. A very poor girl with six brothers and sisters and no father. There was a collection made. I had to give something.

I knew my mother's generous and sympathetic nature for anyone worse off than herself. She'd accept the loss of the half a crown though she might say. 'A shilling would have been enough. After all, you're only a child on small money. Still, let all my bad luck go with it.'

But what, I asked myself, would she say next week when the packet was again opened and my wages short? I couldn't think straight. I couldn't think that far ahead. All I knew was that I had to have the coat. I had to get the docket from Rosie and get to the shop before it closed. The manager was still roaring and raving, walking up and down the rows of machines urging the machinists to sew faster. Then he was called to the office. I seized the opportunity, went to Rosie's bench, offered her the ten shilling note and asked for a docket.

'Is it all right with your mammy?' asked Rosie.

'Oh yes,' I lied. 'She said I can have it.'

'Are you sure?'

'As true as God,' I replied.

'It's a grand fit. Look at yourself,' said the shop assistant, turning me to face the mirror. 'You'd think it was made for you.'

I could hardly breathe with the excitement of owning the coat. Enchanted, I gazed at my reflection. Already I was transformed. Beautiful. 'Wait now,' said the saleswoman, 'let me turn up the collar.' The soft petunia cloth caressed my neck and framed my face. I was intoxicated by the feel of it, by the smell of its newness.

'I'll pack it for you, it's nearly closing time.' Reluctantly I let the assistant help me off with the coat and watched her fold and pack it in a big bag emblazoned with the shop's name.

I sat downstairs on the bus for fear of a careless smoker damaging my coat and I held it carefully to my chest as if it were a new baby and all the while I was seeing myself as I had looked in the shop's mirror. Not until I was off the bus and walking towards home did the enormity of what I had done come over me. And the enormity of what lay in front of me. I had to tell my story about the girl whose wages had been stolen, and tell it convincingly. But before that I had to find a hiding place for the coat. How could I manage that? How could I get the coat inside the house without my mother seeing the bag and asking what was in it. If she saw the brand new coat the lie about the opened wage packet and missing half a crown would be useless. And back the coat would go. She mustn't see it, not for at least a week or more. Not until I'd had time to take off its newness. Not hack it, but rumple and crease it a bit. Make certain the shop wouldn't take it back. During the week while my mother was visiting her sister or seeing my father I'd wear my beautiful coat in my bedroom. But first I had to get it into the house.

4

Realising that wasn't possible, I had to settle for the outside lavatory, hoping and praying that no one would want to use it until I had a chance to smuggle the parcel indoors. I walked on tiptoe into the porch. I could hear the noise of the wireless and water running from the kitchen. My mother, I thought, is washing the delf, so maybe she won't hear the door opening, but I had to be careful. She had ears, or so she said, that could hear the grass growing. I pushed my parcel behind the lavatory pan and went towards the kitchen door. My hand was hardly on it when my mother called as she did every evening, 'Is that you? You're late. What kept you?'

'The buses were full, I had to wait for ages,' I lied, coming in and closing the kitchen door.

'Sit down,' she said, 'and eat this,' putting my dinner on the table. 'Hurry up,' she urged as I dawdled taking off my coat and washing my hands at the sink. My inside was shaking with a mixture of fear and worry. In a minute she'd ask for my wages and I'd have to tell my story. She had piercing eyes as well as good hearing. Sometimes when I was telling a lie her eyes seemed to bore into my brain and I'd think they could see every thought I thought. And there was my beautiful coat in the outside lavatory where, because the door didn't shut properly, tomcats sometimes went in and sprayed their scent. Or my brother might go and use the lavatory and *he* sprayed his pee everywhere. He could soak the bag and destroy my coat.

'Are you not hungry?' asked my mother, watching me toying with the food. Every bit stuck in my throat and I had to force myself to swallow.

'Not very, Ma.'

'It's dried to a stick but that's your own fault for being late.'

'It all right,' I said. 'I'll eat it later on.'

'I'll tell you what,' said my mother. 'Give me your wages and I'll go and get you a One and One. God help you, you've been out since all hours and must be dropping for the want of nourishment. I'll get you a bit of ray, and at this time the chips won't be reheats.'

She cleared away my plate while I took a long time making a pretence of searching my pocket for my wages. When I could delay no longer I handed over the pay envelope.

'What's this?' she asked, looking at the torn packet, shaking the loose coins into her hand. 'What did you open it for and why is the money short? Well, I'm waiting for an explanation.'

I started to cry. 'I'm sorry, Mammy, I know I shouldn't have only there was this girl in work and . . .' The story came out pat. The expression in my mother's eyes was changing from suspicion to pity. She was believing me, sorry for the girl with no father and six brothers and sisters whose wages had been stolen.

5

'You did the right thing,' she said. 'May God forgive the lightfingered one who deprived a fatherless child, that she may never have an hour's luck. But all the same a shilling would have been enough for the collection. Sit over to the fire and I'll go for the fish and chips.'

I let out a sigh of relief when she went, ran to the lavatory, collected the coat and hid it under the bed. I was tempted to try it on but was afraid my sister might come up the stairs nosing around. Far in under the bed I pushed it. There it would be safe, for it was seldom or ever my mother shifted the bed. It would be safe sure enough until such time as I plucked up the courage to confess everything to her.

Then I remembered the mice which every night scurried round the bedroom. No amount of traps could catch them all and as fast as one hole was boarded up they made another. I wasn't afraid of them, nor did I mind the sound of their scurrying. But now all of a sudden I thought – maybe they ate coats! Maybe when I took mine out of the bag the next day it would be a riddle of holes. I was sweating and trembling when my mother came back and couldn't eat the fish and chips. Her face took on an anxious expression which I recognised as worry about my health. In a minute the questions would begin. Did I have a pain in my chest, or in my side near my ribs? Had I been coughing? Why was I sweating? The questions got in on my nerves. She never used to ask them before – only since my father got sick.

I had no pains, nor coughs. Nothing ailed me, I assured her. I just wasn't hungry and silently I prayed that the mice weren't either. 'You want to mind yourself,' she said. 'Nourishment is your best weapon.' I knew she meant against consumption. But that was a word never uttered by her.

I made an excuse to go to bed early, an hour or more before my sister for I had suddenly remembered how I could protect my precious coat from the mice. In my father's wardrobe there was an old oilskin. I rooted in the cupboard until I found it then in my own room took the bag out from underneath the bed. Again I was tempted to try on the coat but afraid of being discovered, didn't, although I couldn't resist peeping inside the bag, convincing myself that the beautiful petunia coat was still there. I touched it lovingly then secured the bag in the oilskin, telling myself that the mice would have a job chewing through it.

I slept and dreamed about the coat. In the dream I was wearing it to Mass and as I walked up the aisle to receive Communion it began to grow so that by the time I reached the altar it was down to my ankles. There was a long line of people behind and in front of me so that although I longed to run from the chapel there was no way I could move except forward. When

6

I knelt to receive, the coat spread behind me like an enormous train. I could hear the laughter and the whispering, even the priest coming along the rail with Holy Communion was laughing. Then my mother came, picked me up and ran from the church telling me over and over not to cry, for the coat was lovely. I had done right to get it.

The next time my mother went to visit my father she took my brother and sister with her. 'Are you not coming?' she asked me.

'I have a headache,' I told her. 'I'll go tomorrow evening on the way home from work.' Knowing that it was the time for my period she smiled sympathetically and told me to take an Aspro and fill a hot jar for my stomach.

The minute she was out of the door I raced upstairs, dragged out the oilskin, undid it and the bag and put on the coat. I wore it until it was nearly time for my mother's return. I sat in it until the back was creased. Stood in front of the mirror with the collar up, then down, the belt fastened, undone, hands in my pockets, posing and twirling round to get a view of the coat's back. It was beautiful. I loved it. I couldn't live without it. I kept thinking as I repacked it but Friday was coming and what excuse could I make this time for another opened wage packet short by half a crown? All sorts of wild hopeful thoughts went through my mind. Maybe a letter would come from an American relation full of dollars and my mother be so delighted she wouldn't mind about the half a crown a week. Maybe we'd win the Sweep. I didn't know if we had a ticket or when the Sweep was, but my mother often said hopefully, 'Maybe one day we'll win the Sweep.' I hoped it would be before Friday.

When I went to see my father the next night I nearly told him about the coat, knowing he would understand, knowing he would make things all right with my mother. But he seemed very tired; his cheeks were flushed and he didn't talk much because his breath was short. So I said nothing.

After that there was nothing for it but to produce the coat and face the consequences. 'Look,' said Maura, my sister. 'Look, Mammy, look at the lovely pink coat Carmel's got on.'

My mother was reading the *Deaths* in the *Herald*. She looked up and took off her reading glasses which long ago she had bought in Woolworths and many times since had repaired with wire or thread. 'Where did you get that?' she asked in an incredulous voice.

So I told her everything. She shook her head. 'I don't believe it. I don't believe a child of mine would do such a thing. Where did you get it? Someone must have lent it to you. You got a loan of it in work.'

I shook my head. 'No,' I said, feeling sick and wishing what she said was

7

the truth, but only for a minute. It was my coat – I didn't want it to be anyone else's.

While this thought was going through my mind, my mother's face changed expression and her look of stupefaction switched to one of anger. 'Take it off,' she ordered. 'Now, this minute! Take it off.' I was crying, praising the coat, its colour, how cheap it was, how lovely it made me look. How desperately I wanted it.

'You deceitful little bitch! You self-willed little bitch. You've no thought for anyone but yourself and you're a liar into the bargain.'

'I have to pay for it tomorrow. I have to give Rosie half a crown.'

'Is that all that's worrying you – Rosie's money? If it wasn't that I don't want you branded a liar I'd be down to the factory in the morning and Rosie'd have her coat back.'

'You can't,' I said. 'I've worn it round the house.'

'You conniving little knat, you thought of everything. But I'll tell you one thing, your lies and deceit will get you nowhere. You'll never put that coat on your back again. I'd reef it up sooner than let you best me. Now get out of here before I lose myself altogether.'

I ran up to the bedroom still wearing the coat, thinking how I'd got off easier than I'd expected. And she was going to pay Rosie and she'd change her mind about letting me wear it. She always changed her mind.

I stayed in my bedroom until Maura was sent to tell me my bread and cocoa was ready. 'I think it's a gorgeous coat,' she said. 'Will you give it to me when it gets too small for you?'

As I knew she would, my mother relented and one Sunday when we were going to see my father she said, 'As I'm paying for the coat you might as well put it on.' My father said I looked lovely and that the colour suited me. I glowed with pleasure at his praise.

Fox six weeks, on Sundays when I visited my father and on the rare occasions when I went out in the evenings, I wore the coat. In it I felt as if I'd changed my old skin and like a chrysalis I was now a gorgeous butterfly. People noticed me in it, women and girls admired me, even my mother said I looked nice in it. If the few boys I knew noticed the transformation in me not one said so. But I felt sure that one day soon, one of them might.

I treasured the petunia-coloured coat. I studied the sky before deciding to wear it. After each outing I brushed it carefully and hung it on a strong hanger which wouldn't let the padded shoulders sag. I stroked it and caressed it, loving it as if it were a living thing and I hoped I wouldn't grow any bigger for a long, long time.

And then one day when I was working I was called into the office. I wondered what I had done wrong: I was never late, I never gave cheek to the forewoman. You were only called into the office for something serious – usually to be sacked. Please God don't let me be sacked, I prayed. Not sacked, not that, please God.

Shaking with fear I knocked on the door and went in. My cousin was there and her eyes were full of tears. She came to me and put her arms round me. 'Your daddy died,' she sobbed. 'Word came after you'd left for work. I've come to bring you home.' We clung to each other. I was crying, broken-hearted and yet aware that for the first time in my life I was the centre of attention. The manager was talking to me, calling me by my first name, telling me how sorry he was. Sending his sympathy to my mother. Someone brought me a chair and a cup of tea. Someone else fetched my brown coat. My father was dead. I shouldn't be thinking of anything else. I shouldn't be aware of what was going on round me. But I was and felt guilty because I was.

When I got home my mother was crying. The house was full of people who were crying. More relations and neighbours kept coming in and as each one spoke to my mother and embraced her they cried in each other's arms. But as the hours passed my mother cried less and was able to answer questions a relation asked: what about the Society money and the funeral arrangements? Was there enough money to buy black?

The aunt and my mother made decisions. There was enough money to buy mourning clothes for her. Armbands were sufficient for the younger children, but I was going on fifteen – I'd have to wear black. A neighbour said she'd run up a dress for me in time for the funeral. 'She'll need a coat as well,' said the aunt.

'She has one,' said my mother. 'It'll take a lovely dye. Bring it down, love. It'll have to go in today if it's to be ready in time.' We looked at each other and she cried again.

I went upstairs and took the coat from its hanger. I laid my face on it then held it against me one last time before the mirror. I swallowed the lump in my throat and ran down the stairs and handed it over. 'Petunia,' said the woman who was taking it to be dyed. 'Petunia's a gorgeous colour. It'll take a grand black.'

Janet's Christmas Party *or* A Kettleful Would Have Been Plenty

Janet read *Nursery World* and *Parents* and had done a course in child psychology, a long time ago, before she was married. So long ago in fact that all she remembered about the course were the Rorschach blots and being asked to interpret a painting of which she could make neither head nor tail. This of course she never mentioned to her friends. But she did mention from time to time her course on child psychology.

Her friends were younger than her. And though they did consider her a bit of a know-all, and sometimes rolled their eyes in exasperation when she started on some favourite topic of child-rearing, it was done with more affection than malice. For Janet was a kind, generous and reliable woman – who gave fabulous Christmas parties with lashings of delicious food and lashings of booze. Everyone gave lashings of booze – it was duty free, but Janet's buffet really was something else.

Two weeks before Christmas Day (on the evening of which she threw her party), Janet always had a coffee morning. 'To tie up the loose ends,' she would explain year after year. Check that everyone was all right for a babysitter. That no one was likely to go vegetarian without her knowledge. Sort out the little odds and ends that made a great party.

At one of these coffee mornings she stood with pencil and list ticking off the queries. Babysitters, OK? No one going on any sort of faddy diet? Down the list she went, ticking as she progressed until she came to Barbara's name. 'Isn't the twenty-fifth the date the doctor's given you, Barbara? Will you be coming, dear?'

Barbara grinned derisively. 'Doctors,' she said, leaving the company in no doubt of what she thought of doctors. 'I am not having this baby on Christmas Day and spoiling it for the children. And I am not, definitely *not*, missing your party! Put a tick by my name.'

'If you're absolutely sure,' said Janet, who was a great believer in doctors.

'Of course I'm sure,' said Barbara.

It snowed on Christmas Eve. Lovely crisp dry German snow that didn't melt and turn to slush as soon as it landed. 'A white Christmas,' said Janet, looking out through the window at the falling snow. Then she returned to filling the home-made vol-au-vent cases. She was justly proud of her light as a feather puff pastry. Before going to bed she put the meringues in the airing cupboard where they would cook to perfection overnight. She lay awake for a while thinking about the party which she was sure would be the best yet. She had prepared for every eventuality.

The guests arrived. The women wore stiletto heels, cocktail dresses and had beehive hairdos. Janet's dress was fashionably short and had a puffball skirt. 'No Barbara,' she said. 'I wonder . . . but surely we'd have heard?' The bell rang. Janet opened the door and there stood a radiant Barbara and her husband. 'Oh, darling, I was just talking about you. I'm so glad you could make it. Let me look at you.' She held Barbara at arm's length. 'What a stunning outfit.' Barbara's great belly strained at the silver brocade smock she was wearing over black toreador pants.

Drinks were handed round. Soon the room rang with laughter. The jokes became more risqué. The men roared with laughter and the women stretched their lips and bared their teeth. The radiogram was loaded with a selection of records and a space cleared for dancing. They danced and sang and smoked and drank and danced and ate. Charades were played and Black Magic. Only Janet and her husband knew the secret of the game. Wild guesses were made as to how they communicated with each other. Once someone came close to guessing the truth. Then Janet quickly suggested another party game. Black Magic was her very own. Once the truth was known it would have to come off her list of party games.

Once or twice during the evening Janet imagined she saw an expression of pain flit across Barbara's face. Then she decided it was all in her mind, for Barbara danced and played the games with gusto and ate enormous amounts of the buffet and drank a lot.

And so the party continued until long after midnight. Then first one woman and then another remembered promises made to babysitters and began working on their husbands to honour the promises. When the men were finally persuaded that the time had come to go, goodnights were said and thanks given for the lovely party. Now only Barbara and her husband, who lived close by, another couple and Janet and her husband remained. He poured another round of drinks. Then Barbara, who was very tipsy, suggested doing the Okey Kokey. And the six of them put their left arms in and their left arms out and Barbara shook her great pregnant belly all about.

Exhausted, they collapsed onto chairs and settees. Barbara's husband suggested it was time to make for home. 'One for the road then,' said Janet's husband and everyone had another drink.

'I told you, didn't I?' said Barbara as she stood on the doorstep saying goodnight. 'I told you I wouldn't have the baby on Christmas Day.'

'You did, you did,' replied Janet and warmly embraced her. 'You clever girl. Now off you go and hurry home, it's freezing and don't slip.' Everyone waved them off.

'A nightcap,' said Janet's husband when they returned to the living room. The nightcap was leisurely drunk. Janet yawned. Her head was spinning and Joan, one of the two remaining guests, sometimes looked decidedly odd, as if she had two heads.

'Last one definitely,' said Janet's husband and, spilling more than he poured, topped up the glasses.

'It's just as well we haven't far to go,' said Joan, finishing her drink and rising unsteadily to her feet. At the same moment there was a loud knocking on the door.

'Who on earth can that be?' asked Janet and her husband went to the door.

She heard the door opening and then the voices, her husband's saying, 'Come in, for God's sake, come in,' and the other shouting, protesting, 'I can't, I can't. There's no time. She's started. *Barbara's in labour.*'

Everyone ran into the hall and there, framed in the door, stood Barbara's husband wearing only his trousers and singlet, his hair full of snow. 'Oh, Janet, come quick,' he pleaded, turned and ran back to his own house. Janet thought she was dreaming. *Wished* she was dreaming. Oh my God, she thought, what am I going to do. I can hardly stand, never mind walk to Barbara's through inches of snow. But she must. Barbara was depending on her. Go she must and at once. She took a few deep breaths, another swig from a glass left on the table and then took charge.

'Put your shoes on, Joan. And you – get our coats,' she ordered her husband. Joan pushed feet that were swollen from dancing and sitting too near the radiator into her narrow pointed stilettos and didn't even wince for the alcohol had anaesthetised her from head to toe. 'Hurry along, everyone,' Janet commanded and out into the snow they went, linking and supporting each other to Barbara's house.

Once there she went to the bedroom where Barbara lay reeking of gin and pickled onion. 'How are you, dear?' asked Janet. As that moment a contraction began and Barbara writhed and roared and Janet decided that she was very advanced in labour. The contraction subsided and Janet told Barbara not to worry about a thing. To keep calm and that she was a good, brave girl. 'I'm just slipping downstairs to send Derek for the M.O. Everything's going to be fine.'

They were waiting for her in the hall, everyone looking expectantly at her. 'Well, yes,' she said. 'Talking from experience I'd say Barbara wouldn't last the eighty kilometres to Hanover. You'd better dash for the doctor, Derek.' As the front door closed she suddenly realised that if Barbara couldn't make it to Hanover then the baby would be born here – and if Barbara's roar were anything to go by, very soon.

Panic seized her. Supposing the M.O. was out on another call . . . What did one do when a baby was born? Well, she knew what one did giving birth – just lay there and pushed. But what if you were assisting? There goes another contraction, she thought, as Barbara made herself heard – and so soon after the last one! Please God don't let the M.O. be on another case. But even if he's not what am I supposed to do? Her expression showed not a trace of the turmoil going on in her mind.

'I've always wanted to see a baby being born,' said Joan and smiled foolishly. 'It's not the same having one yourself – you see nothing.'

The men cleared their throats nervously. Janet's husband said, 'I don't think a drink would do any of us any harm – steady the nerves.'

'Don't you dare!' said Janet. 'Not one drop,' although there was nothing she longed for more than a large brandy – a lot of large brandies and oblivion. And when she had almost reached the point of despair – of admitting to the others that she was as petrified as they, as completely in the dark – she suddenly remembered what to do when a baby was about to be born. *Hot water.* That was it – lots and lots of boiling water. Scene after scene of films she had seen flashed before her mind's eye. Prairie kitchens, slum tenements, suburban semis and home deliveries. The woman went into labour, was put to bed, the doctor sent for and water put on to boil. *Lots* of water. She breathed a sigh of relief.

'Now,' she said. 'Fill all the pots and pans and the electric kettle and put them on to boil. I'm going back up to Barbara.'

She rubbed her back and stroked her hair, listened for Derek's return and from time to time went down to keep an eye on the water. It was doing very nicely. Lids beginning to dance a jig beneath the pressure of steam.

Derek came back. The M.O. was following. Janet smiled benignly and complimented the water attendants. Everything was under control. All would go without a hitch. 'Slip up to Barbara, Derek. She needs you.' Derek, who despite his run to the telephone kiosk was ashen, mumbled something about a woman being better at a time like this. And Janet, wholeheartedly agreeing, silently went up to Barbara, where she consoled and comforted her with one ear cocked for the arrival of the M.O.

13

She heard a knock, went out onto the landing and saw her husband about to answer the door. 'No dear,' she said, hurrying down the stairs. 'I'll go.' And tottered through the hall, the thought crossing her mind that when all was said and done she was a very efficient woman. No doubt the doctor would remark on it and be grateful. Of course, not until everything was over, that was.

The doctor wasn't at all as she had expected. Hardly more than a boy and rather dour-looking. No resemblance whatsoever to the jovial mid-westerners or eager students on tenement deliveries. And as she conducted him upstairs she made her prognosis which he completely ignored. Not as much as one word did he comment. She classed him as not only dour but an ignorant, ill-bred young man.

The kitchen and hall now had the atmosphere of a laundry. Wreaths of steam floated everywhere, wafting up the stairs crowning the heads of Janet and the doctor. Strands of her lacquered hair collapsed and fell limply on her neck and forehead.

'Well then,' said the doctor to Barbara, speaking for the first time. 'So you've started, eh? What time did you have the first contraction?' Janet, despite the M.O.'s rebuff, was on cloud nine. Very soon she would be assisting at the birth of Barbara's baby. How wonderful that would be! Of course, she'd be the godmother. And if it was a girl, maybe even be her namesake. The doctor continued with his questions. 'How often are the pains coming?'

While he asked and Barbara answered he was warming his hands by rubbing one in the other. And then he said, 'Let's have a look,' and pulled down the bedclothes and raised Barbara's nightdress. Gently he probed and pressed and when he was done said, 'Fine, you're doing fine. But you won't go before morning. I'll send for the ambulance and have you in Hanover in no time.'

Barbara was aghast. 'Doctor,' she said, 'she'll never make it, never. And besides, I have everything prepared. Everything – gallons and gallons of water.' She was still protesting as she followed him down the stairs. 'Look,' she said, 'look in there.' He looked. In his line of vision stood Joan and the men, bleary-eyed from drink and lack of sleep. 'That's water, doctor. Boiling water – what am I supposed to do with it?'

'May I suggest that you make coffee, strong and black and lots of it,' said the doctor, proceeding towards the door.

Janet was livid. Such discourtesy! And after all she had done. The doctor picked up his cap. Well, thought Janet, you may have no manners but I never forget mine and she went ahead of him and opened the door. He put on his cap and stood half in and half out of the door and then he spoke. 'You know,' he said gently, 'had it been a home delivery a kettleful would have been plenty.' Then for the first time since arriving he smiled a lovely smile and went out into the night.

All the Angels and Saints

Mary O'Connell died and went to Heaven. From her place among the angels and saints, she looked down to earth and saw her husband and heard the advice he was giving his daughter-in-law. Mary smiled and touched her soft, smooth, radiant skin. Heaven, she thought, did wonders for your skin and sense of forgiveness. Then, closing her eyes, she looked back on her life on earth . . .

'Your skin is soft and smooth, like satin or a peach,' Peter said, stroking her neck and cheeks. Mary sighed with love and delight and thought how lucky she was that Peter, this tall, fine, handsome man loved and wanted to marry her. His fingers left her face and moved to her breasts. Beneath her high-necked blouse Mary's nipples strained against the silk stuff making two erections which Peter's thumbs found and caressed. 'My God,' he said in a breathless voice, 'you'll never know how much I love you. I could eat you, you're that gorgeous. I can't wait till we are married.' He took her in his arms and kissed her so hard his lips hurt hers. She didn't complain, for the hurting was nice in a way.

When the kissing stopped and she opened her eyes, his were looking into them with an expression that was wild and delirious and he whispered all the things he wanted to do, *would* do on the night they were married. And he told her that when her eyes were shut she was like a beautiful sleeping child with perfect skin and roses on her cheeks, and her lashes long and curling the way a doll's did. Then after another crushing kiss he moved slightly away from her. Mary patted her tossed hair and smoothed the front of her blouse – they smiled at each other and said simultaneously that it wouldn't be long now – only three weeks tomorrow. They laughed and she said, 'That's the only reason we're left so long in the parlour without being disturbed.' And Peter agreed.

There was a tap on the door soon after and her mother came in carrying a tray with the best tea things, ham sandwiches and currant cake. 'I was just saying to your father it won't be long now till the wedding.'

'So were we,' said Peter, getting to his feet and moving the occasional

16

table nearer the sofa and helping Mary's mother lay down the tray. 'Three weeks tomorrow,' he said, sitting down again. And the mother and daughter repeated the same thing.

After they were married, Peter and Mary moved into a little house near Baggot Street Bridge. Peter said that in a few years when he was promoted they would have a bigger house, maybe in Rathgar or Ranalagh: 'I'm an ambitious man and I intend to go far.'

'Oh, indeed you will,' said Mary. 'But sure I don't mind if we never move or you never get promotion – amn't I the happiest woman in the world and always will be, please God.'

Every morning after Peter went to the Government Buildings where he was a Civil Servant, Mary sat in her blue morning gown, the one Peter had said was the same colour as her eyes – and counted her blessings. Congratulating herself on having married such a marvellous husband whom she loved and who had given her this wonderful new life. No rushing to the office in the mornings. No more worrying that she might finish up an old maid. She had a gorgeous man, a home of her own, money in her pocket and time to do what she liked. *And* the nights, especially the nights . . . She hugged herself thinking about the nights.

Sometimes an hour would slip by while she sat congratulating herself, then a glance at the clock made her feel guilty. Half past nine and nothing done. The bed not made, the delf not washed, herself not washed. After all the advice her mother had given her, too. 'A man likes his home well-kept. A place for everything and everything in its place. You'll have to mend your ways. You have to have a method.' Mary knew that by nature she was neither tidy nor methodical. With no one to please she could quite happily sit doing nothing for hours and hours. But there was someone to please and above all else in her life she wished to please him.

Once she had shaken off her early morning lethargy she enjoyed doing the housework. Making the bed with loving care, shaking the pillows until they were plump, smoothing the sheets until not the tiniest wrinkle remained and making certain that the hang of the quilt was exactly the same on both sides. She washed dishes and polished brasses. Dusted and swept, found a place for everything and put everything in its place – Peter's pipes, books, magazines and paper spills, into their fretwork rack, wickerwork holder and tall, narrow spill-holder.

Then she had the food to consider – what she would cook for Peter's dinner and tea. Peter was particular about what he ate, very particular. No rinds on his rashers and never too crisply fried. Tender and not browned at all, barely turned in the pan, he had instructed after she served rashers and eggs to him for the first time. There was still an awful lot to learn about his likes and dislikes. He wouldn't eat mashed potatoes nor potatoes in their skins. And she must peel them thinly. All the goodness lay just beneath the skin – apart from the wastefulness of thick peels, he had told her several times. She practised and practised until now her peelings were almost transparent. He liked his fish steamed and his porridge neither thick nor thin and *never* lumpy. Gristle in meat he couldn't abide and his steaks must never be served rare. Mary glowed with pleasure if he praised a meal.

She shopped with him in mind, feeling the hearts of cabbages, squeezing the loaves, sniffing at fish and taking the butcher into her confidence. 'My husband won't eat gristle and his steak has to be well done but tender.'

And the butcher cut her nice bits of round steak and pieces of sirloin, and said, 'Isn't it a changeable oul day,' and told her which meat to stew and which to fry.

Life was grand, she would tell herself as she went home to make Peter's dinner. She watched the clock, counting the time until he came. She knew his footsteps. The thrill it was to see him again! Once he was inside the hall and the door closed she rushed into his arms hugging and kissing him as if their parting had been ages ago. Sometimes after the kissing Peter would stroke her cheek and say, 'Your skin is like a flower,' and Mary would long to stay in his arms and for the kissing not to stop and that he might whisper, 'Will we go upstairs?' Or that she was brazen enough to suggest it. But she knew that in broad daylight Peter would say no such thing. And definitely not at dinner-time, for he believed that meals must not be rushed and that every morsel must be masticated at least forty times. And she would never suggest a visit to the bedroom – it was considered forward and men didn't like that in their wives. Peter had told her so.

After disengaging himself from her embrace Peter hung up his coat and hat and thoroughly washed his hands before sitting to the table. He talked about the weather or people he worked with, mostly in a critical way. Mary listened and served him. Usually he had a suggestion as to how the meal might have been improved – a pinch more salt, a shake less pepper, an extra spoonful of sugar or half a spoon less. 'I'm only telling you,' he would say, 'because you have the makings of a grand cook and with a little more practice would be better still.'

Mary agreed and said she was sorry and would remember the next time as she poured his tea, milked and sugared it as her mother had always done for the men at home.

When it was almost time for Peter's return to work he asked how her morning had been. Eager to talk, for with the butcher and baker, fishmonger or greengrocer she had only exchanged pleasantries, she told him how pretty the canal had looked with the water lilies opening; how sorry she felt for the ducks and must bring bread for them tomorrow; a neighbour had asked her in for a cup of tea. Peter, she soon came to realise, wasn't listening and long before she had finished all she wanted to talk about, looked at his watch. That she knew was the signal for him to wash and brush up, which curtailed what time was left and made their parting brief. One day she watched from the window as he walked away and an awful sadness came over her and she didn't know why.

In the afternoons, after washing up, Mary left the house and walked along the canal to her mother's home, where in the familiar kitchen she shed her responsibilities and newly-acquired tidy habits, leaving her coat on the back of a chair, her handbag on the floor and her hat on the fender. Her mother picked up and hung up and said she hoped she didn't do things like that in her new home. Mary laughed and assured her she didn't, that the house was like a new pin. Her mother made tea which they drank as they ate cakes and biscuits.

Her mother said how well she looked, that married life was suiting her. Mary smiled shyly and blushed. They sat and gossiped about the family, about the neighbours and far too soon her mother was telling her the time and how she'd better hurry, Peter mustn't walk in from work with his wife not there.

Walking home, Mary watched the trees reflected in the still green water of the canal, the valerian growing on the banks and the barges, sometimes pulled by an old horse with a rope around its neck. She admired the Georgian houses on either side of the canal, marvelling that one family owned so much space – marvelling, not envious, for she wouldn't change places with one of them. She was the happiest woman in the city of Dublin. Not, she believed, if you searched the four corners of the earth would you find one happier, nor a husband as handsome and wonderful as Peter. By the time she neared the bridge her thoughts turned toward the night, the time when she and Peter were in bed. Her face became hot and inside herself she trembled with delighted anticipation.

But as the weeks and months followed each other, she became aware of a change that had come over her, a change in her mind when she thought about Peter and night-time. She tried not to encourage these thoughts but all the same they persisted. Peter now seldom uttered the little whisperings that he had when they were courting and first married. It was a silly thing to brood over, she told herself. It might even be a sin – a sin of ingratitude and discontent – and often she said an Aspiration for the thought to leave her mind. But it wouldn't go away. Worse still, she was beginning to think other unkind thoughts about Peter. Peter didn't . . . he never . . . she wasn't quite sure what it was that troubled her about him. Maybe that was how it was supposed to be . . . how would you know something like that? Who could you talk to of such a thing?

Yet the feeling persisted.

All she knew for sure was that when they were in bed she would begin to feel that something marvellous, something magical – though she didn't know what – was about to happen. Something stirred deep inside her, maybe in her soul even, a feeling almost within her grasp, a strange, wonderful indescribable sensation – and then Peter collapsed on top of her, lay for a few minutes then rolled off. It was over. She had lost whatever it was that had been almost there and she felt edgy and sad. Yet at the same time there was in her a great tenderness towards Peter, so that she stroked his back and caressed him and told him she loved him. Sometimes he slept immediately, or made love again – this time so quickly that the feeling she sought never even had a chance to begin. Afterwards it took her a long time to sleep.

When Mary was being discharged from hospital after the birth of her first son, the other mothers bade her goodbye and one laughingly said, 'See you this time next year!' Mary blushed, her soft fair skin taking on the colour of a pink rose, and denied the possibility. The following year the same women said when Mary was brought into the ward from the delivery room, 'Didn't I tell you?'

Her babies were beautiful and thrived. In three years and two months she had one in the pram, one sitting at the bottom of it and one by the hand. Whenever the weather was fine she walked them by the canal and brought bags of crusts for the ducks. People stopped to admire the three little boys, tell her they were beautiful and that God might bless and spare them to her. And Mary asked God and Our Lady to spare her to rear her little children and if it was pleasing to His Will, to let her have a space before she conceived again. Her prayers were answered, for although she conceived, she miscarried three times in a row.

Peter got the promotion he had set his heart on, but complained that now there were so many mouths to feed, much good it did him. 'We'd have had a bigger house if it wasn't for go-carts and all the baby paraphernalia –

never mind what they cost to feed once they're weaned,' he said, once he knew she was again pregnant.

Mary tried consoling him by saying how she didn't mind not moving to a better house. She loved this one. 'Though if God blesses us again after this one, the child will have to sleep in a drawer. There won't be a spare inch for another cot,' she laughed, making a joke of it. But Peter didn't think it was funny.

It was dinner-time when the conversation took place. The table was littered with small plates, spilled mashed potatoes and carrots, and milk that had dribbled from feeding bottles. With a damp cloth Mary wiped and dabbed at the spillages, for she knew they displeased Peter. She still tried hard but knew she no longer followed her mother's maxim of a place for everything and everything in its place. Men expected a well-run home, quiet children with washed faces and combed hair waiting for them when they came home from work. She tried. God knows she tried – but it never worked. No matter how early she got up, no matter how hard she worked, something or other always happened to send her plans astray. A child would fall and cut his knee – bandages and iodine had to be found and time for kisses and cuddles when the iodine stung. A quarrel over a toy had to be settled. There were slaps to be slapped, bumps and knocks to be rubbed better. A neighbour who called for a minute stayed for an hour. And so it went on, day after day, always working against the clock, always trying to restore order before Peter came home. She rarely succeeded.

By the time she was thirty Mary had six sons. At least there would be no problems sleeping them when they grew up, she consoled herself. Though at the present the baby did lie in a drawer. But later on she and Peter would move into the smaller bedroom, for the other would take two beds with no bother.

Often she was very tired, had bouts of breathlessness and her skin became pale. 'You haven't a drop of blood in your body. You're run down. Ask the chemist for a strengthening bottle,' her mother constantly advised. But always when Mary went to the chemist there were things more urgent on her mind than iron tonics. Camphorated oil for the children's chests, Steadman's teething powders, Erasmic shaving sticks, throat pastilles and corn plasters for Peter.

On her thirty-second birthday Mary had twin girls. One was born dead. She wanted to see the baby, know what she looked like, have a face to grieve for. The nursing staff, Peter and her mother said to see a stillborn child was unnatural. No mothers saw their dead babies. She was to put the

21

thought out of her mind. Be grateful one had survived. Pray for the one who hadn't and was in Limbo.

The twin who survived was delicate and beautiful. Once Mary overheard her mother say to a neighbour, 'That child is like a little angel, too beautiful to rear.'

Mary was distraught but kept her fear to herself, devoting almost all her time to minding the baby, hardly leaving her out of her arms, coaxing her to suck, holding her close and gazing at her face, imprinting it on her memory.

When the baby was eleven weeks old she got pneumonia and died. Tears fell from Mary's eyes and milk from her engorged breasts. A fire burned in them and they were tender to touch, so tender that the weight of her nightdress on them made her wince. Her mother brought belladonna plasters from the chemist's – black plasters from which the back was peeled away leaving a sticky surface that fitted over each breast. The plasters were pierced all over with small holes and in the centre of each was a hole large enough for the nipple to protrude. The plasters and doses of Epsom salts, Mary's mother told her, would dry her out.

One night during the drying-out process, when Mary was undressing, her nightdress didn't fall easily into place and for a moment her breasts in their black casings were exposed. In that moment Mary looked up and saw Peter staring, a look of revulsion on his face. Yet once they were in bed and the lights out, he reached for her and prepared to lie on her. 'No,' she said, as his hand felt for the hem of her nightie. '*No*,' she repeated when his hand persisted in lifting her nightgown, refusing him for the first time in their married life. Immediately she was sorry, but not enough to forget the expression on his face when he had seen her exposed, plastered-encased breasts. Then, because she was already feeling guilty as well as sorry, she made excuses. 'I'm too sore, I couldn't . . . When my breasts are better.' He lay beside her and didn't utter a word. Neither did he ever make love to her again.

Night after night Mary lay awake, grieving for her dead babies and longing for Peter to turn to her and take her in his arms. Long ago she had forgotten that once she had imagined something wonderful was about to happen during their lovemaking. She had become satisfied with his want for her, that he kissed and lay on her. She liked the weight of his body on hers, the feel of the parts of his body that touched hers, his entry into her, the relief he sought which her body gave him. She missed all of it with a deep sad longing. There was an ache inside her from knowing he didn't desire her any more.

Getting up in the night to soothe a crying child, put warm oil in an aching ear or oil of cloves on a tooth that hurt, she sometimes caught sight of herself in the full-length landing mirror over which hung a weak bulb. She saw a plump woman, a fat woman in a shapeless nightdress, its pink or blue colour faded from too many washings, the lace edging unravelled, and a face that was pale and puffy beneath untidy hair. She would resolve to do something about her appearance: brush her hair a hundred strokes every night before she went to bed, buy some Pond's Cold Cream and get a new nightie – a stockinette or art silk one. It was nearly time for the gas meter to be emptied. Sometimes there was half a crown or three shillings discount coming back – a huge pile of pennies. You could get a nightdress for three and eleven. She imagined herself in the new nightgown and thought, maybe then when I put my arm round Peter he won't shrug it off.

In daylight, scrutinising her face in a hand mirror, she consoled herself that she still had her soft fair skin and remembered how, years ago, Peter used to rave about it. Thinking of their courting and early married life she made excuses for him. He was getting older, they both were. You couldn't expect things to be the way they were in the beginning. He was a good husband in every other way. He didn't drink and had long ago stopped the pipe. Every Sunday he took the boys to Mass. He was a good husband.

Then she would think – but all the same, wouldn't a little affection in their lives be a grand thing? She was starved of it, starved of someone to hold and love, for nowadays the boys had grown beyond that. If only occasionally Peter would put an arm round her, give her a hug, touch her in passing. Still, he was a good husband. He didn't shower her with money, but gave enough for food and essentials. He was cautious, saving for their old age. You could be too cautious though, Mary believed. A treat now and then would be worth the world. An evening at the pictures, a splash at Christmas. But that wasn't his way. And there was nothing to do but put up with it like all his other little quare ways. He was a good man, for wasn't it his goodness that made him consider their comfort in old age?

She bought two new nightgowns, art silk and lace-trimmed, put cold cream on her face and suddenly, feeling very daring one night before going to bed, opened a bottle of Lavender Water someone had given her years ago for Christmas and splashed some on her breasts. In bed she moved close to Peter and put her arm round him. He let it stay for a minute and hope rose in her, then he moved as far away from her as the bed would allow and soon she heard his snores.

Her mother died. The children were growing up, their demands on her changing. Helping with homework, worrying about them staying out late and what company they were keeping took the place of teething and childish illnesses. She thought less and less about her appearance and had given up approaching Peter in bed. But occasionally a memory stirred and she imagined how lovely life would be if things were different between them. If he didn't sit every night reading, so that their time was spent in uncompanionable silence. If he spoke of things other than shoes needing to be taken to the cobblers, that someone had overwound the clock, that the nights were drawing in or there was a stretch to the days.

One night, when she could stand the silence no longer she said, 'Peter, do you remember when we were courting?' She had to repeat the question before he laid down his book.

'What makes you ask that?' he said.

'I was just thinking how nice it was.'

'We were young, then. Now we're old.'

'Not that old,' said Mary. 'I was thinking about years ago when we were courting, and first married. We were very happy then. You used to say my skin was like a peach. Do you remember that, Peter? "Soft as a peach" – that's what you said,' and she laughed to cover her embarrassment.

Peter stood up and put his book away. 'It's late,' he said, then asked, 'Is everyone in?'

Mary replied that they were and he went round the house locking doors and checking windows, then he wound the clock.

'Can we not talk?' Mary asked, her voice almost a whisper, for there was a lump in her throat.

'About what?'

'Things – us – the way we are.'

'I'm tired. I'm going to bed, so should you.'

'Please, Peter.' She stood up and touched his sleeve. She put her arms round him. 'Please,' she said again. 'Before it's too late. Let's try to . . .' He stood stiffly like a soldier at attention. 'Peter,' she pleaded, 'don't turn away. Look at me.' He kept his head averted. She sighed and let go of him. 'You go on up, I'll just sit here for a while.'

'Goodnight, then,' he said.

'Goodnight and God bless you.'

And so the years passed. Mary's children married and left home. Now and then one of them when they visited slipped her a few shillings. She never expected it – they had enough to do with their money – but she never refused it, either. She saved the small gifts for the rare occasions when she wanted something for herself, like a jar of face cream, a slip or knickers, or her special treat – a visit to the hairdresser's.

Peter retired and supplemented his pension with the savings. He was silent and morose, went for long walks alone, wound the clock and checked the doors and windows before he went to bed. Sometimes a whole day would pass without him uttering a word to Mary.

Sometimes, when the loneliness became unbearable and bitter thoughts entered her mind, she would leave the house, no matter what the weather was like and walk along the canal, looking at the water, watching the ducks. Sometimes there were swans and she'd stare and marvel at their beauty, their grace. Memories came of the times when she used to take her babies, she always thought of them as babies, with bags of bread to feed the ducks.

She'd rest on a seat halfway along the canal and think about herself and Peter and wish they were more companionable. Life could have been grand if he was – just the two of them, able to please themselves now. Going to Mass together, going for walks. Talking about the children. And then she'd think how she could have been worse off. Could have had a drunkard for a husband. One that was violent, or had other women. You couldn't have everything, she'd tell herself as she walked home.

She loved her visits to the hairdressers – the warmth of the salon and the lovely smells of shampoo and setting lotions. The girl who did her hair was very friendly and they had great chats. She knew all about the girl's plans to get married and she'd tell her about her children and what a joy it was to have babies, smiling as she talked and looking at herself in the big mirror while the girl put the curlers in her hair. It was a great mirror, she used to think. It made her skin look soft and smooth with hardly a line at all.

One Saturday afternoon while sitting under the dryer Mary felt extra sleepy. It's the heat, she thought as she closed her eyes. Many times she had a little doze under the dryer. When she woke up she was in Heaven. And as clear as if he was beside her she could hear Peter's voice talking to one of their daughters-in-law. 'My wife,' he was saying, 'the Lord have mercy on her, now there was a woman who neglected herself. When I married her she had a skin that was as soft and smooth as yours. But she let it go to rack and ruin. All dried up and as wrinkled as a fig. Did you ever see a fig – did you ever see the wrinkled skin of it – well, that's the way she finished up. But sure you must have noticed!'

The oul fool, thought Mary, doesn't he know the girl is laughing at him, and she laughed herself. And laughed again when he went on to say, 'There were times when I'd get confused not knowing if it was my mother or my wife I was looking at. Wasn't that a terrible thing for a man! And all through neglect.'

An oul killjoy, thought Mary. Full of fads and fancies but all to suit yourself. As vain as a peacock. What do you see when you look in the glass? Whatever it is it isn't the old man *I* see. God love you. All the pleasure and delight you missed. I'm sorry for you. I can afford to be, for amn't I among the angels and saints with not a worry or care, not a pain or ache. As free as a bird. There's no clock in Heaven and no doors to bolt or lock. And no money – isn't that the marvellous thing? – no money.

No such a thing as time. No such a thing as getting old or sick. No oul cranks. There's another department for them. They're all kept together and can annoy each other as much as they like. There are all sorts of different places in Heaven for all sorts of people. I was lucky I got in this part. I don't know where you'll go, Peter. I wouldn't think we'll be in the same one, would you?

Dickie, Dickie Dout

Matthew said he couldn't remember having lived anywhere else except in the Home but Winnie told him he had. 'Twice,' she said, 'you went away and twice you came back.'

Sometimes Winnie was too busy or irritated by his interminable questions, but not today and never when he asked why he returned to the Home. 'You missed me,' she said, 'that's why, of course!' And she smiled at the little boy with the red hair and pale freckled skin. Poor mite, she thought, he's not what you'd call handsome. His look is too knowing. Puts people off, I expect.

Today she would make time for Matthew. Anything that needed doing could wait until later on. She wanted him kept calm and placid, not in what some of the staff called 'a wobbler'. Matthew in a wobbler wasn't nice or friendly. Sulky and sullen, more like. And that wouldn't do today of all days. Not with people coming to see the children . . . people thinking of fostering. People who fostered sometimes went on to adopt.

Winnie didn't approve of people coming to look at the children, though how else they could choose she didn't know. All the same it was like going to the zoo to look at the poor unfortunate animals who had never asked to be there in the first place. Like going to the zoo or the Dogs' Home to choose a pet, it was.

'Come here,' she said to Matthew and when he came close she tucked in his shirt and as she did so recited *Dickie, Dickie Dout with his shirt hanging out.* When it was all tucked in she said, 'An awful boy you are – six years old and can't keep your tail in.'

'I haven't got a tail,' said Matthew indignantly, his face puckering with annoyance making him look like a cross old man.

'Only teasing I was – of course you haven't got a tail but that's no call for cheek. It's only a silly rhyme. Though some shirts do have tails.' She put an arm round his shoulders. 'So no need to snap my head off.'

Too snappy he was. Always had been. One of the reasons the foster parents hadn't kept him any time. Hard to manage, they had said. And he wore them out with questions. There were other things, too. Winnie smiled recalling them. Mr and Mrs Reynolds – a nice enough couple.

27

First time fostering a child. Great animal lovers, they were. Had a house outside the village where they kept goats, cats and turtle doves – the birds in a lovely painted dovecote in the wide passage of the house. Winnie told herself it was nothing to smile about really but still a smile hovered round her lips when she thought of what had happened: an irate Mr and Mrs Reynolds returning Matthew and him with them only just over a week.

Cruel, they had said he was, putting the cat into the dove-house. Cruelty to animals was a terrible thing, especially in a child. The doves were dead – there was no answer to their accusation.

The next day she had quizzed Matthew as to why he had put the cat in with the doves. 'She was sad,' he replied.

'Sad? What do you mean, sad?' she asked.

'She hadn't anyone to play with. She was sitting watching them for a long time.'

And she thought how often she had watched him sit outside a group, lonely and unwanted. Then she said, 'But cats kill birds, didn't you know that?'

'I do now,' he replied.

'You'd never do anything like that again, promise.'

And he'd looked at her as if she was daft. 'They'd kill them. They'd be all dead,' he said, his tone implying the same thing as his expression. And him only three years of age.

The next couple had him for a month and Winnie remembered how her hopes had risen until the day she answered the phone and Mrs Wallace was speaking. Shouting, more like it – hysterical. He had to be brought back: he'd nearly destroyed her radiogram and only three months paid on it. When Mrs Wallace calmed down she told how coming in from the garden where she had been hanging out clothes, Matthew was in the sitting room with a screwdriver trying to take the back off the radiogram. Winnie's first thought had been, serves you right leaving a child where he could get hold of a screwdriver. But she was all sympathy with the woman.

'It's not only the radiogram,' Mrs Wallace had gone on to complain. 'You tell him to do something and he wants to know why. Why, why, why – that's all I ever hear! Not like a child at all, he isn't. Not like any three year old I've ever known, anyway'.

So back Matthew had come and hadn't been away since. Winnie thought Matthew remembered being sent back. Some children remembered things that happened when they were three. And Matthew had a good memory. Winnie also thought she knew why Matthew pretended not to remember. For all his front he was easily hurt. Not everyone could see that but she could. She'd seen him shrink inside himself when he was

28

made fun of or rebuffed by the staff or older children. Not so that anyone would notice – oh no, he put on a show. Only if you loved him a lot or took a liking to him, as she had done since he first came to the Home, would you notice.

He was a fat baby then, ten months old, his red hair curly and not a sign of a freckle. His mother and father killed in a car crash, poor things. Only twenty they were. And Matthew strapped in his baby seat crying when the fire brigade and police came to cut his parents out. He had to be taken into care while enquiries were made: it took a long time, Winnie remembered. Nothing came of it in the end. There was no one, not a soul to claim him, no will existed to name a guardian for him. Bereft he was and him only a baby. So he came into care permanently.

His curls soon straightened out and the fat fell off him. By the time he was walking you wouldn't have recognised him for the same baby who'd first come to the Home. Winnie often felt it was missing his mother had done it. She'd seen a programme on TV about what happened to baby monkeys taken from their mothers – pined and waned they did, even though you gave them food. Young things and babies needed someone all the time to love them. It didn't have to be their real mother, but someone special for them all the time. You couldn't do that in the Home – there were too many babies, too many changes with staff coming and going all the time. She was the only one left who knew Matthew from when he was a baby. She tried hard to give him what he needed, but there were so many children, all lonely, all wanting someone special.

'Do you know what's happening tomorrow?' she asked Matthew. He was still sulky and didn't answer her. 'Miss Bennet is taking you and Peter and David to the pictures, and guess what's on? Go on, guess!'

His eyes widened, he loved surprises. '*The Empire Strikes Back*,' he said, and hope shone from his face. The reprimand was all forgotten as he launched into what Winnie was sure was the hundredth detailed account of Luke Skywalker and the black knight, Darth Vader. She pretended to be interested. All the pictures and stories there were about space and rockets and crazy things she couldn't and didn't want to understand. The trouble was, she was getting old. She was retiring in two months – then what would become of Matthew with his wobblers? He wasn't easy. In a home of his own with someone who loved him he'd come all right, but there was no denying he was difficult. You couldn't tell him a story any more without him contradicting. The trouble was, he was *too* intelligent. No, not too intelligent, she corrected herself. Intelligence was a good thing – he'd need all of that. Too forward or knowing, that's what he was.

There was a word for it. She'd think of it in a minute. *Precocious*, that was it! She'd once looked it up in the Dictionary: *Someone who was remarkably developed in talk and conduct for his age*, that's what the Dictionary said, and that was Matthew to a tee. He was too grown up for a six year old. A lot of people didn't like that in children.

Sometimes *she* didn't like it – it could knock you off your stride. That had happened last week when she was telling him a story. One of his favourites – *Ali Baba and the Forty Thieves*. To make the story more real, more like life was today she used to add bits, put it ordinary things, but last week that all changed. Just when she was about to begin he'd instructed, 'And don't when you come to the part about the cave say it was full of pop and ice cream and stupid things like crisps and Quavers, 'cos they didn't have them in the olden days.' It had stopped her dead in her tracks. Other mums and dads wouldn't like it, either, so she had told him he was very rude though knowing well what his answer would be.

'I wasn't rude. Rude is saying swear words and telling people to shut up, that's rude.'

And in a way of course she had to admit he was right, though only to herself. They *didn't* have crisps and bottles of pop in the olden days. He had discovered that and was only putting her right – the way he did when she said something about the space films. But grown ups, most grown ups anyway, didn't like that in children. Poor Matthew – he wouldn't be easy for someone strange to love. What would become of him, she wondered. Would he spend all his childhood in the Home belonging to everyone and no one? Well-fed and clothed, his health looked after, his schooling, TV and the pictures, outings, everything but no one special for him.

It would soon be lunchtime – the people who were considering fostering were coming. Matthew was to be considered. 'Off you go now to the dining room and remember to keep yourself tidy and no getting into fights.' He shrugged and half-grinned and went away.

Winnie had her own lunch and then surreptitiously watched the prospective foster parents arrive. Nice enough, they looked, and she knew that they had been thoroughly vetted by the social workers for their suitability as foster parents. Only, some of the knacks for making good parents couldn't be found out in interviews no matter how well-intentioned and clever the social workers were. The hopeful foster parents were kind, good-hearted people – certainly not in it for the money, as some suggested. They were good people wanting to give a home and a bit of individual attention to a lost little child. It was, she supposed, the best that could be done in the circumstances. And she hoped with all her heart that today Matthew might be lucky and find someone who was not

30

looking for a handsome little boy, a sweet, obedient little boy – a boy who wouldn't answer back, argue, contradict and throw wobblers.

There they were now – the ones interested in him. Coming to see him for the first time, come to make friends, invite him out for the day then gradually get to know him and decide if they would foster him. They looked nice if you didn't object to jeans and long hair on the two of them. A pity about that, she thought and about their age, too. Couldn't be much more than thirty. Then she remembered that had Matthew's parents not been killed they would be even younger.

She saw the three of them settle in an alcove. Matthew seemed ill at ease and fidgety. They were talking to him. She couldn't hear what was said but could tell by his face he was bored. She often rowed with him when he complained of being bored, telling him there was plenty to keep him occupied if he troubled to find it. Now she felt like going to him and giving him a good shake. He could be spoiling a chance that might not come his way again in a hurry. She couldn't bear to watch any more, couldn't bear to see the couple pretend politeness and interest and then get up smiling at him, patting his hair, saying goodbye and then heading for the office where they'd make their excuses. They were terribly sorry, but Matthew wasn't exactly what they had in mind – a younger child, perhaps . . . excuses and apologies that all amounted to the same thing – another rejection of him.

She'd go for a walk round the grounds and by the time she came back they'd be gone. Matthew would pretend he didn't care, wouldn't shed a tear – wouldn't even talk about it, although some children did cry something awful, broke their little hearts. Not that anything had ever been promised to them – no one had even hinted that they might be fostered. It was a very careful, gradual process. But the children knew. Some of them had been there for years. They weren't blind or stupid and from time to time saw their friends go away with the people who had become regular visitors. Some returned after weeks, months, even years and the fortunate ones never. Yes, she'd leave Matthew for a while before going near him. Then remind him of the treat tomorrow – the visit to the pictures. That would take his mind off things . . .

When she got back, to her delighted surprise Matthew and the couple were still in the lounge and he was talking excitedly and pointing to pictures in one of his space books. Still keeping out of sight she moved closer. They were arguing. Arguing the way Matthew did, cheeky-like. But the marvellous thing was, the man wasn't annoyed! She could see him wait for a chance to get a word in then explain reasonably some point in Matthew's argument with which he didn't agree. And then to her

31

amazement, Matthew spoke less and she heard him question the man and listen attentively to his answers.

The man, she thought, must be one of them astronauts to impress Matthew, for no one impressed him. She stepped a little nearer and could hear what the man was saying. 'You've got a great grasp of it, Mat. How old did you say you were?'

'Six,' replied Matthew.

'Well, that's really something. Only six – did you hear that, darling?'

Smiling at the two of them his wife said she had heard and that Matthew must be very clever.

'Let me show you,' said the man, turning again to Matthew. 'This is what really happens at blast off,' and he tore a sheet of paper from a notebook and started drawing, talking as he did so and pointing to parts of the sketch.

'Please God,' prayed Winnie, 'don't start, Matthew. Don't you be rude and start a contention. Don't be precocious.' And when he did she almost screamed aloud, 'You've done it now, spoiled your chance, you have!' But to her amazement the man and his wife didn't seem a bit put out. And she thought hopefully that maybe there *were* people who understood boys like Matthew – who saw his intelligence, his quick enquiring mind and who were able to put him straight without putting him down. She hoped so, with all her heart she hoped so.

She watched for a few moments longer then, intrigued to see more, she ventured a little way out of her hiding place. And there was Matthew leaning against the man, watching him draw. Matthew was the least demonstrative child Winnie had ever known. To get a kiss or a hug from him was as rare as snow in summer. But sometimes in passing he would touch her. A stranger could have seen the touch and thought it accidental – but she knew it was intentional – a little touch, no more, to show his affection. That's what he was doing now, leaning against the man. Pretending it was necessary to get close so as to watch the drawing. Wanting to show affection – but always on guard in case of being rebuffed.

There were things she had to see to – other children needing her attention. She turned to go. Then looked round for a final glimpse of the little group. The man was tearing another sheet from his notebook and offering it to Matthew. He could draw well, especially anything to do with space. She watched him accept the paper and pencil, saw him bend over the paper and his tongue come out between his teeth the way it did when he concentrated on drawing or painting, and begin with his quick strokes. And over his bent head she saw the man and woman exchange glances and smile at each other. And Winnie went away thinking – hoping, praying – that today this might be Matthew's lucky day.

A Summer's Day

Hannah and I sat on the curb making piles of the summer dust that collected in the gutter and planning to murder John-Joe Durkin. John-Joe was three and a half and I hated him. He was small and pale, the front of his trousers was always wet and he kept kicking over our carefully-made mounds of dust.

'After we murder him we'll chop him up in bits,' I explained to Hannah and she agreed. A dray went past on its way to Fitz's pub. Great big horses pulled it – horses nearly as big as the elephants in the zoo. Long hair grew around their hooves almost touching the ground. One lifted its tail and steaming dollops of manure fell onto the road. As if by magic bluebottles and flies appeared. Murdering John-Joe was forgotten as Hannah and I found two sticks, ran into the road and upended the shiny brown balls from which pieces of undigested bran poked. The disturbed flies flew away.

'Get off this road before I tell your mothers!' a passing woman shouted.

If she did, which she might, my mother would be roaring and shouting from the window for me to come in and threatening what she would do to me when I did. So I said to Hannah, 'we'll go and watch the barrels going down the hole.'

'All right,' she said and we follyed the dray to the public house. John-Joe started whinging to come with us but I wouldn't let him.

The grating was up and the men in aprons already lowering the barrels into the cellar. It was very dark down there. I stood near the edge and peered over. Thick dust like dirty grey wool clung to the sides of the walls and sweet and Woodbine packets littered the cellar floor and the smell of porter was everywhere.

'Mind outta the way or youse'll be kilt,' said a man in an apron. We ignored him. 'Get outta the bloody way before I clatter the pair of youse.'

'I know,' I said to Hannah when the man threatened us again. 'We'll go down the Alley and have adventures.'

The Alley was a narrow lane which ran along the back of my side of the street. The shopkeepers threw their rubbish there and sometimes there was treasure in the rubbish. You might find it. Once I found half a crown. And my mother said, 'May God bless you, that's after getting me out of a hobble.' Apples and oranges were thrown in the Alley, only a bit mouldy sometimes.

'I'll get into trouble if I go in the Alley again,' Hannah said.

'Ah, come on. Only for a few minutes. Sure your mammy won't know,' I coaxed.

'No, I can't. Me mammy says I stink of fish when I've been in the Alley.'

'Well, anyway, I'm going. And if you tell I'll scrawb your eyes out.' I ran off and left her.

The Alley was cool and dark. Battered ashcans overflowed. The Alley smelled of overripe fruit and rotten fish. I poked about looking for something or anything. A half-empty vinegar bottle lay on its side amongst a patch of stinging nettles. I picked it up, pulled out the cork and drank it. I loved the sharp taste. My mother said you shouldn't drink vinegar, it dried up your blood. A child she knew that drank vinegar had a terrible end – all dried up, her body like a sheet of brown paper. I didn't care. I drained the bottle and threw it over the wall.

Halfway down the Alley was a hill, only a small one. I climbed up and sat on the top. Pee the beds grew there and nestling amongst the yellow flowers and ginny joe seed heads that you could tell the time with by how many puffs it took to blow away all the seeds, was a dead fish. It must have been there a long time. The skin was coarse and dry. I turned it over with my foot. The underneath was moist. I poked a stick through, breaking the skin, and saw thick white maggots wriggling. The fish looked like a moving rice pudding.

Hannah had changed her mind. I could see her now timidly walking down the Alley, carefully stepping over the rotting vegetables. I hooked the stick inside the fish and flung it towards her. Clumps of maggots flew through the air. The fish missed her, hit the wall and landed on her white runners. She started to cry. 'I'll tell my mammy so I will. I won't play with you any more.' She ran sobbing from the Alley.

On top of my hill I danced and chanted, 'Cry baby, cry baby.' I was sorry when she went and stopped singing. Then consoled myself that after dinner we would make friends again. I'd send someone to ask if she was 'spin spout, or black out'. If she said spin spout we would be friends, but if the answer was black out I'd have to try again.

I climbed down the hill and started for home. I walked slowly with my eyes down, looking for treasure. Two seagull feathers lay on the tarry road. I dashed into the road and picked them up. Now I could play Indians. As I neared my hall door, John-Joe sidled up. I stuck the feathers in my hair and did a war dance. His vacant pale eyes, bulging like gooseberries, stared at me. I stuck my tongue out and raced up the stairs.

My mother was at the gas stove cooking dinner. 'Where have you been? And what's that you have in your hair?' she asked, looking round at me. 'I've been calling you for hours. I've never met such a child in my life. You're never where you should be. Where were you?' She didn't really expect an answer so I kept quiet and went to the window to watch for my father who would be coming home in a minute. I moved the lace hangings to get a better view.

'Leave the curtains alone!' my mother shouted, looking round again from the stove and again noticing the feathers in my hair. 'What's that you have in your hair? Take it out.'

'It's only feathers. I was playing Indians.'

'I'll give you Indians – take them out immediately.' I raised my hands and pulled at the feathers. They fell forward over my face, the quills bending, but the ends remained stuck in my hair, glued there by the tar. 'Will you take them things out of your hair. You've been down the Alley! Look at the cut of you! And wash your hands – they're like pig's paws. Take them out. How many more times do I have to tell you!' My mother's voice was louder.

I tried again to pull out the feathers, wincing at the pain in my scalp. My mother crossed the room, looked at my hair and hit me a stinging slap. 'Sweet Jesus, what have you done to your hair – it's full of tar.' A smell of burning filled the room. The drained potatoes left over the flame to dry had caught. She ran back to the cooker and removed the saucepan while still giving out about my hair. 'You've destroyed it. What am I going to do with you? I'll kill you, so I will.' She got a big pair of scissors and came towards me, cut the feathers out of my hair, snapped them and threw them onto the fire. 'Let me catch you putting anything else in your hair and see what you'll get.'

Clouds of blue smoke began to fill the room. The frying pan had overheated and the smell of burning fat also filled the air. 'Now look what you've been the cause of and your father walking in the door,' she said and slapped me again. The more I cried the more she hit me. I cried louder, hoping my father was coming and would hear me. 'Stop that crying,' she shouted. 'Stop it, d'ye hear me.' Then with a final slap she pushed me away saying, 'Now you've got something to cry for.' Her face was creased and red and her eyes glared.

'I hate you, I hate you. I wish you were dead,' I said again and again to myself.

'That's him coming now,' said my mother. 'Stop that crying before he comes in.' I cried louder. My father would be on my side. He loved me the best.

He opened the door and blue haze enveloped him. 'Jesus Christ, what happened?' he asked.

'What happened is that that one came in full of tar and feathers. Look at it. Look at the state of her hair.' She banged the iron pot on the stove trying to dislodge the burnt potatoes. 'And it's all your fault,' she continued. 'You have her ruined. I can't get good of her.'

'She's only a child. You're always on at her.'

I sidled up to him, rubbing my face against his sleeve, forcing out the sobs. His coat smelled lovely. He ran his hand over my hair.

'Sit down and leave your father alone,' my mother ordered. 'Sit down now this minute.'

My father had the top potatoes which hadn't scorched. Some of mine were burned but I liked the crispy bits. My mother as always had only a little dinner on a saucer. After the meal I asked, 'Mammy, can I go out and play?'

'Wait first and have a cup of tea, it'll be drawn in a minute.'

Her anger was forgotten. She cut bread and buttered it, talking to my father at the same time. I ate bread and jam and sipped the hot tea. My father gave her five shillings – tips he had made – and me twopence.

'Now can I go?' I asked again, finishing the last of my bread.

She was engrossed in what my father was telling her, looking happy smiling at him. 'Yes,' she said, 'go down but stay where I can see you.'

I shouted my agreement as I went through the door, raced down the stairs and out into the sunlit street – the slaps, tears, tar and feathers all forgotten. John-Joe was sitting on the curb by the shore dropping stones into the water. I sat beside him, pushing him up a bit so I could throw stones into the grating too. 'Have you seen Hannah?' I asked. He shook his head. Sometimes he answered you, sometimes he didn't. 'Will you go to her house for me?' He looked sullen and shook his head again. 'Ask her if she's spin spout or black out, go on.'

'I won't,' he said.

I gave him a good, hard shove and he started to cry. I stood up and ran away shouting 'John-Joe Durkin is no good. Chop him up for firewood.'

I wandered down the street stopping to look in the shop windows, deciding how to spend my twopence. In the end I settled for Ma Doyle's toyshop where I bought a gelatine doll and a balloon on a bamboo stick with red feathers on the mouthpiece. When I came back there was still no sign of Hannah. If she didn't come soon I'd be stuck with John-Joe for the rest of the day.

I sat beside him and started to blow up my balloon. I blew hard and the red rubber swelled, the colour paled and the balloon grew into a big rose-pink ball. I took it out of my mouth. The air rushed from it with a squeaking sound. John-Joe laughed and reached for it. I turned away from him and started blowing up the balloon again. John-Joe clapped his hands as it grew bigger and bigger. 'Me have it, me have it,' he chanted, pulling at my arm. I stood up, trying to shake him off, but he clung on pulling harder on my arm. I jerked it to dislodge him. The balloon shot out of my mouth and sailed into the middle of the road squeaking as it went. It landed and did a lot of little hops as the air escaped. John-Joe with a squeal of delight ran after it and straight into the path of a speeding sand lorry.

His body was lifted and thrown towards the grating. He fell with his head hitting the curb and his blood, the same colour as the balloon, ran down the drain. All the people came running from everywhere. Mrs Durkin came running down the street screaming. I ran away, around the corner into the Alley. I climbed the hill and lay down in the grass that grew near the top of the wall.

I kept seeing John-Joe's blood going down the drain. He was dead and Hannah would tell everyone I had murdered him. My mother would kill me. I still had the gelatine doll. One of its legs dangled on the thread elastic. I pulled it off and threw it away.

I lay for a long time. It seemed a long time, anyway. It began to get dark. My mother would be looking for me, calling me. She might think I was dead and be sorry for me. I was hungry and I wanted my tea. I pulled some stalks of grass and chewed them. I wanted to go home but I couldn't. I could never go home again. I would have to stay here all night. I would be put in prison and have bread and water for ever and ever.

I sat up and looked down the Alley. It was nearly dark now. Cats were prowling, searching for fish-heads. Two started to fight, spitting and snarling at each other. I thought about the dead fish I had thrown at Hannah and imagined the maggots crawling up the hill to eat me.

Then I heard the whistle. It was my father, whistling the way he did to call me in. Then I heard him call my name. His footsteps came nearer. I could see him now. My sobs grew louder, each one hiccupping through my body, choking me so that I couldn't call out. He saw me and started up the hill. 'Thank God, oh thank God. I've looked everywhere for you.' He wrapped me in his coat and carried me down the hill. I clung to him and cried all the way home.

My mother was at the hall door. She ran to meet us. 'Thanks be to God you're all right.' She rubbed my hair where the feathers had been and hurried us up the stairs, saying, 'Where were you? I was demented not

38

knowing where you were.' She talked all the time while she made me hot milk, repeating her fears and worries for my safety.

'Tell her what happened to John-Joe, Mammy,' my brother said. 'Tell her, Mammy.'

I closed my eyes, I didn't want to hear. I squeezed them shut. Maybe she'd think I was asleep, take the mug from my hand and carry me to bed.

'Poor little John-Joe,' she said. 'But wasn't he lucky all the same.'

I opened my eyes. 'What happened to him?' I asked.

'He was knocked down after dinner, but someone was praying for him. His head was split open – fourteen stitches he needed – though thanks be to God he's going to be all right.'

The mug slipped from my fingers on to the hearth, smashing, the milk trickling across the oilcloth. The cat lapped it.

'Why the bloody hell can't you be more careful! I never knew such a child, always smashing and breaking something.'

Everything was all right. I was home. I was safe. Everything was normal. 'I'm tired,' I said. 'I want to go to bed.' Everything was all right. I went to bed.

A Good Bint

She came to me with a reference carried in a flat, 50-Players' tin – her place of safe-keeping for important and precious papers. From head to ankles she was draped in black, only her face, hands and bare feet visible. She handed me the single sheet of paper and I read the recommendation.

'Fatima is a good bint. She is honest, hard-working and has a Garrison pass guaranteeing her free from infectious disease.' The reference was signed by her previous employer, an army wife about to leave Egypt. Her one eye smiled as I looked up from the recommendation and made my decision. 'Yes,' I said. 'All right. Come on Monday.' Neither working conditions nor pay were discussed. Bints washed and ironed clothes, scrubbed floors, lifted and beat carpets, swept and swilled steps and verandahs and whatever else their employers required for five shillings a day.

'Why do they call them bints?' I asked my husband when he came home from work.

'I'm not really sure. I suppose it's an Arabic term for women. That's what the British call them, always have. You know the song?'

I said no, I didn't know the song, so he sang a verse: 'Sayida bint I'd like to meet your charming mother. I'd wash her in carbolic right away and then my little Lena, she'd be ten times bloody cleaner. You're my little Gypo bint, you're quois keterre.'

He grinned. 'Derogatory in a good-natured sort of way – like calling the men, any native, a wog.'

On Monday morning I watched from the verandah for Fatima's arrival, experiencing a mixture of feelings. Excitement at having for the first time in my life someone to work for me. A little fear and apprehension that the servant was foreign and black, and a great curiosity as to how we would get along.

Just before seven o'clock when the sun was already hot I saw the group of bints come into the compound, each one in her flowing black so that the group resembled a flock of assorted birds. Some were sleek as blackbirds while others resembled fat untidy waddling crows and rooks. Across the hot golden sand they came on splayed bare feet making as much noise as a

40

garden of quarrelling starlings, loud-voiced, gesticulating. In the centre of the compound they stopped and stood still for a moment before dispersing and walking to their different houses. Calling to each other as they went, 'Fatima, Aisha' and strings of Arabic words which I supposed were farewells, messages, or maybe having the last word.

Up the steps and onto the verandah Fatima came, her head held high, her walk regal. I greeted her, talking English loudly, almost shouting. I introduced my two small daughters. The oldest was unresponsive, but the youngest smiled and ran to Fatima, who beamed and holding out her arms lifted her up and said, 'Ah, that girl, that girl.' Not many weeks later a photograph of 'that girl' was added to her flat 50-Players' tin.

In the kitchen she unwound her wrap, folded it neatly and placed it on a box on the verandah. She wore a dark blue cotton frock sprigged with small white flowers. The material reminded me of the pinnies worn by elderly women. The dress hung from her shoulders to her ankles – no breasts, hips or belly showing to alter its shapeless line. On her short, tightly curled hair, she tied a kerchief garishly embroidered and beaded at the edges then organised the lighting of the four-burner primus stove on which the water for the laundry was heated.

'Well,' asked my husband that evening. 'How did it go?'

'She's fantastic. The house is gleaming! She cleared all the ironing, never stopped except for a cup of tea.'

'That's good. Will you keep her?'

'I think so,' I said. Not adding that I found it disconcerting to have a black woman in the house. That her smell was strange. That somehow I wasn't able to identify with her as another woman. She seemed more like an exotic pet trained to perform. She would take getting used to, but I liked her – her good-humoured face, the silent grace with which she moved about. I liked her and I would be kind to her, treat her well – and feed her. That above all. She needed flesh to cover bones barely concealed beneath her grey-black dry skin. I'd feed her until she looked like a sleek black cat.

'What about her English?' my husband enquired.

'She has enough for what I want. After all, we won't be having conversations.'

'No,' said my husband, 'I suppose not.'

The next day I began the fattening-up process – making beef sandwiches for Fatima's break. 'For you,' I said, handing her the plate.

'Meat?' she asked.

41

'Yes, beef. Lovely roast beef.'

She shook her head and smiled apologetically. 'No meat, Missus. Fatima no eat meat in English house.'

'But why? It's good for you. It'll make you fat.' To illustrate my point I pinched up the flesh on my arm.

'Egyptians fat,' Fatima said. 'Egyptians eat, eat. Egyptians very fat.'

'But you're Egyptian,' I said.

'No!' There was no mistaking her indignation. 'Me Somali.'

She handed me back the plate of sandwiches. I knew that as a Mohammedan she wouldn't eat pork but beef – was that also forbidden as it was for Jews unless it had been slaughtered in a certain way? I asked her this but she wasn't able to explain. I had to wait until later to find out that my plan to feed up Fatima was doomed. All the meats in my house were forbidden, and as she had made clear her abhorrence of fat it wouldn't do to stuff her with cake and sweet things.

I began to think of her in a different light. Like me she had a religion which she obeyed. She was vain about her body and proud of her nationality. She wasn't a pet who would obey my every command.

As the weeks passed I found myself looking forward to her arrival each morning. It was nice to have another woman about the house and I was no longer aware of her smell being different. I wanted to know more about her. How old she was. Was she married? How had she come to live in Egypt? And by degrees I did have answers to most of my questions.

I never did find out her age. Perhaps I didn't make the question clear, but having discovered one of her vanities I suspected another was responsible for her not revealing her age. For she wasn't young and wasn't married, though she had had a 'sweetheart', her word for the Lascar seaman who had sailed to Liverpool and never returned. 'Did he die?' I asked. She didn't know. I was intrigued about her romance. And having already learned that she had left Somaliland to go to India as the servant of a British family, it occurred to me that he might have returned and couldn't trace her. I suggested other reasons as to why they never met again but either my shouted questions and attempts at mime failed, or Fatima had revealed as much as she wanted to.

The closer we became, as is often the case with friends, I found that certain things about her irritated me. Her taking of the children's part, for example, and their great affection for her. The former I saw as an attempt to usurp my authority and the latter made me jealous. Sometimes I would act the part of mistress and Fatima retaliated by showing her contempt without uttering a word. Turning her back on me and stalking from the room with head held high.

In time I came to realise that her defence of the children was well-justified. If they broke ornaments or painted the walls with lipstick and nail-varnish it was as she said, 'No baby's fault, missus. Your fault, missus. No leave where babies can touch.' I also came to understand that their affection for her was well deserved. She was never cross or bad-humoured and had a gaiety as child-like as their own.

One day I decided to make known to her that I was Irish, not English, so beckoning her into the living room where two pictures of Dublin were hanging I began. 'Fatima,' I said, pointing to a view of O'Connell Street. 'Ireland, Dublin.' She nodded. 'Ireland, where I come from. *Dublin*.'

'Dublin,' she repeated.

'Where I live,' I said, my voice rising as it always did when I didn't think I was getting through.

She smiled obligingly and moved in closer to the picture, her good eye peering intently. Then turned and shrugged her head. So I moved her to the other picture – a view of Trinity College – and began again. 'Ireland, Dublin.' I was now shouting. The children came to see why and I sent them out to play. I was determined to make Fatima understand what I wanted her to know. 'Where I come from,' I said, laying a finger on Trinity's imposing façade. 'Where my mammy lives.'

I saw the dawning of understanding wreathe her face with smiles and she said with obvious delight, 'Your mammy's beautiful bungalow. Ah, Dublin. Beautiful bungalow,' and her finger joined mine at the entrance to Trinity.

'Well,' I said, and was about to try to put her right when I remembered all the years she had lived with the Raj. So I left her believing that Trinity was my mammy's beautiful bungalow. And dined out on the story for many a night until once when I was relating it I remembered that Fatima could make herself understood in English and French *and* could speak fluent Urdu and Arabic while I needed to shout and mime in the only language I possessed. I never told the story to amuse again.

She cleaned my house and helped to rear my children. I loved and hated her by turns depending on my humour. She smuggled for me – eggs and onions and anything else unobtainable in the NAAFI when the Egyptians placed an embargo on certain goods coming into the Garrison. Arriving in the morning she would do a twirl and a shower of golden-skinned onions cascaded to the floor from the parts about her where she had secreted them. Eggs she carried in a nest of cloth on top of her head covered by the black wrap.

Her delight at having outwitted the authorities in her village reminded me of my mother when she had done something similarly audacious.

There were many times when Fatima reminded me of my mother. In her strict adherence to the fast during Ramadan – more demanding than the fasting imposed on Catholics during Lent – but followed with the same unquestioning faith. During the forty days when between dawn and dusk she could neither eat nor drink I would try to make her work easier, but with no success. And sometimes as I watched her emaciated body lift and beat the carpets and knew the torment of thirst even more than hunger that she must be suffering I would think – as often I did about my own faith – supposing it isn't true, any of it? Supposing at the end there is nothing . . . And then she might smile and her face had about it as my mother's had the serenity of people who have a simple unquestioning faith. And I felt the poorer for my doubts.

She loved my daughters. But I knew that had I had a son, he would have been worshipped. Boys, she used to tell me, were good. Very good to their mammys when they were old. To their mammys and daddys and to sisters who never married. And I remembered that she shared the home of her married brother. 'Boys in England good to their mammys?' she asked.

'Some,' I said. Then, seeing the look of uncomprehension on her face, I lied and told her yes, boys were always good to their mammys and daddys. And remembered how it was the highest accolade paid to a son that he was good to his mother – and all the disappointed mothers there were. But perhaps in Fatima's culture western ways had not caught up.

A summer passed, spent swimming in the buoyant waters of the Bitter Lakes and lazing on French Beach beneath shady umbrellas, waited on by Egyptian men. And I thought of how not one Arab man, woman or child was allowed to use the beach. And I also thought of other appalling inequalities. The water supplied to the Garrison purified to such an extent that tablets had to be added to remove the taste of the purification process. Meanwhile, the Egyptians collected theirs in old gerry cans from the Sweet Water Canal, where the carcasses of dogs floated and on its banks people defecated and dipping their hand in the water, cleaned themselves. The Canal, of which it was said that if an English soldier fell in, he was hospitalised and injected against all known diseases. And I heard the strident voices of English army wives call, 'Boy! Come here,' to men old enough to be their fathers or grandfathers. And patiently they came, smiling.

And then I thought of Fatima walking five miles a day to and from my house to clean and scrub, wash and iron and beat carpets – and all for five shillings a day. Man's inhumanity to man, I thought. And resolved that in future I would keep the house tidier, not allow the children to pester her, make her life easier. But it never crossed my mind to do the one thing that would have had an immediate effect on her life – raising her wages. And as is the way with so many good intentions after a while they were forgotten and the burden of the house became hers again.

When I told her I was expecting another baby she almost hugged me, but not quite – perhaps another hangover from her days with the Raj. And then she informed me that she would have all the women in her village pray that I would have a son for 'her master'. Rosaries and novenas would also be offered up once the news reached Dublin. There the prayers would be prefaced or ended with the acceptance of God's will, whatever He sent. As I'm sure they would have also been begun or ended in the village.

God and Allah chose not to send a son for Fatima's master. I wondered how she would react when I brought home my new daughter. However, I didn't have to wait that long. The day after the birth when I was resting with no prospect of interruption except afternoon tea, Fatima came sailing down the ward, her black drape flowing behind her, accompanied by several other woman in the uniforms of cooks and orderlies.

My first thought was a selfish one. As a soldier's wife I was subject to military discipline. I'd get into trouble. The hospital staff would think I had encouraged her. Then I thought of her – how much she had risked by coming. How much her companions, employees of the hospital, risked by bringing her in through some back entrance, for no Arab was allowed across the hospital threshold without having the most intimate and humiliating tests performed on them. Fatima risked losing her Garrison pass and her accomplices their jobs, yet here they all were beaming at the new baby and congratulating me. What more could they have done for a boy, I wondered.

She helped me rear the baby – a cross baby who slept little and cried often. 'No leave baby cry, missus,' Fatima would admonish, picking up the child and nursing her, soothing her and singing to her until she slept. What would I do without her, I often wondered. How could I possibly manage on my own without my friend, my story-teller, my children's adored Fatima. The healer of my husband's horrible foot infection, which had defied the dermatologist's treatment.

On seeing the blistered weeping feet for the first time, Fatima declared, 'I know how to make better. All policemen in Ishmalia have same. Tomorrow I make better.' And the next day she came with herbs which she ground and beat into a paste, pungent-smelling and the colour of curry powder. Then, like Mary Magdalene kneeling at her master's feet, she washed and dried them and annointed them with her ointment and bound them in strips of torn sheet. For three days she repeated the

45

treatment and on the fourth when the bandages were removed his feet were whole and healthy.

Sometimes she and I cried together. Once because of a story she told me – one that I now know is common to many cultures but at the time it was my first hearing of it. The story told of a young wife jealous of her mother-in-law and constantly demanding proof that her husband loved her more than his mother, finally demanding that he must kill her and bring the heart to her. Running with it to his wife the young man stumbled and fell and the heart asked, 'Are you hurt, my son? Are you hurt?'

We sniffed and dabbed at our eyes but our crying was short-lived – after all, it was no matter how moving only a story. The other story, however, was true. Fatima had witnessed it on her way to work and arrived distraught. A young English soldier guarding an army lorry bringing supplies from Port Said and driven by an Egyptian was surrounded as the lorry entered Fatima's village. The soldier was overpowered and dragged from the vehicle.

'They beat him and kicked him,' she cried. 'The poor boy. His poor mammy in England. They beat him and kicked him and the women threw sand in his eyes. Poor boy, poor dead boy. His poor mammy.' We consoled each other as best we could but the memory of the murdered soldier lingered for a long time.

Inevitably the time came when we were posted back to England. When I told Fatima that we would be leaving in a few weeks she said, 'You go to Liverpool, missus. I come with you to Liverpool, missus.' I thought of her Lascar seaman as I said, 'No, not Liverpool. Another place far away from there.' She shrugged and smiled philosophically. And I wished with all my heart that it had been possible to take her with me.

She reared a duck for our going-away present: a bony bird that tasted of its muddy pond and was impossible to eat. I lied about its succulence. She was pleased.

I never found out what age she was, nor her second name. Nor what became of her when she placed her new reference in her flat 50-Players' tin and I watched her walk away. Watched until the proud, black-robed, bare-footed figure pushing my discarded pram piled high with the rubbish of our leaving walked on and out of the Garrison and out of my life.

Cassie's Wedding

Always in September the fair came to town. From hundreds of years ago it had been coming, people said, but maybe this year because of the War it might not. Everything was different because of the War. So in the second week of September when the horse-drawn painted waggons were seen making their way to the fair field everyone was delighted. The women because they could buy good flannel for the shirts their husbands and sons wore to work; soft thick flannel that soaked up the sweat that poured from them in the Tin Works. The men were pleased, for the fair put in an hour for them after the pub. Riding on the merry-go-round they felt like kids. There were coconuts to win and shooting galleries where you could imagine you were giving Fritz a run for his money and still go home for supper.

Tessie O'Brien and her friend Cassie were also delighted to know the fair was definitely coming to town. They wanted to have their fortunes told. The day it was set up Tessie said to Cassie, 'We'll go and maybe she'll tell you if Tom wants to marry you.'

'We're not supposed to – it's a sin for Catholics to go to fortune tellers, but if we went when it was dark no one would see and be able to clech to Mam!'

'We'll go tonight. I'll meet you at the top of the road.'

'All right then,' said Cassie.

From the end of the road they could hear the music, see the naphtha flares lighting the booths and stalls. And as they got nearer the young men and women riding two to a Hobby Horse cwytched into each other as round and round they went to the strains of the *Gold and Silver Waltz*. And Cassie and Tessie, exhilarated by the sounds, sights and smells of the fair caught hands and did a few gliding steps as they walked along the dusty path to the fortune-teller's tent.

There was a poster outside which read: *Madam Helena famous fortune-teller. All the way from Poland. A gypsy princess from the city of Cracow. Admission sixpence.*

'From up the Rhondda, Mam says she is and puts on the foreign twang, she does,' Tessie whispered to Cassie as they waited their turn to have their fortunes told. Cassie went first, reminding herself she didn't believe in fortune-tellers but at the same time remembering tales she had heard of things foretold by gypsies that did come true. A man at the tent's entrance took Cassie's sixpence and said, 'Go on in, love.'

The tent was draped in swathes of red and purple velvet. Madam Helena sat at a small table also covered in velvet which looked more black than purple in the dim light. Its skirt was spangled with silver cut-out stars. On the table was a pack of cards and beneath a square of velvet what Cassie guessed was the fortune-teller's crystal ball.

'Sit down, child,' said the gypsy, beckoning Cassie to a chair in front of the table. 'You have a lucky face,' she said then held out her hand and asked for silver.

'But I paid the man outside. Sixpence I gave him,' Cassie protested.

The woman shrugged. 'For that you get not much, only a glance in the crystal ball. For more there's the cards. I make a marriage bed. I read your palm.' She took the cover from the crystal ball. 'I see,' she said, bending and gazing into it, 'a dark man. He's with you, in a big building – a chapel, a church. You know a dark man?'

Spellbound, Cassie looked into the gypsy's eyes and nodded.

'This dark man has a great regard for you. In the church or the chapel I see a wedding. Then I see the dark man in a uniform.'

'Oh, no, you're wrong there. He's not a soldier or a sailor,' said Cassie with the utmost certainty.

Again the fortune-teller shrugged and began to cover the ball.

'Is that all?' asked Cassie.

'You want to spend more money?'

Cassie shook her head. 'I haven't any more,' she said.

'Then that's all,' said the gypsy.

'Well, what did she tell you?' asked Tessie when Cassie came out from the tent.

'About a dark man and a wedding,' Cassie replied.

Tessie shrieked with laughter. 'That's you and Tom – he's going to ask you! Don't forget I'm going to be your bridesmaid.'

'It mightn't be him. She said the man was wearing a uniform – a soldier or a sailor – that's not Tom.'

'You wouldn't want to take everything she says seriously. Make up the half of it, they do. Most of the men in the country are in uniform – playing it safe she was,' Tessie said, then noticing the look of disappointment on

Cassie's face quickly added 'But about you and Tom getting married, that's bound to be the truth.'

'I hope so,' said Cassie then asked, 'What did she tell you?' She linked her arm in Tessie's and as they walked home Tessie told her.

It was to be a quiet wedding, Mam said, none of that old nonsense. And Mam's word was law so Cassie's pleading for the filmy wedding dress and fine veil with a wreath of flowers that looked like privet blossom had been in vain. 'Spend your father's hard-earned money on something you'll never put on your back again? Well, indeed I won't.'

'But Mam, it's only ten pounds,' Cassie had argued, remembering the bags of sovereigns her father earned trimming.

'Ten pounds!' exclaimed Mam. 'Do you know how long it takes him to earn ten pounds slaving like a black in the hold of a ship and the coal dust choking him? You'll have something serviceable. A costume – a velveteen costume, maybe a brown one. Brown would be very becoming.'

So Maggie Murphy made the brown costume and a matching hat with artificial roses on its brim. It was the first thing Cassie saw when she opened her eyes on her wedding day. It hung on the wardrobe door and the hat irreverently draped the head of Our Lady's statue that had stood for as long as Cassie could remember on the press.

Old nonsense, she thought, nestling in the feather bed. What Mam meant was that I couldn't have the dress and veil nor a cab to the church but her and Dada and all their cronies, all the big fat men and women, will drink gallons of stout and bottles of whiskey. No sprag on the drink. A big Irish wedding and them in Wales this long time – they still have to have that. And someone else will have the lovely dress, the dress in Abel Jones' window that I looked at every day for a week and imagined myself wearing.

She stretched in the unaccustomed luxury of the double bed from which her sisters had been banished the night before. From now on it was hers, and tonight she would share it with Tom. It was a lovely bed, only she wished it wasn't next door to Mam and Dada's room. And thinking about Tom she forgot all about the bridal dress.

She smiled, remembering how the fortune-teller's words had come true. How at Christmas he had asked her to marry him, and she had said yes, but that they had better wait until after her birthday in April for she didn't think Mam would agree until she was eighteen. And they'd say nothing for the time being – keep it a lovely secret. Now the secret was out and after nine o'clock Mass this morning she'd be Mrs Tom O'Hara. 'Mrs Tom O'Hara', she repeated aloud and smiled, recalling the first time she had seen him. Well, not the first time, for she and Tom had gone to the same school, but the first time she had noticed him. . .

All the girls were talking about Tom O'Hara, the Yank home on holidays. He was a great swell, they said and had gold, real gold in his teeth. So after Mass she had hung about the church porch pretending great interest in everyone except him but taking in everything about him, and she had to admit he wasn't bad-looking. And the clothes on him – enough stuff in one leg of his trousers to make two skirts. She went to the dance that night in the church hall and he asked her to dance and he never went back to America. Even though in the steel mills in Springfield, Indiana, he was earning two hundred dollars a month, rolling. Into the Tin Works in town he went instead and they started courting. She hugged herself as she thought about him and how from now on every night when he wasn't working they'd be here together in the double bed. And because he was a Rollerman he would never have to go to the War even if they brought in conscription. Rollermen were special – in a 'reserved occupation' they called it. She loved him so much and Mam and Dada liked him even though Dada had said the first night he came to call, 'There's a bloody packman at the door wanting something.' And afterwards excused himself by saying, 'Well, how was I to know he was Dinny O'Hara's boy in that get-up?'

From downstairs Cassie's mother called, 'Do you know what hour of the day it is? Are you up yet?'

'I'm up, Mam. I'm up,' Cassie shouted back and swung her legs over the side of the bed, made stamping sounds with her bare feet on the oilcloth-covered floor then got back into bed, settled herself against the pillows and continued with her thoughts. . . recalling with amusement her mother's question when she told her that she and Tom wanted to get married. 'What's your hurry, Miss?' she had asked, with that searching expression in her eyes.

'What do you mean, Mam?' she had answered, although she knew full well what her mother meant and had said to herself, 'Fat chance of anything like *that* happening to me, God forbidding all harm. If it wasn't for the tumps on the beach, it's little I'd have known about courting with Mam pushing open the parlour door every five minutes when me and Tom were on our own.'

She turned on her side and looked at her reflection in the big mahogany looking glass on the chest of drawers. Dark red hair curled over her broad forehead and fell in ringlets to her shoulders. She wound a curl round her fingers, liking the texture of the hair but hating its colour. 'Copper knob, ginger nut!' she heard again the taunts of the children when she was in school, but Tom loved the colour of her hair and pretended to warm his hands on it.

She studied her profile, hating her long high-bridged nose as much as she loathed her hair. She liked her pale skin and green eyes and was glad she didn't have freckles and gingery eyelashes like her sister Mary. 'If it wasn't for my nose and the colour of my hair I'd do,' she said aloud. Then the sound of footsteps on the stairs made her leap from the bed just as her mother pushed open the door and came into the room.

'I might have known it,' she said. 'I've never known such a girl in all my life. But you're going to have to change your tune – you'll have a man to look after, now. Your days of lolling about are over.' She put a jug of water on the washstand and began to make the bed. While her hands smoothed the sheets, shook the bolster and plumped the pillows, she scolded, 'It's airing the bed should have been this hour or more.' Then eyeing Cassie's round belly pushing against her flannel nightgown, she said, 'And make sure you wear your stays otherwise you'll look like a sack tied up in the middle.'

Cassie's clothes lay in the heap she had stepped out of the night before. Her mother bent and picked them up and scolded again. 'You're a terrible child so you are.' Then quickly and shyly she kissed the side of Cassie's face before going from the room.

Cassie took the costume from the wardrobe door, laid it on the bed and returned to stand before the long mirrored door. Taking off her nightdress she looked at herself in the mirror and thought, Mam's right, I am fat. With her two hands she pushed in the folds of her belly, turned sideways and admired her new shape, then turning to face the glass again she stuck out her tongue, made a face at herself and let go of her belly.

I'd better wash myself, she thought and poured warm water from the jug her mother had brought into the basin. Thoughts of Tom swirled in her mind like the water swirling over the basin's cracked glaze of pink roses: thoughts she shouldn't be thinking, sinful thoughts about tonight and the bed. A flush as pink as the roses on the washstand set suffused her cheeks.

In the soap dish lay a cake of buttermilk soap. The soap was new. Letters on it spelled *Buttermilk*. It was the colour of Cassie's skin when she wasn't blushing. She washed and soaped herself, enjoying the unaccustomed warmth of the water. Sliding her hands over her body, smelling the scent of the soap, making bubbles between her thumb and forefinger and standing naked, blowing them round the room, she felt as light and airy as a bubble herself, happy and excited that this was her wedding day. The bubbles sailed round the room, some as high as the

51

ceiling, and she watched them with delight. And was sorry to see them vanish as one by one they landed or touched any surface.

She dried herself and put on her new underwear. The skirt of her petticoat was edged with a flounce of lace and her camisole threaded with ribbons. Then she got into the brown velveteen costume and for a moment remembered with regret the dress that had been the talk of the town while it was in Abel Jones's window. She ran a comb carelessly through her hair, twisted it into a coil which she secured with a couple of hairpins, picked her hat from the Virgin's head and ran down the stairs calling, 'Mam, Mam, I'm ready!'

The kitchen was full of the smell of boiling ham and her mother's friends come to see the bride and drink strong tea laced with whiskey. They blessed her and kissed her and said she looked lovely and was a fine girl, and a lucky girl to be getting a man like Tom O'Hara for her husband. A man that everyone in town knew the seed, breed and generation of. A man with a good job that would keep him from the War.

'He'll be tired this morning after coming off nights,' one of the women said. And another, taking advantage of Cassie's mother being out of the room, nudged the first woman and said, 'Not half as tired as he'll be tomorrow, Ellen.' Cassie was almost married and from now on she would be included in the women's talk. It was all right for her to laugh and acknowledge the reference to her and Tom's first night. So she laughed and at the same time silently thanked God for Tom not having to go to the War. And she thought of all her friends who had gone, some in reserved occupations, too, but they had volunteered. And the telegrams coming and the prayers and Masses that were said for their souls, and the mothers and wives and sweethearts left to pray and cry for them.

'Mother of God Almighty what way have you done your hair and you going out to be married in a minute!' Mary with the gingery eyelashes had come into the kitchen and with her good-natured criticism banished Cassie's sad thoughts. 'Sit down on that chair and let me fix it.' She obeyed and sat while Mary brushed and combed her hair and patted and pinned each glorious tress into place, then carefully placed the hat on them and pushed home the two pearl-headed hatpins. 'Now take a look at yourself,' she said, handing Cassie a mirror. All the women sighed and said she was gorgeous.

Soon afterwards Tessie arrived and it was time for them to go. In the early morning sunshine they walked through the narrow streets, past the Tin Works with the noise of its clanging, clattering rolls, over the bridge and past the paper shop with placards announcing the success of the spring offensive in France. Not until the spire of the church came in view did Cassie realise the seriousness of what was about to happen. Soon she would be a married woman forever and ever. Suddenly she felt very nervous. Supposing she didn't like being a married woman forever and ever? Or worse still, supposing Tom didn't. Supposing he didn't really love her. Supposing he wasn't at the church! She longed for Mam. Longed to be at home. She kept walking and then she was entering the church and Tom was there with his best man, getting to his feet, looking over his shoulder, smiling at her. Her heart was filled with joy, her fears fled and on feet that felt as if they were winged she walked up the aisle.

It had already been decided that after the service Tom and Cassie with Tessie and the best man would go to Swansea, eat there, have their photographs taken and come home early for the hooley in the evening which would go on until the early hours of the morning. They went to Swansea by train. Tom said, 'First the photographs and after that we'll eat, all right?'

Everyone agreed.

On the way to the photographer they stopped to look in the shop windows and Cassie thought of all the nice things she would buy when she and Tom had a home of their own. And how she would get up early when he was on mornings or coming off nights and cook his breakfast. And always cut him a nice box and never ever leave her clothes in a heap on the floor. Then Tom said they had better get a move on and find the photographer's.

The photographer's was up a flight of stairs over a shop. In the studio there were paper mâché pillars and a balcony with artificial flowers festooned over it. The photographer arranged Cassie and Tom in front of this with her sitting on a chair and Tom standing, his hand resting on her shoulder. 'Smile,' said the man. 'That's good – hold it!' then his head disappeared beneath the black cloth covering the camera. Another photograph was taken of the group.

In the café they had sandwiches and cream cakes. The waitress brought the pastries on a two-tiered silver-plated cakestand. Cassie didn't know which one to choose and Tom told her to have as many as she liked. Imagine, she kept thinking as she ate cream puffs, I'm a married woman. She felt like standing up and shouting it out so that everyone would know but of course she didn't want people to think she was daft. Instead, she kept raising the hand with her wedding ring on it to fiddle with the pins on her hat. The sun shining in through the window made the gold of her ring gleam and her hair shine like the burnished copper kettle on the window sill.

They ate and drank and ordered more sandwiches and cakes and laughed and talked a lot. And Cassie knew that this was the happiest day of her life and that she would always remember it. And that all her days with Tom would be happy ones. Then from the street came the sound of newsboys shouting, 'Stop press!' Men and women went rushing out to buy a paper and Tom and his best man went, too. Cassie lolled against her chair waiting for them to return. Tessie watched the goings-on through the window, while Cassie's thoughts returned to the morning's events. She thought about the women in the kitchen and the jokes they had cracked. She was one of them now, a married woman. She saw Tom's eyes, the way they had looked when he placed the ring on her finger. It was all so wonderful, the day and being married and loving Tom the way she did. And then to her mind came another thing, the sight of the photographer going beneath his black cloth. The cloth reminded her of something. . .

It was a minute before it came to her, then as clearly as the copper kettle Cassie saw the gypsy fortune-teller, heard her saying, 'A dark man in uniform, a soldier or a sailor,' and she remembered the black cloth covering up the crystal ball. For a moment it seemed to Cassie as if her heart had stopped, so cold did she feel and so dark had everything become. From far far away she heard voices that came nearer; one she recognised as Tom's asking if she was all right and she saw that he was back and the other people who had run out of the café were back and all had newspapers. And gradually the cold dark feeling left her and in her head she heard another voice saying, 'You wouldn't want to take everything she says seriously. Make up half of it, they do.' Tessie was eating an eclair, her chin and lips covered with chocolate and cream. She smiled at Cassie and Cassie smiled at her and reached for another cake while Tom and his best man sat down at the table and read the latest news about the War.

'Talk to him – he may be able to hear you'

Sophie was afraid she was losing Michael. Michael, she believed, no longer loved her. He had grown tired of her because she was too old for him. And so every morning since these suspicions had taken root in her mind, she rose before him, having willed herself to do so the night before by repeating silently over and over again the time at which she wished to waken.

After rising she went to the bathroom where she stood looking into the mirror: a haggard face with puffy eyes looked back at her. There were lines around her mouth, one beneath her chin, others fanning out from the corners of her eyes and her skin was slack and blotchy. Mistaking the mask of fear for her true likeness, despair would overwhelm her and tears trickle down her cheeks as she thought how terrible it was to grow old. If only she had money for plastic surgery she would endure as many nips and tucks as were needed to make her young and beautiful again. But there was no money, only a miracle could transform her and long ago Sophie had stopped believing in God and therefore miracles.

Tears continued to fall from her eyes as she regarded her face and she told herself that she would sooner die than lose Michael. She would kill herself. And then she would shake her head and smile sadly and talk to herself, saying, 'Killing yourself needs a madness or courage you don't possess. You have to keep on fighting for him, do the best you can to keep him loving you.'

Already her spirits were lifting and after a warm shower, a cold pack for her eyes and with a becoming bathrobe wrapped around herself, she returned to the looking glass: with pots and tubes, brushes and blushers she painted on a face for Michael when he woke.

One morning after such a ritual when she and Michael were having breakfast together, a letter came for Sophie addressed in a hand she didn't recognise and with a London postmark.

'Anything interesting?' asked Michael, sitting to the table in his old soiled dressing gown, his face stubbled and his eyes bleary.

'Alex is dying,' said Sophie and beneath the blusher her face had

55

paled. 'He's in a hospice. I can't believe it. It's from a nun – he's asking to see me. She says there's not much time. What'll I do?'

'Go and see the poor sod. It's the least you can do after walking out on him.'

It sounded like an accusation. Had he forgotten the part he had played in her 'walking out', Sophie thought, and wanted to remind him but she said nothing. Nowadays she never provoked Michael, although there was a time when she would have, but not now. Not even when he drank too much, squandered what little money they earned occasionally selling one of their pictures – not even when he stayed away for hours, sometimes all night. Once she would have screamed and cursed, thrown and smashed things, hurled accusations at him. And he would fight back – sometimes laughing at her outbursts, goading her to further outrage, but always their rows finished in bed, their lovemaking fired by the passion of the quarrel. Their differences were resolved by the time they lay exhausted and at peace in each other's arms, her head upon his breast, his hand lazily stroking her back. But not any more could she risk a scene. Not any more rely on how it would end. Michael didn't desire her as he once did. He thought of her as old – she didn't want him to think her a shrew as well.

'How did the nun know where to send the letter?' asked Michael, wiping butter from his chin.

'What? What did you say?' enquired Sophie, who had been far away in her tormented thoughts.

'The nun – how did she know where you lived?'

'Alex must have told her.'

'You wrote to him?'

'Yes, a long time ago. You were away, I was lonely. I remembered it was near his birthday and I sent a note. The address must have been on it.'

'Poor old Alex,' said Michael. 'I liked him. He was a nice bloke. I'm sorry he's dying although I suppose he must be a good age.'

'Sixty,' said Sophie, and remembered Alex at forty when she had married him, how ancient he had seemed to her twenty years. Now she was forty and the gap didn't seem so great. Not nearly as divisive as the ten years between her and Michael.

Again Michael's voice interrupted her thoughts. 'Will you go over?'

'I'd be afraid. I've never seen anyone dying. And in any case, we've no money.'

'Use the Visa.'

'You lost it.'

'I only let on – trying to stop us spending.'

Take the Visa! How flawhool he is all of a sudden. He wants to get rid of

56

me. He has someone else. He's hoping I won't come back. I don't want to go to London, I don't want to go anywhere. I don't want to throw him into the arms of her, whoever she is, waiting out there.'

Michael left the room and came back with the credit card. 'Here,' he said, offering it to Sophie. 'Take it and go. He's still your husband. You were married to him for ten years. The least you can do is see him before he dies.'

'I'm only still his wife because I had the misfortune to be born a Catholic and like a good one came home to get married.'

'It never showed.'

'What didn't?'

'The Catholic bit – you were never a Child of Mary exactly.'

'Being a Protestant you wouldn't understand.' The exchange was good-humoured and for the first time since getting up Sophie smiled. It was a long time since Michael had teased her about being a lapsed Catholic who couldn't completely lapse.

'Seriously though,' he continued, 'you ought to go. If you don't, later on you'll crucify yourself with guilt.'

Sophie sighed and said she supposed he was right. Her carefully applied make-up was smudged from where she had held her face in her hands while she contemplated her decision. A blonde streak of hair fell over her forehead. Michael came to her and tenderly smoothed it back. She leant against him. 'I love you,' she said and hoped he would bend and kiss her, say as once he would have done, 'Let's go back to bed.' Instead he put a hand on each of her shoulders and squeezed them, saying, 'Come on now. You have to go. Get dressed and I'll ring up about flights.'

'But,' said Sophie, still reluctant to leave him, 'if he dies I'll have to stay for the funeral – it could cost a fortune.'

'Ah,' said Michael, letting go her shoulders and beginning to walk towards the door. 'What's money at a time like this?'

Sophie arrived at the hospice in the early afternoon. A nun showed her to the cubicle where Alex lay propped up on pillows. It was ten years since she had last seen him. He was sick and she had expected his appearance to be altered, but nothing could have prepared her for such a drastic change. She found him repellent and was unwilling to approach the bed. Had the nun not been in the room she would have kept her distance.

'He has cancer,' the nun explained. 'A quick one, thanks be to God. He isn't in any pain.'

'He wanted to see me,' said Sophie, moving closer to the bed. 'He's sleeping, is he?'

'He's in a coma. He deteriorated rapidly.'

'Will he waken up, recognise me? Talk to me?'

The nun shook her head and smiled. 'Please God he won't. They seldom do, And even the conscious ones rarely make the farewell speeches you hear about. Dying isn't easy – it doesn't often allow for farewells. Sit by him. The staff will come in from time to time to see to his comfort. There's a bell,' she indicated it. 'If you want anything or are worried that there's a change in his condition don't hesitate to ring, though I think he won't go before night or early morning.'

The nun left the little room. Sophie remained sitting by the bed growing more accustomed and less afraid of the tortured face struggling in great loud gasps to breathe. A young girl with a sympathetic smile brought her tea and sandwiches. Later, two nurses came with a trolley on which there were basins and dressings. Sophie moved away from the bed while they drew curtains round it – pretty curtains, she noticed, with yellow sprigs of blossom on them. She heard the sound of water pouring into a basin, the rustle of disturbed sheets and smelled the smell of urine – and all the time there was the sound of Alex's breathing.

A little later, after the nurses had left, the nun came back. 'You should talk to him,' she said. 'No one really knows about comas – he may be able to hear you. And if there's a Special Intention you have, ask him to intercede for you. Soon, you see, he'll be in God's presence. Would you like me to have more tea sent in?' She smiled cheerfully and left the room.

Nuns, Sophie thought – what made them like that? Able to talk about bells and tea and death and God's presence all in the one breath. The awful and the ordinary – never separating one from the other. Not only here in the hospice, where she supposed being with the dying could make a person callous, but in school they had been the same. She remembered beautiful summer days sitting on the convent lawn making daisy chains, playing and laughing, a blackbird singing, the heat of the sun on her back. And then a nun would come to join them and comment on the lovely day, but sooner or later she would turn the conversation to God's goodness in giving all the beautiful things on earth and would talk of His great love for everyone – everyone who deserved and earned it. Earned it must be – for only then when we died could we be sure of being with Him for ever and ever. And then for Sophie the day was spoiled. The sun didn't shine so brightly nor the daisies seem so wondrous. She saw the visions of Hell painted by the nuns daily in the religious instruction class and the bodies of friends and relatives her mother took her to see laid out on their beds or in their coffins.

She came to dislike nuns and when she left school, stopped going to

Mass and stopped praying, except in moments of fear or despair, when she slipped into the habit of childhood. Yet when it came to marrying Alex she couldn't face the Register Office wedding he suggested. Unlike Michael he didn't point out the incongruity of her – a non-practising Catholic – insisting on a church wedding. He was a kind, understanding man.

She forced herself to sit by his bed and to talk to him as the nun had suggested. 'It's me,' she said. 'It's me, Sophie. I'm sorry you're sick.' There was only the sound of her voice and Alex's breathing. No hospital noises – no indication that there were other patients nearby or visitors, nuns, kitchens, telephones – an unnatural silence which emphasised the loudness of her voice, the banality of her words.

Poor Alex, she thought, I wish it was true for your sake. You deserve the Heaven I was taught about. She studied his face, the mouth which had never learnt to kiss a woman expertly now sucked into a toothless purse struggling to inhale each breath and she looked at his fingers which never knew how to stroke her flesh, transparently pale laced in one another. She felt such sorrow for him, and wished for Life Everlasting for his sake. He hadn't had much of a life. He'd been used, exploited, and more cruelly by her than anyone else. She longed to believe again in God so that she could go down on her knees and pray for Alex. Pray for him to be received into Heaven. Pray for him to have all the reward he was denied on earth . . .

At that moment the day, which had been overcast, suddenly brightened. A shaft of sunlight pierced the window pane and the room was flooded with light. It was a sign, Sophie felt, but instead of continuing to think of Alex and interpret the sign in his favour her mind became filled with thoughts of Michael. Thoughts of what the nun had said about the dying hearing your spoken pleas and interceding for you in Heaven. She would ask Alex, tell him of her love for Michael. How without him she would rather die. Beg him to speak for her – ask him for a miracle.

She almost spoke the words, then recoiled at the thought of using the man on whom she had inflicted so much pain to salve her own. The sun went behind a cloud. The room darkened and Sophie told herself she had become hysterical. It was the effect of this place, of the nun. Here she was, allowing herself after so many years to become involved in the claptrap of miracles and prayers and Life Everlasting. Intercession, supplication, litanies, relics – she had finished with all that a long time ago. There was no miraculous power to help *her* – she had no prayers to say for anyone. She wanted out of this place, away from her dying husband, from nuns and all the claptrap. She would in a minute ring the bell, summons the nun, tell her she had a place to catch. She almost touched the bell. . . her fingers were about to touch it when Alex's breathing changed tempo. She leant over him and began to talk, naturally this time. Unselfconsciously as she might have to a sick child. 'It's all right, I'm here. I won't go. I'll stay until you fall asleep. Don't be afraid, I'm here. I won't leave you.'

Perhaps he heard her. He seemed a little easier. She stopped talking and watched him. Thoughts of Michael again filled her mind. Questions and fears. Where was he at this minute? Who was he with? What would become of her if he left her? Was she being punished for what she had done to Alex? Was there a price one had to pay for everything? Again she spoke to the dying man. 'I'm so sorry. I never meant to hurt you, but I did. I know now what you must have suffered. I couldn't help it – and I never pretended to be in love with you. I told you. You said it didn't matter. You said . . .' then, remembering his dear kind face when he had said he loved her enough for the two of them she cried, letting the tears run unchecked down her face.

'It was your fault – you introduced us. "A nice chap, an Irishman", you said. A painter who couldn't sell his work, you explained. He had come to work in the agency: would I mind having him in for a drink? I could show him my paintings, you said. And of course I didn't mind, half out of my head as I was with boredom. With your kindness and gentleness and constant concern for my welfare. Fussing over me like my mother. I'd have agreed to have anyone in for a drink. You were so trusting, so naive. He was so handsome, so gorgeous. Another man would have seen the danger. I could no more help what happened than I could breathing. Oh Alex,' she laid her hands on the clasped ones, 'I love him so much. The way you loved me, I suppose. I'm suffering the way you must have suffered. It hurts like a real pain. Oh God, please forgive me. I shouldn't talk about real pain – not here, not to you, Alex, who have had real pain. I won't talk any more. I'll only sit here and hold your hands and you go to sleep.'

It got dark. The smiling-faced young girl who had brought Sophie tea now brought dinner. The nun came again and said Alex wouldn't last the night and for Sophie to ring the bell if there was any change. 'We like to say the prayers for the dying.'

'He isn't a Catholic,' Sophie said.

'I know that. We talked about it many times. He had a great admiration for Catholics and made me promise that at the end we would say the prayers. Forgive me – I'm just a curious old woman – you're his wife, aren't you?'

'Yes,' replied Sophie, trying to sound nonchalant, determined not to be made to feel guilty by the nun's question and presence, but all the same flushing red.

'I thought so. He spoke to me about you: he forgave you, and when he asked me to send for you he left a message in case he wasn't well enough by the time you got here to tell you himself.'

'Oh,' said Sophie, but couldn't bring herself to ask what it was that Alex had told the nun.

'He wanted you to know that you gave him the happiest years of his life and that he didn't think badly of you for what happened. He forgave you and I know he'd want you to forgive yourself.

'Poor Alex,' said Sophie. 'Poor kind Alex.' She wanted the nun to go. She wanted no more talk about forgiveness. She had never suffered a moment's genuine guilt for having left him – how could she, when she loved Michael so much? But it wasn't the sort of thing you could admit in the presence of the dying man and the nun, who fervently believed that by relaying Alex's message she had lifted a burden from her. The goodness, the innocence of her – that wonderful ability which earlier and all her life she had scorned in nuns, to deal with death and tea and ringing bells – the awful and the ordinary. That was life and they didn't shy away from it.

Moving towards the window, she turned her back on the nun and stood pretending to look out. 'I'm very grateful,' she said, keeping her face averted. 'Thank you for telling me and for looking after him.'

'It's what we're here for. And now I'll leave you again. You know where everything is?'

'Yes,' replied Sophie. 'Yes, thank you.'

After the nun had gone she went back to sit by the bed and think and wonder about Michael. Remembering her flight from the comfortable stultifying home Alex had provided for her. Preparing a meal for him which she had left laid out with a note beside it telling him she wasn't coming back. She was returning to Dublin: he wasn't to try to get in touch with her. And then the lies. . . How sorry she was. She would never forget him. A part of her would always love him. There wasn't anyone else – he must believe that. Something inside her had changed – she had to go back to Ireland. She had wronged him terribly by marrying him. She was going home. She would find work. He mustn't worry about her.

She had propped the note against a glass and gone to Waterloo, where she caught a train to Tooting Broadway and the flat Michael shared with a group of design and fashion students. It was a big flat – a warren of little bedrooms, a huge communal living room and a kitchen where at all hours of the day and night someone was making mugs of instant coffee or eating takeaway meals, while in the living room dresses were being tried on tailor's dummies, swathes of materials were draped over chairs and settees and pins and snips of thread obscured the carpet's pattern.

She slept in a single bed in Michael's arms under a window draped with a swatch of brilliant green dress-net; the traffic roared by and drunken Irishmen and women quarrelled and cursed in the street below then went on their way. In the morning Michael brought her fresh rolls and a peach, which he told her he had bought from a barrow pitched at the corner next to the baker's. They had their breakfast then he kissed her and left for his last day in Alex's office.

'How was he?' she asked when he returned in the evening. 'Did he say anything?'

'Nothing out of the ordinary. I was so screwed up with guilt it's a wonder I didn't give the game away. I wish I hadn't gone in.'

'You had to collect what was coming to you,' she said dismissively. Then reminded him that Tooting was a long way from Euston. If they wanted to catch the boat train he wasn't to get too relaxed on the bed and fall asleep. Going to him and hugging him she said, 'Just imagine – we'll be home tomorrow! We'll be back in Dublin, isn't that fantastic?'

'Yes,' said Michael.

'Well, look a bit more cheerful for God's sake.'

He sighed. 'I can't help thinking of that poor old bugger. Are you sure he never suspected about us?'

'Not for a minute,' she said confidently.

Now, sitting beside the dying man she wasn't certain of anything any more. Maybe he *had* suspected. Maybe while she had lain with Michael in Tooting he had lain in his bed that had been theirs and cried and cursed himself for the fool that he was to bring Michael into their lives. Well, she thought now, you've had the last laugh. I'm being dumped just as you were. Right at this very minute Michael may be moving out and moving in somewhere else. And what am I going to do then? How can I bear it? I'll meet him with *her*. Dublin's so small you couldn't avoid that. I'll be walking down a street, turning a corner, going into a café for a cup of coffee – and they'll be there. Holding hands, smiling at each other. Oh dear God how will I bear it.

Alex's breathing altered; a longer pause separated one gasping breath from another. Sophie became petrified with fear. Death was in the room. Fearful and as superstitious as when she was a child she looked round the room. She saw nothing except the curtain billowing at the window, which was opened at the top. The nun – she must call the nun, ring the bell. Have the prayers for the dying. *Dying*. Now – it was happening now! His face had altered in minutes, had grown longer, the flesh fallen from his nose, its bridge raised. She thought of pictures of the dying Christ. No longer afraid, she bent close and kissed his cheek. Water was seeping from his eyes. She thought it was tears. *He knew she was there.* She spoke his name. His eyelids twitched. *He could hear.* The nun was right . . . Soon he would be in God's presence. Unbidden the thought came to her mind and with it the nun's words . . . 'If there's a Special Intention you want . . .' Such an Intention that it was. Such a Special Intention. Again she found herself believing in the possibility of Life Everlasting of Heaven, prayers and Intentions granted. And again was tempted to ask the dying man to intercede for her. And again resisted and put Michael from her mind.

She put a hand beneath and above her husband's clasped ones. 'Don't cry, Alex,' she said. 'Go to sleep. It's all right.' Then she remembered something. Alex had liked her to stroke his face last thing at night. She had seldom obliged but now, letting go of his hands, she did so and whispered, 'Hush now, go to sleep. Everything's going to be all right. I'm here.' He opened his eyes and she thought he recognised her and that he smiled but later she couldn't be sure. Then he sighed as though he was weary, blew out a little breath and died.

Only then did she remember not having rung for the nun. Once again she had deprived him of something precious – even now in the last moments of his life she had cheated him. 'I'm sorry,' she said, bending to kiss his cheek. It was still warm and his hair when she brushed it with her lips smelled as it always had. She sat by him for a while longer before ringing the bell, wondering where was the Alex she had known. All that was him – his kindness, intelligence, his awkwardness and shyness, all the things that made him different from anyone else – his personality, his soul – where were they? 'Somewhere, they are somewhere,' an inner voice told her. And she believed it. So fervently did she now believe it that she knelt by the bed and for the first time in years, prayed. For Alex, for his soul, and for herself: that peace of mind would be granted to her, and courage to go on living no matter what the future might hold. When her prayers were finished she rang the bell.

The nun came and more prayers were said. When they were done and Sophie made a move to leave, the nun asked if she had a place to stay, telling her it was very late and she could find a bed for her in the hospice for the night. That Sophie didn't want and so she lied about a hotel booking but asked if a taxi could be called and enquired when the funeral would be.

'The arrangements are all made. Mr Chern before being admitted saw to them himself. It will be a cremation at Golders Green, but this being London it may not be for at least a week.'

'I couldn't stay that long, not for a week. Maybe I can come back.'

'Maybe so,' said the nun. 'I'll arrange for the taxi... Five to ten minutes,' she said when she returned from making the phone call. 'Come into the sitting room and wait. Would you like a cup of tea or some coffee?'

Sophie thanked her but refused. They sat each side of a small round table and Sophie noticed for the first time how old the nun was, and thought how tired she must be.

'I'm glad you could come. It's a sad lonely thing for those who die alone. You'll have given him great comfort in his last hours.'

'I hope so,' said Sophie.

'That's the taxi I hear.' They walked towards the door. 'I'll remember you in my prayers.'

'I need someone's prayers.' Sophie shook the nun's hand and thanked her. 'You're wonderful, you and the staff and the hospice – you're all wonderful.'

'Go now, it's very late and the taxi is waiting. God bless you, child, and say a prayer for me sometimes.'

The taxi driver knew of an hotel where she would get a booking. He often took relatives there late at night from the hospice. It was a small, family-run business, warm and comfortable and though she thought that she would lie awake all night she fell asleep almost at once.

When she woke in the morning, at first she didn't know where she was. Then she remembered and thought about Alex, how terrified she had been at the prospect of seeing him dying and how, in the end, it wasn't like that. Were all deaths thus, she wondered. She was sorry he had chosen to be cremated. Alex, who loved the country, grass and flowers and birds, should have been buried in a small country churchyard in a grave that was tended and to which people brought flowers. But who would have visited, and who would have laid flowers over him?

She wished she could go to the funeral, but where could she stay for a week? How could she afford it? How could she bear to wander round London, not knowing what lay in store for her in Dublin? She thought about that, about the possibility of Michael having moved out of the flat before she returned, and found she was able to consider it more calmly than she would have believed possible. It amazed her, this serenity, this ability to consider life without Michael. Sadly, with regret, but without despair.

There were things she must do. She must ring Aer-Lingus and find out about a flight then telephone Michael. It was too early yet. She made tea with the kettle, cups and tea bags provided, feeling rested and relaxed. She thought again about Alex and decided she would have flowers sent to the crematorium. A florist could contact the hospice for the date of the funeral and have them delivered.

There wasn't a flight until late evening. She disliked flying at night and booked one for the next day: one more night on the Visa wouldn't make much difference. The hotel switchboard rang to ask if she wanted breakfast. She told them no, but rebooked the room.

She rang Michael, and counted the rings. She would hang up after ten. She counted and in her mind saw the deserted flat. A note, maybe, telling her some lie. He thought of himself as kind . . . He would try to let her down gently. On the tenth ring she heard his voice, blurred. He had just got up, she guessed.

'Oh God,' he said. 'I've been waiting and waiting for your call. How is he?'

'He died last night.'

'I'm sorry. Poor old Alex. The Lord have mercy on him. When is he being buried?' She told him about the cremation and the delay with burials in London. 'Will you hang on then? Do you want me to come over?'

'No,' she said. 'It could be a week, ten days even. I'm coming back.'

'When?'

'Tomorrow.' She explained about the night-flight and told him the time of the other one.

'I'll be there,' he said. 'And Sophie, I love you. I'll see you tomorrow.'

'He loves me,' she said to the empty room. 'He says he loves me and I believe him. My mind isn't in turmoil any more.' She bathed and did her face and the face that looked out of the mirror was her face, her forty year old face and she found it acceptable. 'I'm me, I'm forty. I'm at peace with myself. I'm glad to be alive. I've gone through a period of madness, of depression but I'm all right again. I'm glad to be alive. Michael says he loves me. I believe him. I want him to. I want to stay with him for the rest of my life but now I feel within me that should he *not* mean what he said, I won't go under. I'll cope. I'll start again. I'll make a new life for myself. Life, that's it. Maybe having seen how quickly it is snatched away I'm appreciating being alive. Or maybe it's more that that: maybe I've been given the gift of faith again. Please God, let it be that. Let it be faith and let me keep it forever and ever. Let it be the miracle I didn't believe in.'

She ordered the flowers for Alex, had lunch in a small Italian restaurant and went for a walk in the park. The hours passed and soon it was time to eat again, watch a little television, sleep and then get up and go to Heathrow. On the flight home she looked at the clouds and remembered how as a child she had believed that God and Heaven were up there with the souls of the faithful departed. Now she didn't know where they were – but that didn't matter. They were there somewhere.

Michael was in the arrivals lounge and he embraced her. Knowing him as she did, she could tell he was ill at ease. They said little in the taxi on the way home but something ailed him deeply. He was bursting to tell her – and for a moment her newfound serenity deserted her. She looked out through the window and watched the approaching city and breathed deeply until she felt calm again.

'Listen,' he said when they were in the flat. 'Before you do anything I have something to tell you. Don't take your coat off, don't do anything. Just listen. What I have to tell you is fading from my mind like when you've dreamed something and bit by bit it vanishes. We'll have a drink.'

He poured two whiskies. She gulped half of hers. 'Well?' she asked, her hand gripping the glass to stop its trembling.

'I nearly didn't meet you.'

'Oh,' was all she could say.

'I nearly walked out the night you went. I thought you'd done a runner. Invented the whole thing about Alex. Got someone to write that letter and post it from London.'

'Why would I do that? What made you think such a thing?'

He shook his head. 'I don't know. I mean, I don't know why I thought it. Well, in a way I do. You'd been peculiar for months. Distant-like, as if you were going off me. Fed up with our life. Trying to make the break and not knowing how. Things had changed between us. You were always doing youself up – I was sure you had someone else. So when the letter came, I thought – this is it: she's fixed it, she's doing a runner. And that's when I decided to go. I was making it easy for the both of us. If you came back for anything, to collect something, I wouldn't be here and if you didn't – well, I wouldn't know.'

'And what were you going to do with everything – the pictures, your clothes, all the things you've accumulated over the years?'

'Not worth a tosser. Anyway, I was in such a state I didn't think that far ahead. I didn't care what became of them or me.'

'Oh Michael, and I thought you didn't love me, that you felt I was too old. We could have lost each other and never known the truth.'

'I know,' he said. 'We could have been destroyed through suspicion and not opening our hearts to each other. But let me tell you what happened. And don't laugh or say I was drunk. I know you don't believe in these things, but as true as I'm sitting here this really happened. I was packing my shaving things and a few odds and ends and then I lit a fag and sat down, right there where you're sitting now. And then it happened. At first

66

I thought I must have dropped off and was dreaming, but the match was still in my hand, there was hardly a puff out of the cigarette, no ash, nothing. I *hadn't* dropped off. My mind was all crazy. I even thought someone had left the front door open and he'd come up the stairs – that maybe the flat door was open.'

'Who, Michael, who? For God's sake tell me who came.'

'Alex. Alex came. He was here in the flat as large as life, not a bother on him. I knew then for sure you'd made it up about the letter, because Alex was in the whole of his health. You'd done a runner and by a strange coincidence he was visiting Dublin.'

'What time was that?' asked Sophie, and her voice was no more than a whisper.

'Late. Midnight, or round about then.'

'And you're sure it was the first night, the day I'd gone over?'

'Of course it was. Let me finish. It all happened in a flash – him there, me thinking this and that: the door was open, the flat was open, you'd left and he'd come. And then all of a sudden something came over me. I went cold. I knew none of the doors had been left open, knew I hadn't dropped off. *Alex was appearing to me.* I was quaking, drenched in a cold horrible sweat and my heart going like the clappers. And then he spoke, his voice the same as always, quiet and reasonable. "Be kind to Sophie," he said. "She loves you. Never doubt that, Michael. Treasure her all her days." And he vanished. He just disappeared. The cigarette had burnt down and was roasting my finger. Look at the blister.'

He held out his hand and Sophie bent to look and she was thinking, I didn't ask him. I never voiced the words but all that time, that night when he was dying, they were in my mind. All my energy was concentrated on them. But how did Alex know? He was dying, in a coma. Did he pick them out of my mind? Was his love for me that powerful that he manifested himself to Michael?

'And the queerest thing about it,' Michael continued, 'was that suddenly I was no longer frightened. I felt so calm, so peaceful – as if something very special, very beautiful, had happened to me. And I knew that all the things I had imagined about you, your being distant, running off with someone else, they weren't true, only part of some crazy imaginings.'

He came and sat beside her on the settee. 'Wasn't it the queer happening? Like one of your Catholic miracles, only you don't believe in them.'

'I'm not so sure of that any more,' she said, and her voice was muffled for she was crying, 'but that Alex came to you I have no doubt. Love is such a powerful thing. I have seen so much love in the last days – such love and caring, such goodness. And Alex was all those things. He loved us both. He wanted us to be happy.'

'You must be starving – will I get you something?'

'I have everything. I have you. I want to go to bed and lie in your arms and sleep. While she got ready for bed she prayed for Alex, thanked him and thanked God.

Michael held her close as she drifted off and when she was almost gone she heard him speak. 'When did you say the funeral was?'

'In a week or ten days.'

'Ring the hospice and find out exactly. I wouldn't let him go without being there. We owe him that.'

'We do,' agreed Sophie. 'We owe him that.' And as sleep overcame her again she thought that one day – maybe tomorrow, maybe after the funeral – she would tell Michael about Alex's last hours. Tell him about her temptation to ask Alex to intercede as the nun had suggested. And how she couldn't, couldn't bring herself to utter the words. And how, after all, they weren't necessary. For where there was love such as Alex had had for her, everything was possible . . .

Before the Revolution

The baby's crying woke Hetty. Six-thirty am, the bedside clock said. She pulled the bedcovers over her head to drown out the cries. She couldn't get up – she was too tired. She was always tired. For years and years she had been tired. And more so than usual this morning because last night Peter had come home late from another function in the Mess. She had waited up for him – he liked her to wait up. She liked waiting up. Peter drunk was pleasant – talkative, even though some of it was nonsense and repetitive. Still, it was talk, and talk was something they seldom did nowadays. On the nights when Peter was at home he liked to read and there were amendments to make to his textbooks but on the nights when he came home pleasantly drunk they talked and laughed, were silly with each other. It was lovely – like it had been before they married.

She could still hear the baby's cries. He was standing up in the cot – she knew because he was rattling the bars. Like a prisoner, she thought. If she could steel her heart for a few minutes more maybe Peter would get up and see to him. The bliss that would be . . . to stretch out in the double bed, hear the crying receding as Peter carried the baby downstairs. The luxury then of closing her eyes and sleeping for another half hour.

Accidentally on purpose she nudged Peter. He grunted, turned over and reached for her. Without opening his eyes his mouth searched for hers. The baby screamed with hunger, anger, discomfort and frustration. Peter's hold on Hetty tightened. He liked to make love in the mornings. He liked to make love anywhere, any time. So did she – except when a child was screaming.

It was a forlorn hope, her extra half hour's sleep. Why, she asked herself as she pushed Peter away and got out of bed, do I torment the baby when I *know* Peter never gets up and never will? She put on a dressing gown and went to her small son.

'Hush, darling. Hush, love. Mummy's sorry.' His hands were held up to her. She lifted, kissed and hugged him, inhaling his early-morning soaking wet piddly smell. 'My poor little love,' she said as she carried him downstairs, where she continued talking as she took off his napkin and nightgown. 'A soaking wet piddly pup, that's what you are, a soaking wet

69

piddly pup.' She bent her head and kissed his belly. He gurgled with delight. There were tears clinging to his long dark eyelashes. Carrying him to the sink she bathed his bottom, dried it, kissed it and said before putting on a napkin and securing him in the high chair, 'I could eat you.'

Then she put on the kettle and milk for the baby's rusks. The dishes from Peter's late-night supper were in the sink, congealed egg and bacon fat clinging to them. They accused her of being a slut. A few minutes was all it would have taken to wash them the night before. But she excused herself that she had been too tired and Peter insistent on her going to bed. She smiled, thinking of his appetites.

She drank strong coffee and fed the baby his rusks in between sips. After the second cup of coffee and a cigarette she felt a surge of energy. From experience she knew it would be sufficient to get the other children up, make breakfast and take them to school. Do a bit of shopping, get back, make the beds, do the dishes and then maybe eat something. Skip the beds perhaps, for Gisella was calling for her at nine-thirty. Today being Thursday they were going to buy the pork.

She liked going with Gisella to buy the pork once a month. The meat was from pigs reared by a regiment in the garrison – fresh pork, more delicious than the NAAFI's frozen stuff and cheaper than the German butchers. There was a small thrill about the expedition. The walk was out of the ordinary, it being a once a month only occurrence and the gamble as to whether or not you would get a choice cut. A fillet, loin chops, even half a shoulder and you felt you had competed and won a prize. And besides, because it was a long walk, herself and Gisella had lengthy conversations as they pushed their prams.

The baby shoved his dish away. Before putting it into the sink she spooned out the remains of the pap and ate it, thinking as she did so that she must remember to tell Gisella about her nightmare. She had forgotten it until this minute and the recollection made her shiver. But she put it from her mind and measured out the children's porridge, giving it a quick stir. She took the cereal bowls from the cupboard, stirred the porridge again, laid out the dishes. And so, doing two and sometimes three things at the one time, she set the table, arranged Peter's sausage and bacon on the grill, talked to the baby and kept an eye of the porridge.

From upstairs the morning noises were beginning. Voices called, 'Mummy, Mummy!' Long ago she had learned when it was safe to ignore such cries. Then another voice called, one not to be ignored: 'My shirt – where is it? I can't find my clean shirt.'

She went to the bottom of the stairs and called back, 'On a hanger – in the wardrobe.' But even as she spoke her foot was on the first step.

'It's not. I can't see it!'

She went and found it where she had said it was – where his clean shirts always were. 'You're worse than the children,' she said affectionately to Peter, handing him the shirt.

He grinned back. 'What sort of a day is it?'

Hetty pulled back the curtains. 'Not bad – it hasn't snowed yet.' Peter, engrossed in his dressing, said nothing. She went into her daughters' room where the small girls were struggling to pull up their strumpfhosen. She adjusted the coloured woollen tights, turning their toes to where they were supposed to go, smoothing them up the girls' calves and then telling them they could manage the rest. In the other room her toddler was still sleeping. She closed the door quietly hoping he would continue to sleep a little longer – at least until she had cooked Peter's breakfast.

He came to the table immaculate in his uniform. Her face was unwashed, her hair uncombed and her dressing gown splashed with milk and rusks. No one except herself seemed aware of her sloppiness. She served Peter's breakfast and poured her own tea. 'It will be freezing outside so eat up all your porridge,' she encouraged her daughters, and gave the baby, who was still secured in his high chair, a buttered crust. Then from upstairs came a wail. 'Bring him down,' she told one of her daughters, 'before he gets going, otherwise there'll be no pacifying him.'

He always woke liverish. For five minutes he had to be ignored by everyone except his mother. After being held by her for that long he became human. Holding him in one arm she dished out his porridge and when she felt it was safe to do so, sat him to the table.

'That was very nice,' said Peter, shifting his plate to the side. 'Any more coffee?' Hetty poured him a cup. After drinking it he left with *The Times* under his arm and went upstairs to the lavatory. His going reminded Hetty of the urge in her own bowel which she was suppressing. Suppressed it would have to remain for a while longer. Sometimes it was after lunch before she found the time to go.

She made toast for the children and cleared away the cereal bowls. 'Hurry up, girls,' she exhorted her daughters. 'I have to do your plaits before I get dressed.'

Peter came down from the lavatory as the last tress was being plaited. He put his cap and swagger-stick handy, lit a cigarette and studied the crossword while he waited for his landrover. It arrived. He bent his face for the farewell kisses, told the children to be good, kissed Hetty, pinched her bum and went. They stood at the window watching him go and waving.

In a frantic rush she washed and dressed herself, the baby and the

71

toddler. Then told the girls to hurry, to wrap up well. The baby and the toddler were jammed into their siren suits. She put the pram down the two steps, lifted the baby into it, the toddler onto it and Hetty and her family set off on the walk to school.

Her belly rumbled with hunger. She ignored it. There wasn't time to concern herself with the workings of her stomach, only to get to school, deposit the children and do the shopping. She was exhausted by the time she got back to the house. The beds would have to wait but the dishes she'd have to do – and without taking off her coat. 'Shit,' she said, when her cuff went into the bubbly water and it ran up her arm. It was almost half-past nine and Gisella would be here any minute. She settled for a glass of milk instead of the bacon sandwich and tea that she craved.

Gisella rang the bell. 'OK,' Hetty called and put on a woollen cap and wrapped a thick scarf over it. 'I'm coming!' Her toddler had settled himself with the Lego and was reluctant to leave it. A small battle ensued which Hetty won by picking him up and carrying him screaming his protests through the door. The baby slept on in the pram where she had left him.

The women greeted each other then set off on the three-mile walk to the garrison butcher. Both women had toddlers whose hands were put on the prams' handles and they were told to walk with a promise of a ride later. To have let them ride would have been quicker but the way was uphill and the children hefty. Hetty and Gisella wore flat, fur-lined suede boots and slacks and thick woollen gloves. They were good walkers. They had to be – there was no transport for the wives in the camp. When it snowed they pulled the children on sledges to school and to the shops. In all other weathers they walked and pushed their prams: across the palms of their hands were callouses from pram-pushing.

It was a bright, bitterly cold day and windy. The silver birches were stripped bare of their leaves. The rowan berries were fading and the wild cranberries from which the women would make the sauce for the Christmas turkey had not yet begun to ripen.

'I hope we're in time for a decent joint,' said Gisella.

'I don't mind if it's chops – they'd cook in time for lunch. Peter loves chops.' Hetty yawned as she spoke and thought regretfully of the bacon sandwich she might have had. The milk hadn't given her back her energy.

They were passing the place where their garages were – Bill's and Peter's. For the first time ever she thought of the cars – a Ford Consul and Bill's Citroën – snug inside their shelters, their bellies full of anti-freeze and their bonnets covered with brown army blankets secure and snug, protected from the vicious wind which was tugging at her headscarf.

Stopping the pram while she tucked in the scarf she said, 'Gisella, don't you ever wish you could drive?'

'Sometimes,' admitted Gisella as they set off again.

'Imagine the bliss of bunging in all the kids, towels, rubber rings, sandwiches, feeding bottles, vacuum flasks, everything – the lot – and driving off to the swimming pool.'

'Today!' said Gisella with mock irony.

Hetty laughed. 'But seriously, wouldn't it be marvellous? Nipping the kids to school. No more mountains of shopping to lug home. Going to the doctor – the dentist. Remember last year when you had all your bottom teeth out? It was a freezing day like this and you were petrified of getting a draught in your gums. Imagine all the things we could do, the places we could go and never have to bother the men. Peter hates having to drive at the weekend.'

'So does Bill, but he won't let me drive. I did suggest it once.'

'I did too,' said Hetty. 'Peter said he didn't think it was a good idea. He says the accident rate on the autobahn is very high. I tried explaining that I wasn't thinking of going on the autobahn but it was no use.'

'Bill felt the same way. I suppose they're right. And you don't see many women driving in the camp.'

'Only a few officers' wives,' Hetty said.

They were going uphill now. Bent over the prams and encouraging the toddlers who were grizzling to walk a little bit further. Past the playpark they went, ignoring changed pleas to ride the see-saws or go on the swings. To stop now would spoil their chances of a good cut of pork and worse still, they would not have their husbands' lunches ready in time.

'I meant to ask you if Jane got the job in the NAAFI,' Gisella enquired when there was a lull in the children's pleas and protests.

'She did. She started on Monday.'

'So what happened with Derek? He didn't want her to take it.'

'There were rows when she first applied. He said he'd be a laughing stock in front of the men. I expect she got round him. Anyway, she's working and loving it.'

'She must get good money as a secretary.'

'Marvellous – but what she likes most is not feeling stupid any more. Derek used to make her feel stupid.'

'That's a horrible thing to do. Bill has never done that.'

'No,' said Hetty, 'neither has Peter. Mind you, I like Jane but she does hold forth a bit. I'd never argue with Peter about politics. She does – with any of the men.'

'It's probably because she has more time to read than us – you know, with not having children.'

'I wish I had time to read the papers. I try to make it but somehow it never works out and especially on Sundays with all the children home, a roast dinner to cook and making sure everything is ready for Monday. Peter starts them with breakfast, and again when he comes home from the Mess at lunchtime. He'll spend the afternoon with them. Sometimes he'll call me to listen to something funny.'

'I don't want to read the papers. The Wall and the Bomb – I don't want to read about them.'

'You broke my dream,' said Hetty. 'I had the most horrible nightmare last night. It was about the Bomb. I don't know if it had been dropped or was about to be dropped – you know how dreams are all mixed up. But the balloon had gone up anyway and our men had left for their stations. It was so real. This terrible feeling that the end of the world was coming, that we'd all die. But do you know what the worst thing was? It sounds funny now but it wasn't in the middle of the night. That little Quartermaster was the only man left in the garrison. He was in charge of seeing that all the women and children got back to England, I suppose. He was lecturing us. One minute we were all on the square and the next minute I was in the house and he was telling me what to do. I had to take all the army blankets I could carry, all the first-aid stuff, feeding bottles and dried milk. And I was arguing: "How can I? I have to carry the baby. I can't carry blankets as well." Imagine if something *did* happen, having him in charge. It was so horrible.'

'I thought you only had nightmares about the Bomb in the summer,' said Gisella.

'I do. I hate the summer – the sound of machine guns and shells going all day. I hate the summer and the practice camps. And wakening up at night to hear the tanks rolling past the perimeter. I have a nightmare at least once a week then. I hope last night was a one-off thing.'

'I've heard them all before for real,' said Gisella. 'Maybe I know the difference and that's why I don't have nightmares.'

'I don't know how you survived living through a real war. I'd just die of fright.'

'You don't have any choice,' said Gisella.

'What's so awful is having no say in what happens to you. I'd like to join the CND. At least you'd feel you were doing something.'

'It's not allowed,' said Gisella.

'I know,' said Hetty. 'I don't suppose Peter would agree even if the army did. Any time I try to talk about the Bomb or the Wall he tells me I mustn't worry, that everything will be all right. I suppose being a soldier he's bound to know.'

The toddlers finally rebelled at having to walk. Gisella's little boy let go of the pram handle, lay down on the path and howled, and Hetty's also let go and refused to move. They were hoisted up on to the prams and their mothers continued their journey.

Gisella began to talk again about Jane going to work. 'She'll have money of her own now, that'll be nice.'

'Marvellous,' repeated Hetty. 'I'd give anything to have even a pound that was mine. Peter doesn't keep me short. I know Bill doesn't, either, but you always know that the money is theirs.'

'I know,' agreed Gisella. 'That's what makes me feel guilty if I buy lipsticks, or rubbishy things because I fancy them.'

'I'm exactly the same – so was my mother. I remember how sometimes she'd scrimp and save out of the housekeeping to buy a dress or a blouse; it could be anything that wasn't really needed, but that she wanted for herself or us. She'd hide it for months before bringing it out and if my father noticed, tell him lies. Say he'd seen it before – that it was ages old. He was kind and good-natured but like me and you she didn't feel the money was hers.'

'Wouldn't it be nice if women had wages for having and minding children.'

'Lovely – but who'd pay them?' asked Hetty and they both laughed.

Passing the converted bathhouse which was now a Catholic church, Hetty made the sign of the Cross and thought as she did so how Gisella had once been a Catholic, long ago when she was a child before the war. She had told Hetty about it on one of their walks to the butcher's. 'My family always went to Mass. Then, not long after I made my First Communion, an SS man came every Sunday and stood in the back of the church. It wasn't always the same one, you know, but always there was an SS man. To me it meant nothing but before long my father became frightened. Strange, terrible things were happening in Germany. It was safer he said, not to draw attention to yourself. And so we didn't go to church any more.'

Hetty had asked her if she missed going to church and Gisella had replied that no, she didn't think so. Her mother had been very upset however, crying and arguing with her father but in the end she had to agree that he knew best.

'And what about now? You're a grown woman and the war's finished – do you ever regret it?' Hetty had enquired.

'Sometimes,' Gisella said.

Not long after this conversation, a missionary priest came to the camp. During one of his sermons he told the parishioners that if they knew of a lapsed Catholic, it was their duty to do everything possible to encourage him or her back into the church. Hetty thought of Gisella and the damnation of her soul and told her friend what the priest had said. 'All you'd have to do is go and see him, he would arrange the rest."

For a while Gisella considered the idea, then shook her head. 'Too many complications,' she concluded.

And Hetty said, 'Like what?'

'Like Bill. He wouldn't allow me – not that he's religious – but he wouldn't want me becoming a practising Catholic and wanting the children brought up as Catholics.'

Hetty understood completely. And told Gisella so. 'Yes, I can see what you mean. Peter would go spare if it was me in your shoes.' They never mentioned the subject again but every night Hetty said a prayer for Gisella, asking God to forgive her. Telling Him that it wasn't her friend's fault for not being able to go back to church.

Hetty's little boy kept nodding off to sleep so that she had to keep hold of him with one hand and push the pram with the other. 'I think I'd better lay him down,' she said, stopping the pushing. She arranged him on top of the apron and placed his head under the hood beside the baby, who woke and cried and woke the toddler who cried as well.

They arrived at the butcher's heralded by screaming children. The prams had to be left outside and the little boys brought in. The young soldier wearing white overalls on top of his khaki said, 'Another few minutes and there'd have been nothing but a pig's head.' He picked up a pig's tail and waved it at the little boys, who weren't amused.

'What do you have?' asked Gisella.

'What would you like?' he replied. Hetty thought he fancied Gisella. Once she had said so to her and Gisella had blushed and said of course he didn't. 'I put this under the counter,' he said now, bending and producing a piece of loin. 'How about that – three thick chops apiece, ladies.'

They expressed their gratitude. 'Anything for two nice girls,' replied the butcher as his cleaver chopped through the loin of pork. They paid their money and took their leave.

Now the walk was downhill. They went quickly, not talking so much, conscious of the fact that the lunch must be ready before their husbands came home. They passed the church and Hetty again made the sign of the Cross. This time her thoughts were not on the lapsed Catholicism of Gisella but whether she would have sufficient time to make a certain pudding that Peter liked.

She did, and the pork smelled delicious. It was the first thing Peter commented on when he came home. Then he told her, 'It's bloody freezing out.'

She was happy and contented placing the meal before him. The walk had given her a good appetite and she enjoyed her food. She helped the baby to eat his dinner in between forkfuls of her own and coaxed the toddler to eat some more of his.

'That was gorgeous, darling,' Peter said as he left the table. 'Oh, and by the way, you won't forget to iron my Van Heusen will you? There's a Mess meeting tonight.'

'I'll have it ready,' Hetty promised. 'What do you want – tea or coffee?'

Peter said he would have coffee. Hetty made it and brought it to him. After drinking it he stretched out in a chair and dozed for a few minutes, something he did every day after lunch. It set him up for the afternoon. Hetty put the baby down for his nap and took the toddler on her lap, showing him pictures in his favourite book.

The landrover came. She woke Peter and told him. He rewarded her with a kiss, and one for the little boy. She carried the child to the door, where they waved Peter off. All of a sudden she was overwhelmed with tiredness which she blamed on having eaten too much. She looked at the kitchen clock. It was ten minutes to two: an hour before the children were to be picked up from school. She put down the child and prayed a little prayer that the baby would sleep for at least half an hour – time enough for her to make the beds and wash the dishes. The draining board was piled with them and the pots and pans.

She would make a start on them. Her legs ached and her lips were chapped from the morning's icy wind. She washed and scoured and thoughts went through her mind... what she would make for the children's tea. Now and then she hated Mess night meetings – they could go on until all hours. How long and lonely the evenings were when you were alone. How lovely it would be if her children or Gisella's were old enough to be left on their own. Then she and Gisella could visit each other on the nights the men were out.

A piece of steel wool from the pad with which she was scouring a pan jabbed her finger. She knew from bitter experience that if it became embedded in her finger she could get a nasty infection so she left the washing up, sterilised a sewing needle and probbed for the wire wool. And another thought came into her mind. *How nice it must be to be a man.* She dismissed it for numerous reasons and went back to the washing up.

The Stone

'You should see the stone they have over their father and mother,' Kitty Minogue was in the habit of saying to her family when she came back from the cemetery where she often went on Sunday afternoons. Once, the children used to accompany her on her visits but now they were growing up and refused to go. Her husband Tom had always preferred other ways of spending Sunday afternoons, earlier in their marriage coaxing Kitty to have a lie down with him and when, because of growing children, that was no longer possible, settling for reading the papers and dozing by the fire.

Kitty liked fresh air and a chance to stretch her legs after a morning spent in the kitchen. It was a pleasant walk to the cemetery and peaceful browsing amongst the gravestones, reading the names of people she had once known and murmuring a prayer for the repose of their souls.

In the summer, many graves had flowers growing on them. She admired the flowers and the relations who had thoughtfully planted and attended them. Once, a long time ago, the cemetery had been a private demesne whose owner had brought back from his foreign travels strange and lovely trees. One had thorns five inches long and legend had it that it was a slip from the tree that made the crown for the crucified Jesus. Kitty blessed herself whenever she passed it. Walking on, she marvelled at the exotic blossoms and variegated leaves of the imported trees and in the autumn, scuffled through their fallen foliage. In spring she didn't visit the graveyard. With the trees burgeoning and plants sprouting and birds nesting, the cemetery made her feel uneasy. And in winter, with an east wind of freezing rain graveyards, she believed, were best avoided.

It wasn't until she grew past middle age that Kitty felt a sense of loss and regretted that the graves of her parents and grandparents were unmarked. She knew where her mother and father lay for their grave was close by a wall and near a stone hut in which gardening tools were kept: as long as the wall and shed remained she would have no trouble finding her parents' plot but as to the whereabouts of her grandparents, she had no idea. She grieved to think of their mouldering bones lying with no stone to mark the spot, and then feared that a time might come when the resting place of her parents also became obscure.

In the cemetery she was surrounded by granite and marble crosses, angels, obelisks and the old-fashioned tombstones. Names, ages, dates and prayers were chiselled into the stones making a permanent record of those beneath them and a testament to the love and respect in which they had been held. She longed for such a monument on the grave of her and Tom when their time came. If he went before her she would see to it – but Tom wasn't a believer in wasting money on such things, that she knew for a fact. Money was for the living, was his maxim. But the children, they might take the hint. And so on Sundays after returning from her visit she would say, 'You should see the stone so and so have over their parents.'

Sometimes the children ignored her comment, for often they were engrossed in listening to the wireless but on other occasions one of the girls would say, 'For God's sake, Mother, don't keep on about graveyards and tombstones. You're very morbid, so you are. And in any case you and Daddy have years in front of you, please God.'

She wasn't morbid, she didn't want cheering up. She wanted all of them, or one of them, to say, 'God forbidding all harm if anything happens to either of you you'll have a stone that everyone will stop to admire and say, "Look what that family thought of their parents".'

She wasn't resentful that the promise wasn't forthcoming, Kitty would think as she took off her hat and coat and began preparations for tea. Nor morbid, either. Death had its place and should be prepared for like everything else in life. It was as natural as being born. As natural as her children's comments on gravestones, for what concern of youth were tombstones? By the time the tea was ready her thoughts had turned to other things. Where were the children going tonight? To the pictures or dancing. Would they be late in ? She would leave out sandwiches in case they were.

There were times when Kitty was overwhelmed with guilt as she recalled the promises she and her sister had made when their parents had died. She'd say to herself, 'God knows it wasn't that we didn't love and respect them. We did and we always meant to get the Stone only at first there wasn't enough money. We'd talk about it: "Next year," we'd say. "Definitely next year – for their first anniversary. The grave will have settled by then. It takes a year to settle." ' Only next year, we were engaged to be married and saving up. Then we were married and the children came along. Time passed so quickly. Another year gone, more babies and the money being swallowed up faster than it was earned. Your thoughts were less and less on tombstones. The wants of the dead slipped into the background and the visits to the grave were seldom. That's how it is when you're young. There's always tomorrow.

The years passed. Kitty's children grew to men and women, married and had children of their own. She and Tom grew into old age contented with each other and thankful for their good health. In summer and autumn Kitty still made her afternoon visits to the cemetery, admired the graves and was more determined than ever that a Stone would mark her and Tom's grave. 'If he goes before me,' she'd say to herself, 'I've plenty of policies, but God spare him for many a year yet.'

God answered her prayers and spared Tom for many a year while inflation ate into the insurance policies so that when he did die there was only enough money to pay for funeral expenses. Kitty's children consoled her as she wept because their poor father like so many before him would lie in an unmarked grave. 'It'll be all right,' they said. 'Next year we'll see to it. Next year definitely. In any case, the grave won't have settled until then.' And down the years Kitty heard her own and her sister's voice saying the same things. Next year, she thought, the child with the buck teeth will need treatment. And there's another one said to be musical with his mother's heart set on a piano. Her children's intentions were of the best, as hers and her sister's had been – and like them would come to nothing.

After Tom's death Kitty went oftener to the cemetery and on each occasion vowed that one day she would raise a monument over him. Provide it she would – how, she didn't know but succeed she would – otherwise another generation would lie until the Last Day when God called them from their unmarked graves. She would find a way. God would direct her. Morning and night she prayed for His direction, for a solution to her problem. Then one evening her prayers were answered. She remembered the wash-stand. The wash-stand which she had bought secondhand when she wasn't long married. For years it had stood in her bedroom. For years she had treasured it until the girls grew up and got ideas about what was fashionable. 'Ma,' they said, 'this is 1940. Nobody has wash-stands any more. You should get a bedroom suite – they're gorgeous.' She let them persuade her and bought a bedroom suite made of shiny veneer which she never liked, but the girls loved it and were forever admiring themselves in the dressing table's triple mirrors, saying, 'Weren't we right – aren't you glad you threw out that oul gazebo of a wash-stand?'

Only she hadn't thrown it out. She had such affection for it and believed that if you kept something for seven years you'd find a use for it. So she had made Tom, with her help, carry it down to the shed. It was a terrible weight and Tom said he'd be lucky if he didn't rupture himself. Poor Tom, she thought, little did you know to what use it would be put.

She was impatient to see it again, but it was already growing dark and there wasn't a light in the shed. Her impatience would have to be curbed until morning. In the meantime she could puzzle her brains as to where she'd find a stone cutter, how much she could afford to pay him and what inscription to put on the Stone. Years ago there used to be stone masons in every street. Now she couldn't recall having seen a yard for ages. There'd be firms, she supposed, but they'd be in business in a big way and asking high prices. Somewhere in the city there must be one of the old kind left, a man with a yard, working on his own, one who wouldn't fleece her.

Kitty was happy and excited sitting by the fire thinking of all she had to do the next day. The money – that was the first thing. She had five pounds in the Post Office and with the help of God that would be enough. If it was and she found a stone mason the rest would be plain sailing. Then a disturbing thought occurred to her – supposing the slab of marble on the wash-stand had been damaged when it was moved to the shed. Supposing there was a crack in it! 'Please God, no,' she prayed. 'Don't let it be cracked. Sure You wouldn't do that, not after directing me to it.' All the same she wished morning would come quickly so that her mind might be put to rest.

Before the night was out she had decided that if the marble was sound what she wanted for Tom's tombstone was a Celtic Cross. A lovely Celtic Cross with a nice inscription and room left for her own name to be added when she died. But she wouldn't have their ages on the Stone. There was no need for everyone to know your business and she had always been put out by being the few years older than Tom.

'I won't close me eyes with thinking about tomorrow,' Kitty said to herself as she went to bed. 'I haven't been so excited this long time – I'll be awake all night, but I won't mind for my thoughts will be joyful ones.' Before she knew it she fell asleep and it was morning.

While the kettle was boiling she went out to the shed. The padlock was red with rust. It took a while to wrestle it open then she was in, stumbling over boxes, an unwound garden hose, bumping into bundles of bean poles and pea sticks festooned with spiders' webs. Undaunted she made her way to the back of the shed and there, shrouded with old coats and sacks, stood the wash-stand. Kitty peeled off the layers of sacking and cloth, disturbing families of wood lice, earwigs and myriad insects she couldn't identify to reveal the slab of grey and white mottled marble. She ran a hand over it. There was dirt and dust but otherwise not a blemish on its surface. It would make a beautiful Cross to lie over her and Tom. In her mind's eye she could picture it, see the passing people stop to admire it and say a prayer for those beneath it. And she could hear the voices of her grandchildren and *their* grandchildren saying, 'Look, that's it – that's the family grave.'

After a hasty breakfast Kitty set off to find a stone mason. She walked a long way, down many back streets and little cul-de-sacs where small businesses were, but of stone mason's yards there wasn't one. Tired and footsore she was on the point of giving up her mission at least for today when she turned a corner and there was what she was seeking: on a high double gate was a card which said *Michael Magher Stone Mason*. Through the gates Kitty saw a yard with some slabs of granite propped against a wall; smaller slabs of marble leant there as well and hanging on the wall was the defaced head of an angel and beside it a Holy Water font. On the lefthand side of the yard was a small cottage from whose chimney smoke rose in the still air and next to the cottage was what appeared to be a little work-shed.

Kitty put her hand on the latch of the gate, opened it a little and as it creaked a big brown and black Alsatian came running and barking furiously from the shed. He was by the gate in a flash. Terrified, Kitty pulled it to and quickly moved her hand further up the gate, far enough she hoped to miss the dog's flashing teeth if he leapt at her. Her instinct told her to let go and run – but reason warned her that she hadn't latched the gate. If she let go, the dog could prise it apart with his nose and pounce upon her as she fled. The dog barked and snarled and leapt. Kitty's arm was going numb from holding the gate upright. When she thought she could hold on no longer to her relief she saw a man come from the shed, shout something to the dog and tell it to go to heel.

'What do you want?' asked the man abruptly.

'I saw the sign,' said Kitty, nodding towards it. 'I wanted something made.'

'Come in then,' said the man uninvitingly.

'Does he bite? Does the dog bite?' enquired Kitty, still holding the gate shut.

'Only if I tell him,' replied the man in such a manner that Kitty couldn't tell whether he was being serious or not.

'He's all right,' said the man, 'Come on in.'

Slowly Kitty opened the gate and warily made her way into the yard. The dog lying at the man's feet ignored her.

'What were you wanting made?' asked the man, pushing his cap back to reveal a balding head.

82

'A stone for my husband,' explained Kitty.

'I don't do them any more. I haven't done a tombstone for years. It's the rheumatism – I'm not able for the stones any more.'

Kitty felt her heart drop in her breast and her voice was choked with disappointment as she said, 'But I saw the slabs and the sign – I thought you were still working, still making things.'

'Only small things like plaques, stone flower vases and Holy Water fonts. The back won't let me do the stones. Granite I couldn't handle at all – there's a desperate weight on granite.'

'It wasn't granite I had in mind,' Kitty said eagerly. 'No, not granite. Marble – that's what I was thinking of. Do you see, I have this wash-stand and it has a grand marble top with not a mark of it. As sound as a bell it is. I was wanting a Celtic Cross.'

The mason scratched the exposed part of his head. 'A wash-stand you have. How big is it?'

Kitty spread her arms. 'About that size.'

'Three, maybe four feet?'

'I'd say so. I'd say that's about it, three or four feet.'

'I might be able to manage that,' said the man. 'The finished Cross wouldn't be very big though, we'd lose some of the length in the working.'

'I wouldn't mind that. If you could see your way to making it I wouldn't mind that at all.'

'I'd have to have a look at it first.'

'Whenever you like. It's in the shed at home. I'm there all day so any time you like would be convenient.' Then Kitty looking at the old man remembered the weight of the wash-stand and warned him, 'It's very heavy and I wouldn't be much help to you.'

'There's a young fella who'd push the handcart and give me a help with the slab.'

'May God Bless you, sir.'

'Now I'm not promising anything, ma'am. I'll have to have a look at it first.'

'Of course, I understand that. But with the help of God you'll be able to take it on. If you only knew how much it means to me. Tell me this though, if you can see your way to making the Cross what would you be thinking of charging?'

The stone mason thought for a few minutes then said, 'Two pounds ten. That's thirty shillings for the Stone, a few bob for the young fella and there'll be the expense of erecting it.'

It was for nothing, Kitty thought even with the tip of ten shillings she'd

83

give him for all his trouble and making her dream come true. The mason agreed to come to the house the next day and made a note of Kitty's name and address.

After examining the piece of marble he said he would make the Cross. Kitty could have thrown her arms round him so delighted was she. 'It'll be ready a week Monday and if the weather holds I'll erect it before the following Sunday – how's that?' She couldn't answer him for a minute. She was too full up, afraid that her joy would spill over into tears. When she could trust her voice she thanked him, made tea for him and the boy and insisted on paying half the price in advance.

She was tempted to let the girls know – she was longing to share her happiness. Then she decided against saying anything until the stone was on the grave. She'd ask them to come to the house on Sunday and then suggest a visit to the cememtery. If they reminded her that she usually went alone she'd let on that she didn't feel too good and would be glad of their company. And then the surprise they'd get! How delighted they'd be. They'd laugh afterwards about the wash-stand – at her cleverness in not throwing it out. She counted the hours and minutes until the Monday when she would see the finished Cross and as she went about the house thanked God and talked to Tom. 'Didn't I tell you I'd have a Stone over you? I know you never cared one way or another and no doubt you'll be laughing at me now, thinking, "Kitty and her cemeteries and tomb-stones. . ." but all the same you'll be delighted.'

The finished Cross was a lot smaller than she had imagined and she felt a pang of disappointment. 'Well?' asked the mason. 'What do you think of it?'

Already she was getting used to the size, and everything else about it was what she wanted. 'It's beautiful,' she said. 'May God bless your hands. You've made me a happy woman.' Then she opened her handbag. 'I'll fix up with you now,' she said, counting out what she owed him and adding an extra four half-crowns.

'Ah, not at all,' said the stone mason, 'there's no need for that.' It was the form in any transaction. Kitty said her line, 'You will so,' and the man his: 'You're a terrible woman,' before accepting the tip. After pocketing it he asked which cemetery the Cross was to be erected in.

'Mount Meldon. How did I forget to mention that – the most important thing of all,' said Kitty.

'Not Mount Meldon! That's very unfortunate, ma'am. Mount Meldon's very unfortunate indeed.'

'I know it's a bit out of the way but haven't you the handcart and the young fella?' For an instant Kitty wondered if he was trying her out, wanting extra money, using the distance as an excuse, but a look at his face told her it was more serious than that. He had gone a bad colour and the hand lighting his pipe was trembling so that one after another the matches went out.

'What ails you?' she asked. 'What's wrong with Mount Meldon?'

'They won't let you bring in a Stone.'

'Of course they will,' said Kitty dismissively and wondered if the man was in his dotage. 'Amn't I there every Sunday of my life and isn't the place full of tombstones?'

'Indeed it is, ma'am, but every one of them is made on the premises. The stone masons there have a monopoly and not for God Himself would a monument they didn't make be allowed through the gates.'

'You mean,' said Kitty, as her head began to reel and her legs feel weak, 'you mean Tom's Cross can't go in?'

'Sit down. You don't look well. Here, sit on this oul crate and I'll get you a drink of water.'

She sat down but refused the water. 'I can't believe it,' she said, over and over again. 'To think I let it go this far and never mentioned where Tom is buried. A fool, an old doddering fool, that's what I am.'

'Ah now,' said the man, 'don't be hard on yourself. Wasn't I as much to blame? Wasn't it the first thing I should have asked you?'

'What am I going to do! What in God's name am I going to do?'

Taking pity on her the stone mason told her a lie. 'There's maybe a chance. I know a hearse driver. He might be able to smuggle it in. Then on a dark evening I could go and erect it. It's a small chance but worth a try.'

He saw hope come back to Kitty's eyes and heard her say, 'I wouldn't mind if it took a while, so long as one day it could be got in.'

And he felt very guilty knowing from a previous experience that no hearse driver would risk smuggling a gravestone into the cemetery. He hadn't the heart to tell her the truth straight away and so he said, 'Leave it with me and I'll see what can be done. Come in next week and maybe I'll have better news for you.'

For three weeks he kept her hopes high with more lies. On her first visit she heard that the hearse driver had a bad dose of 'flu. The next week the 'flu had turned to pneumonia – but with God's help he'd be on his feet in no time. He was on his feet by Kitty's third visit, back in work and had tried smuggling in the Cross but was spotted. There was a terrible row, a threat to tell his employer, his union, the relatives of the dead person who were paying for the hearse in which he was doing his smuggling.

Kitty heard him out on the third week and as he came to the end of his story said, 'I don't think we'll ever get it in.'

'Ah, now, I wouldn't say that. Sure, anything could happen – the rules might be changed. Don't lose heart about getting in the Cross. But it won't be easy. No, it won't be easy, that I won't deny.'

The Cross was propped against the wall. She had long forgotten that it ever seemed small. She saw it as a thing of great beauty. Its place was over Tom, not in a strange yard with that oul dog sniffing round and maybe worse. She was not leaving it there. If it could not lie in its rightful place she was taking it home until such time as it could.

'Well, if that's what you want, ma'am,' said the mason looking at her as if she had lost her mind. 'In the house, under the bed. Right you are, then, I'll deliver it.'

'There's only one thing,' said Kitty. 'Would you not bring it till after dark. I wouldn't want the neighbours to think I've lost my mind.'

She cried for a week after the Stone was brought home, for now it seemed as if it would never reach Tom's resting place. Gradually, though, hope returned. When she died the girls would find it. By that time the monopoly in the cemetery would surely have finished and wouldn't they be delighted to have it all ready made for them? There would be only another inscription to be added. Sometimes she was tempted to tell them, to see the surprise on their faces, then she'd think they mightn't take it the right way. They might feel that by having it made herself she was accusing them of not having made their promise. Either that or they'd say she was mad and morbid keeping a tombstone under her bed. She knew she was neither. She had done a wise thing, ensuring a monument for her and Tom and saving her children money. The only thing she regretted was having had the Cross pushed so far under the bed, for there were times when she would have liked to look at it and rub a duster over it. But no matter how hard she tried, she never managed to budge it an inch and as she grew older and more feeble, she gave up the attempts.

Kitty died one night in her sleep. When eventually the time came for clearing out the house her daughters, looking under the bed, saw something they couldn't recognise nor pull out. One of them went to the head of the stairs and called her husband who came and dragged out the Celtic Cross. 'Sacred Heart of Jesus!' exclaimed one of the girls. 'A tombstone under the bed!'

'She must have lost her mind,' said the other sister. 'Who ever heard of such a thing?'

'It's desperate-looking – what'll we do with it?'

'Throw it out.'

'Where? Can you imagine the binmen if they found that in the morning!'

'Leave it to me,' said the husband. 'I'll get it down in the yard and give it a few bangs with the sledgehammer then we can scatter it.'

'That's a good idea,' said his wife. 'Then next year we'll club together and get a decent stone for the grave.'

'Yes,' said the other sister. 'We'll do that next year definitely.'

A Bit of a Consequence

Chrissie and grandmother sat at each side of the range. Her grannie was drawing together a hole in the heel of a white cotton sock.

'This is a stab-all of a needle – all it's doing is reefing the sock further. Have a look in the drawer for a finer one.'

Chrissie went to the drawer and pulled it open, then searched through years of accumulated odds and ends. She pushed aside half-filled reels of thread and several empty ones, round wafer-thin boxes of healing and drawing ointment, corn paste tins, empty matchboxes, assorted buttons, empty Coleman's mustard tins, broken rosary beads, safety pins and hairpins then gave up her search.

'I couldn't find a needle,' she said, returning to her chair.

'This'll have to do, then,' said her grannie and continued with the big thick needle to cobble the hole in the sock. 'It's a mystery to me where needles vanish.'

'I wish,' said Chrissie, 'I had never left school.'

'You were fourteen – you had to.'

'I know that. I'm only saying I wish I hadn't. I loved school and I hate working.'

'You couldn't wait to leave and you're not working.'

'No, I'm not,' Chrissie said and laughed. 'I wish you could have seen McGurk's face. I thought he was going into a fit. He was puce and had spit on his lips. For a minute he gave me a terrible fright. But I don't care. I hated the job.'

'You could have had worse. You could have been scrubbing for someone – working for five shillings a week cleaning a house from top to bottom and having to keep an eye on a crowd of children as well. The money was good, and for habits you don't have to be particular about fit or finish. I'd love to have seen that oul fella's face. Tell me again all about it.'

'I let on to be dead.'

'Why?'

Chrissie laughed and shrugged. 'For a laugh, I suppose. Anything to take my mind off death. I never got used to what it was I was making, the feel of that stuff and the colour. That awful brown – everywhere you looked piles and piles of brown habits with crosses stitched on their fronts and you knew each one was for a corpse. The others didn't mind or maybe they only let on. They were always tricking and joking, holding habits up to them and saying, "How do I look in this, d'ye think it suits me? Would I get a fella in it?" ' Making habits didn't seem to take a feather out of them. Always laughing and singing and tricking they were. . .

'So I thought maybe I'd do the same, joke about the habits and get used to them. I dressed up in one. It was lunchtime and the others had gone into the kitchen to eat their sandwiches and make the tea. Ellie said she'd help me. We took a habit and went down to the lav. I put it on over my clothes and Ellie tied the tapes down the back. It was miles too long, tripping me up. But we fixed that with a piece of string.' She stopped talking for a minute and her grandmother urged her to go on with the story.

'We were laughing and giggling going up the stairs and afraid of our lives we'd meet someone coming down. But we didn't. Ellie opened the door a crack and peeped in. "Quick," she said, "they're still in the kitchen. Quick, get up on the cutting table. No, wait! You have to have flowers, there's always flowers near a corpse." And she took the paper ones we had on the May Altar.

'I got up on the table and stretched out. Ellie tucked the habit in round my back and pulled it down over my shoes. "You have to shut your eyes and keep them shut and join your hands," she instructed. "No, not like that, not pointing up. Corpses' fingers are laced in one another." Ellie's terrible bossy. She was getting on my nerves with all her orders: "Beads, you have to have rosary beads. You never see a dead person without beads in their fingers. I'll get mine. Now you're ready. Remember, not a move out of you." Then I got a fit of the giggles like you do in the chapel sometimes. You want to laugh out loud but know you mustn't. I had to keep it in and I nearly wet myself. And then for a minute it was lovely just lying there with the sun shining in through the skylight right down on my face. I was grand and comfortable. I think I could have gone to sleep.'

Her grannie put down the sock she was mending, rose and went to the range and with a ladle tasted the soup that was simmering in a big iron pot. 'I'll give you a cup of that in a minute,' she said, returning to her mending. 'Go on now and tell me what happened next.'

Chrissie felt a great surge of love for her grandmother. She was so kind. Other grannies or mothers would have given out yards about her losing the job in the habit factory. 'Well, what happened was I kept squinting through one eye, only barely open it was so that I could watch the girls coming out of the kitchen. Lizzie was the first out. I told you about Lizzie.

She's old, older than you and very cranky. Always giving out yards to the young wans. She's the wan who told me I was too big not to be wearing a bodice. I don't think she knows about such things as brassières. Anyway, she let out such a scream when she saw me laid out. All the others laughed and Lizzie kept saying," It's no laughing matter! It's a disgrace, that's what it is." I could hear them coming up to the cutting table. "Lord have mercy on her," one of them said, as if I was really dead. And someone else said, "She didn't suffer, she looks beautiful," and they all started laughing again. Lizzie was still giving out. Someone else said, "Look at the flowers – aren't they beautiful?" And another girl said, "There's no Holy Water to bless the corpse. We have to have Holy Water." I guessed what was coming. There was whispering and giggling and I knew someone would go to the kitchen for a cup of water and I'd be "drownded". And then everything went quiet, there wasn't a sound. I was thinking I'd better open my eyes and make a joke of it then I felt a breath on my face. I knew who it was immediately – I could smell the porter on him. He hissed in my ear, "Get up. Take off that habit. Go to the office and get your cards. You're sacked!"

' "Ah, but Mr McGurk, she's only a child. She didn't mean anything, she was only tricking. You can't be so hard on her. She's no mother or father. Give her another chance." It was Lizzie sticking up for me. Lizzie's the only one not afraid of him. Lizzie's like you, not afraid of anyone.

'But it was no use. "Lizzie," he said, "respect must be shown to the dead. No one is too young to learn that. This girl has to be taught a lesson." Then he rang the bell and lunchtime was over. That was all. I got my cards and came home.'

'The oul shite, the bloody oul shite. You were harming no one. God knows the dead wouldn't have minded what you were doing. And it wasn't even in his time you were doing it. "Respect for the dead", indeed. I hope he takes that into consideration when he robs their relatives with the price of his habits, the bloody oul hypocrite. But don't mind him. You'll get another job, please God. And the girls, God bless them, were very decent taking up a collection for you. Here,' said her grannie, 'the sock's done, the other one is there, so put them on and go for the paper. There may be something in it. You're not cut out for the sewing. Your writing's like copperplate and you're a great speller – I'm sure you could get an office job. The nuns would give you a grand reference. We'll have a look in the Situations Vacant. Go on now and the soup'll be ready when you come back.'

Chrissie put on her shoes and socks. The one that had been mended was lumpy at the back so she undid her shoe and pulled it down from the toe and doubled the sock beneath her foot.

'Now it's inches shorter than the other one,' said her grannie. 'Leave it as it was, it'll only work its way up again and sure no one will be paying any attention to you.'

But someone might, Chrissie thought, for it was nearly time for the boys to be coming home for their lunch and she might meet *him*. She hoped she would. She didn't want him seeing the big lump on her sock. 'I'll pull the other one down so they'll be even. Look, Gran, they're all right now,' she said when she had finished arranging the good sock.

'I'll buy you a new pair when I get my pension,' said her grandmother. 'Are you going for the paper?'

'In a minute. I'll just tidy my hair, it's a show.'

Chrissie got an old handleless cup, put a spoon of sugar in it and poured water from the kettle that sat on the range, always singing. She stirred until the sugar dissolved. Her grandmother watched as she combed her hair with the solution, pressing waves into it and arranging two kisscurls to fall on to her forehead. 'What are you tidivating yourself for and you only going to the corner for the paper?'

'I like my hair to look nice – does it?'

'You've beautiful hair like your poor mother's, the Lord have mercy on her. Now will you go for the paper or every job in it will be gone.'

'Where's the money?'

'Here,' said her grannie, handing her a penny, 'and here's one for yourself.'

Chrissie took the twopence and quickly kissed her cheek. Her cheeks were lined but felt soft to her lips and about her was the sweet clean lovely smell that no one else in the whole world had except her grannie. 'I'm going,' she said, and again felt a surge of love for her and was sorry for all the times she had thought and said to herself, 'I hate you, I hate you, you're not my mother.' And she made up her mind that never again would she think or say such things.

She ran down the stairs from the two rooms in the big tenement where she and her brother and sister lived with their grandmother. Her mother had died on the birth of her sister when Chrissie was three and her brother two. Six months later her father died. She didn't remember him but sometimes thought she remembered her mother. There was a photograph of her on the mantelpiece. She was very pretty. Once she had overheard a neighbour say to her grannie, 'Chrissie's the fine girl, God bless her, but she'll never be the beauty her mother was.'

Since she was fourteen Chrissie had taken down her mother's

photograph oftener than ever before and studied her face. She was smiling when the picture was taken. Her lips were parted and you could see her teeth: white and even, beautiful teeth like her own. Her face was round with a dimple in one cheek – not like hers, which was long and thin and without dimples. Her mother's eyes were big and blue, her grandmother had told her. 'Blue as a blue bag,' she described them. 'It was the first thing you noticed about her, her lovely blue eyes dancing out of her head.'

Chrissie's eyes were a queer colour, not blue nor green nor grey. A duckety mud colour was how she saw them, and when she gazed into the looking glass they never danced out of her head. But her hair was soft and fine – brown hair with a glint of gold in it like her mother's, her grannie was always telling her. 'Hair you can do anything with. A bit of spit, a twist of your fingers and it's how you want it.' Chrissie was always delighted when her grannie said that about her hair.

The sun was shining when she reached the street but there was a cold wind blowing. Winter was coming, and she wished she had worn a coat instead of her cardigan but her coat was shabby and she didn't want to meet Art while she was wearing it. The first time he had spoken to her was in the summer and she had been wearing a pretty cotton dress. She knew who he was. He palled up with a crowd of boys from the Parade. They all went to Synge Street School. They would all go on to college. He was riding his bike round and round in circles at the entrance to the Parade and as she went to cross, he had to brake suddenly. 'You could have knocked me down. You should mind where you're riding that thing,' she had said, letting on to be angry.

He had grinned and said he was sorry, got off the bike and wheeled it at the edge of the kerb beside her. 'Do you live around here?' he asked. It was on the tip of her tongue to say no, to pretend she lived somewhere else other than the tenement house but then she saw her grannie standing at the hall door and had to tell him the truth.

'I'll see you then,' he said, getting up on the bike and riding off.

'Who was that?' her grannie asked.

'I don't know his name, he hangs round in the Parade.'

'He's a nice-looking young fella. Come on in now, your dinner's ready.'

She saw him around. When he was in a crowd he just called out hello but sometimes he was on his own and they talked. She told him she had left school and was looking for a job. He said she was lucky – *he* had another three years in front of him. And all the time they were talking she was watching his face and thinking how gorgeous he was. His name, he said was Art. 'Is that short for Arthur?' she asked.

'No,' he said. 'Art – that's it. My father's a lover of ancient Irish heroes. I got away lightly – it might have been Finn.'

'What's your other name?'

'Maguire. Art Maguire. Maybe we could go out some time – hiking in the Pine Forest or Bohnabreenagh.'

'I don't think my grannie would let me.'

'Hurry up and get a job, then once you're working you can go anywhere. Haven't you noticed that the minute anyone starts working they can go anywhere they like?'

After thinking about this for a minute Chrissie said, 'I suppose you're right. I know a lot of girls who left school when I did, they're working now and go to dances on a Saturday night. But you don't work so how can you go hiking?'

'Ah, well,' he said, 'I am nearly sixteen and hiking's not the same as dancing. It's supposed to be good for you, all the exercise and fresh air.'

The next time they talked he told her where he lived. She knew the street. Lovely red-bricked houses. Guinness' houses: his father must work in the brewery. She asked him and he said, yes, his father was a cooper. She was impressed – coopers were the top tradesmen in Guinness'.

Once she saw him going into Mass with his mother. She had on a lovely coat and hat and kid gloves. They were in the porch in front of her – maybe they would sit near her. But his mother put threepence on the plate and she and Art went into the side chapel. Chrissie only had a penny and for a penny you were only allowed into the body of the church. That was something her grannie was always giving out about – different prices for different parts of the church. God, she said, had never intended that. That was the priests' doing. There were a lot of things about some priests that she was sure God had never intended. The big bellies and jowls on them from all the whiskey they drank. Stall-fed they were, and half the people in their parishes in want. She couldn't imagine Mrs Maguire talking like that about priests. She looked very religious. She wouldn't curse, either, not like her grannie who was always cursing. It was supposed to be a sin using bad language, and you shouldn't laugh at it, but all the same Chrissie almost always did laugh when her grannie cursed. She was very funny – you couldn't help it. People like Mrs Maguire wouldn't think it funny, though.

The next time she saw Art was just before the summer break. He told her he was going down the country for his holidays and she knew without a doubt that they must be very comfortable. She had never gone away anywhere, nor her grannie either, nor anyone in the house. He was the first person she had ever known who was going away for his holidays.

'Good luck with the job and I'll see you when I come back,' he said before riding off.

She hadn't seen him since, but maybe she would today, after she had bought the paper. She delayed in the newsagent's pretending interest in the comics and magazines – soon they would be coming out of school. She would love to see him, talk to him, even just catch a glimpse of him.

When she left the shop she dawdled by others near it, looking in the windows apparently studying pork chops, sausages and a cobbler with his mouth full of nails sitting before his last. Reflected in the windows she saw boys from the school riding past, some two abreast, talking, laughing and others walking – but not Art. She waited until no more boys passed and thought that perhaps he had gone home another way. Then that he might be sick. A fever ambulance drove past and she got a feeling of dread in the pit of her stomach. He could be in hospital, dying with diphtheria, and she'd never know. He could die and she'd never know. Every day people died with fevers. 'Please God, don't let him be dead,' she prayed in her mind as she began to walk home. 'Please let me see him again. Please, God.'

'What the bloody hell kept you? The dinner's nearly boiled dry,' her grannie said when she came in. She lied about the crowd in the. newsagent's. 'You look perished. You should have put on your coat, you'll get your end going out half naked. Sit over by the fire and I'll give you your dinner on a tray. Look at your legs they're blue with the cold. Pull your chair nearer the fire.'

After she had served her, her grannie said, 'I put my glasses out of my hand a minute ago and now I can't find them.'

'You're always losing things. If it's not your glasses it's your snuff box,' said Chrissie bad-humouredly. 'They're on the press.'

'God bless your eyesight,' her grandmother said, getting her spectacles and sitting opposite Chrissie with the paper. 'Let's have a dekko.'

The food and warmth were restoring Chrissie's equilibrium. He didn't have fever. He wasn't dead or dying. He might have missed school or just gone home another way. And she was sorry for having snapped at her grannie even though she hadn't noticed. She looked affectionately at her, at her head bent over the paper, her lips silently forming the words she was reading. Then, looking up from the paper she said, 'Here's one that seems made for you. Listen to this: *'Wanted. Young girl, school-leaver with good handwriting, good at figures and of neat appearance'*. Your handwriting's like copperplate and you can do sums.'

'Where is it? Is there an address or one of them box numbers?' Chrissie asked.

Her grandmother returned to look at the advertisement. 'Well, God blast them anyway, the bloody cheek of them! It shouldn't be allowed.'

'What? What shouldn't be allowed?'

'This,' said her grandmother, holding the newspaper out to her and pointing with a finger to the last line of the advertisement. Chrissie read, '*Only Church of Ireland need apply.*' 'Protestants', she said, 'that's what the Church of Ireland means, isn't it?'

'You can forget it, you're not a swaddler. Bad luck to them and their job. But never mind, love, you'll get another one please God. Don't let your dinner go cold.'

When the dinner was finished and the dishes washed they sat up close to the range drinking tea and eating thick slices of homemade seed cake. 'Slip off your shoes and put your feet up on the fender. They'll be warmer there, love.' The heat from the opened door of the range spread from her toes and gradually all over her. She was pleasantly drowsy. Her grannie was reading the paper, studying the Deaths column, sometimes exclaiming when she recognised the name of the deceased, calling down blessings on them, relating anecdotes about them. Chrissie only half-listened, for her mind was full of thoughts of Art. Conjuring up imaginary meetings, outings, conversations, declarations of love. Her grannie put away the paper and sat silently for a while then, as if her mind had tuned into Chrissie's thoughts, she asked, 'Did you ever see that young fella again?'

Pretending ignorance she asked, 'What young fella?'

'The one on the bike. What was it you said his name was?'

'Maguire. I saw him in Mass the other Sunday with his mother I think.'

'What was she like?'

'Low-sized, very respectable looking, with red hair.'

'That's her. I knew the name was familiar. Was she footy?'

'How would I know – I wasn't looking at her feet. Why, do you know her?'

'Her and everyone belonging to her and they were all footy.'

Knowing that when her grannie started passing remarks about people being footy, knock-kneed, gunner-eyed or having any physical imperfections, she would have more to say about their character, Chrissie changed the conversation and asked about her grandfather. 'How old were you, Gran, when you started going out with Grandad?'

'Fourteen. The pair of us were fourteen. I'd just started in the laundry and he had a job with a scaffolder.' Her eyes shone and became soft and smiley as they always did when she talked about her Jack.

'Were you in love with him? At fourteen did you know you were in love with him?'

'You didn't talk about being in love. That's all from the films, from America and books. But I knew I liked him and he liked me better than anyone else. It was a long time before we talked about love.'

'And was he the only one you ever went out with?'

'The only one,' said her grannie. 'He was a beautiful man. Every time I'd see him my heart would leap in my breast. We never had a cross word, not in earnest. He could make me laugh. I don't suppose we'd have married for years if it hadn't been for the war. Everyone was going, all the fellas from the street. In droves they went – the poor fools.'

'Is there going to be another war, Gran?'

'According to the papers.'

'And would everyone have to go again?'

'We're a Free State now. If it's England's war they shouldn't have to, but then,' she shook her head, 'they didn't have to last time. There was no Conscription yet they went. A madness takes hold of men when they hear the drums. Please God it'll never come and if it does we can be thankful there's no men in the family.' Chrissie thought of Art and hoped her Grannie was right. 'Bring me over the photograph. 'Chrissie fetched the picture and stood beside her grandmother looking over her shoulder at the young man in uniform and the slim pretty woman holding his arm. 'We were eighteen when it was taken and had been married three months. He was going to France the next week.'

'I think I look like him,' said Chrissie.

'There's a resemblance,' her grandmother admitted. 'He's still a boy. He never grew old like me. He never saw your mammy but he knew I was expecting her. That was the last letter I had from him – telling me how delighted he was with the news. He was killed two weeks before she was born.'

Chrissie had heard the story many times but never before had she felt such an emotion of sorrow, of terrible loss. To love someone so much, to be married to them and then for them to die. 'Oh Gran,' she cried and tears ran down her face, 'how could you bear it?'

'You have to,' said her grannie. 'Sure, what else can you do?'

'I love you,' Chrissie came from behind her grandmother and put her arms round her. She knelt down and put her head on her grandmother's lap who began stroking her hair and comforted her until she stopped crying.

'Remember him in your prayers. Now, put the photograph back on the press and I'll lie down for half an hour.'

Alone, Chrissie's thoughts returned to Art and she wondered how soon she would see him again and knew that she loved him just as her grannie had loved her grandfather when she was fourteen. If she objected to her going out with him she'd remind her of that, but she wouldn't. She was kind and understanding. Then Chrissie remembered the way her grannie had talked about Art's mother. What objection could she have to her? Her grannie knew everyone. She must have known his mother's family. She said they were all footy, too. Maybe it would be as well if she did meet Art again and if he asked her to go with him, not to let on to her grannie for a while.

She'd have to get another job. Be a grown up. And in any case, it wasn't fair that her grannie had to keep her with only her Army pension to live on. At fourteen you were supposed to keep yourself. Once she had a job she would make it up to her. Buy her everything she liked and seldom had – packets of high-baked water biscuits, bags of nutty toffees. Packets and bags instead of the ounces and two ounces which was all she could afford. And soft slippers that didn't hurt her bunions. And a string of jet beads like those she wore in the photographs.

She kept looking for a job. She wrote letters painstakingly, in her best handwriting and had no replies. With her heart in her mouth she went to shops and factories asking for a vacancy and there were none. And every day when she went to the corner to buy the paper she hung round hoping to see Art. A month passed before she did. At the sight of him her heart leapt just as her grandmother's had each time she saw her grandfather.

He stopped by the kerb. 'Were you wondering where I'd got to?' he asked, smiling at her.

'I never gave you a thought,' she said, her voice flippant but the expression in her eyes belying the tone.

'I was sick,' he said, 'a touch of pneumonia, but I'm grand now.'

Chrissie remembered how she had imagined him having diphtheria – pneumonia was as dangerous as that. She had had a premonition. You only had premonitions about people close to you, all the old women said that. 'Pneumonia,' she said, 'that's very dangerous. Are you sure you should be out in this weather?'

'Ah,' he said dismissively, 'it was only a touch, I'm grand now. Would you like a ride on the bike?'

'But it's the lunch-hour. What about your dinner?'

'I've a half-day – me ma will keep it hot.'

She had never ridden on a crossbar – it looked a dangerous thing to do – and she hadn't yet bought the paper. She couldn't go with him on the bike, not here on the South Circular Road. The neighbours came here for their messages: one of them was bound to see her and tell her grannie.

97

She considered all the reasons why she shouldn't accept his offer of a ride on the crossbar and one by one dismissed them for the urgency that possessed her to be in his company. 'I will,' she said, 'if you wheel the bike to the corner of Stamer Street and we'll ride round the back streets. You'd never meet anyone there.'

He wheeled the bicycle in the gutter. He was taller than her so that she had to look up at him when she spoke. She told him of all the jobs she had tried for and hadn't got. And the ones where only Church of Ireland could apply. 'I think I'll be idle for the rest of my life.'

'It's all a question of who you know. Isn't there anyone who'd put in a word for you?'

'Not really.'

'Go back to school, then. You've more of a chance with a few exams behind you.'

'You had to leave our school when you were fourteen. I'd have to go to the Tech. now.'

'Do that, then.'

'I might,' she said, knowing she wouldn't. You had to pay for the Tech. Her grannie couldn't afford that and in any case, at fourteen you should be paying your own way. They had reached the corner of Stamer Street. 'It'll be all right here. We can ride round the back streets, but not for long.'

He got on the bike and held it steady while she manoeuvred herself on to the crossbar and settled her coat so that her legs wouldn't be exposed. Smoothing down the shabby coat that in the excitement of seeing him again no longer embarrassed her.

'Right then,' he said, 'we're away.' The bicycle wobbled under the extra weight. Its unsteady movement threw her closer against him. He smelled of soap, lead pencils – his breast-pocket held a quiver of them – and peppermint sweets. The wind blew her hair against his face. Her heart beat quickly and despite the cold wind she felt warm all over with a glow that went from her toes right up to her face. He had control of the bicycle now and their progress through the narrow streets was smooth and steady.

'Will you stay in when you go home?' she asked, for the sake of something to say.

'Not for long,' he said. She was very conscious that one side of her body was leaning against his. She closed her eyes and imagined laying her head on his shoulder. 'After my dinner, I'll be back. I'm seeing the lads in the Parade. Maybe later on we could go for a walk or something.'

'Yes,' she said, 'a walk or something would be lovely. I'll let on I'm going to see Ellie, Ellie's my friend. But I'd have to be in early.'

'Half-five then. I'll meet you then. Do you want to go home now?'

She didn't. She wanted to go on riding, go on leaning against him, smelling the soap and peppermint, feeling his breath on her cheek forever and ever. But at home her grandmother was waiting for the paper. Wondering where she was . . . what had delayed her. 'I suppose I'll have to. Ride me back to where we started from and I'll see you there this evening.'

Her cheeks were flushed and her eyes shining. 'What kept you?' asked her grandmother, looking long and hard at her. 'You look as if you've been running.'

'I was talking. I met someone.'

'Who?'

'A girl. A girl I used to work with – Ellie. Remember I told you about Ellie? Well, she had lots to tell me. Mr McGurk had a stroke and Lizzie gave her notice in after what happened to me. Ellie's a scream, she had me in fits. I said I'd see her tonight, go up to her house after tea. She's working in a new place making ties. She might be able to get me in.'

While she told one lie after another her grannie's eyes never left her face. She could feel them boring into her, seeing into her mind the way they did when she was a little girl telling lies. Then she always lost the battle and lowering her eyes would confess the truth. But now too much was at stake. She had to brazen it out, she wasn't a child any more. Her grannie couldn't see into her mind. All she had to do was stare her out and unblinkingly she did so until her grandmother, looking away, asked for the newspaper.

'Can I go to Ellie's?' she asked when her grandmother was settled by the fire with the newspaper.

'So long as you're home by half eight, not a minute later. There are plenty of women looking for "generals", but no office jobs, nothing,' her grandmother said as she finished reading. 'What's a general?' Christie asked.

'A slave,' said her grannie. 'A skivvy. I'd keep you for the rest of my life before you'd go to that sort of work. Let's have a look at the Deaths.' As usual she made comments as she recognised names of people she had known. 'Another one gone to her long rest, the Lord have mercy on her. I only saw her last week and she looked hale and hearty. It's the weather. The cold is killing them like flies.' She put down the paper, opened the door of the range and picking up the poker drew the burning coals that had spread as they were consumed into a pile, tore a piece of cardboard from a box by the grate and fanned the pile into a flame. 'I'm short of firing. I've never let it get so low before. I'd go out for a stone of coal only my bunion's gone septic and I can't get a shoe on my foot.'

From the dream world where Chrissie walked with Art, his arm round her waist, her head upon his shoulder, she heard the voice with its hint that coal was needed. Before today, to go for a stone of coal was no different from fetching a stone of potatoes, a sack of sticks, a pillowcase of the day-old bread which for some reason she could never understand was called 'fancy': they were the messages which frequently she brought for her grannie. She pretended she hadn't heard.

'It'll be out before the evening.'

Still she said nothing.

'Did you hear what I said? There's coal wanted and I can't go for it.'

'Let the others get it when they come in from school. I'm too big to be going for coal. I'd die if anyone saw me carrying a coal sack.'

'Since when,' asked her grannie, 'did you ever object to doing my messages?'

Chrissie saw herself with the sack, coal dust leaking out of it, her hands black, dragging it behind her for fear that if she carried it in her arms it would destroy her clothes. And just as she came to the Parade Art would be there, Art and the crowd he went round with. They'd all be on a half-day. They'd laugh or worse, talk about her behind her back. 'That's a grand mot you have there. A fine big girl – look at the muscles on her.' She'd die. There on the spot she'd drop down dead.

'I'm grown up now, I'm fourteen. I shouldn't have to go for coal. I'm too big.'

'And the others are too small. They'd be stuck with a bag of slack and not have the gumption to say anything.'

For the first time in her life Chrissie refused to do something her grannie asked her. 'I'm not going for coal. I won't. I don't care. I'm not. Supposing someone saw me.' She waited in trepidation, not knowing how her grannie would respond to the refusal but determined that no matter what happened she wasn't going. Not even if it meant her grannie forbidding her to go to Ellie's. She would rather not see Art at all than meet him while she dragged a sack of coal behind her.

'Who's suddenly going to see you who hasn't seen you before bringing a message for your grannie?'

'Anybody. How do I know? Anybody could see me. I'm not going for it and that's all.'

'There must be strangers in the locality all of a sudden. Someone moved in that's made an impression on you, that's all I can think. But sure – don't go. Your arse'll freeze sooner than mine, I've more flesh on me.' And with that her grandmother returned to the newspaper.

'I'll go in the morning, first thing in the morning.' It would be safe in the morning. He'd be in school. Early in the morning she'd get the coal.

100

'Do that then,' said her grannie without looking up from the paper.

'Is it still all right for me to go to Ellie's?'

'Why wouldn't it be? Hasn't she said she might get you a job – don't miss that opportunity.'

Chrissie couldn't understand any of it. Her grannie never usually let the coal run out. Her grannie seldom took no for an answer, not that she'd refused her before, but she'd heard her with the others when they didn't want to do a message. It was all very peculiar. And her bunion hadn't been that bad before she went for the paper. She had a feeling her grannie was hatching something but what, she couldn't fathom.

Her grandmother seemed engrossed in the paper – another unusual thing, for after reading the Situations Vacant, the Deaths and a glance at the front page she would sling the paper, saying, 'There's never anything in that bloody thing.' But she had said she could go to Ellie's so there was no harm in getting ready. She washed her face and hands, put on one of the new pair of socks and then got the handleless cup to make up the sugar and water solution for her hair, unaware that every now and then her grannie looked over her glasses to watch her tidivating.

Then suddenly without rearranging the paper she let it fall to the floor and announced, 'I'm dying for a pinch of snuff. Have a look for my box like a good girl.'

Chrissie again sensed danger. Her grannie had something up her sleeve. She only snuffed when she was vexed or agitated. 'Where did you have it last? 'She asked.

'If I knew that I wouldn't be asking you to look for it.'

Chrissie found the small mustard tin which served as the snuff-box in a work basket amongst black woollen stockings waiting to be darned. Between finger and thumb her grannie inserted a pinch in each nostril and inhaled with an audible sniff. From her pocket she took a large brown-stained hankie and waited for the head-shaking sneezes to begin, afterwards replacing the tin and the hankie in her pocket.

Now, thought Chrissie, she'll start. Tell me what she really thinks of me refusing to get the coal and stop me going to Ellie's. She's in a bad humour when she snuffs. But to her amazement when her grannie did speak it was about Art's mother. 'A bit of a consequence, she is.'

'Who?' asked Chrissie unsuspectingly.

'That young fella's mother, Lizzie Fagan.'

'I don't know who you're talking about.'

'That young fella – Maguire, wasn't that his name? Lizzie's his mother. Lizzie Fagan is the name she was reared with. Betty she is now'. She laughed. 'Betty how are you! I knew everyone belonging to her. Reared begging they were. Her father was a little slither of a man never without a dewdrop on the end of his nose. He sold papers at the corner of Bride Street until he fell in for the money. In through a plate glass window in O'Connell Street during the Rebellion and came out with hatfuls. A daylight robber. People were shot for looting but not that oul shite, he slithered away.

'They went to hell with theirselves then. No holding them. A cacky-eyed little gouger that got his hands on a fortune. Before you knew it Lizzie was in the private part of the convent, him with a newsagent's and tobacco shop and they bought a house. Put a begger on horseback and they'll ride to Hell. You'd do well to keep from any of that man's seed, breed or generation.'

'I don't know why you're telling me all this,' Chrissie blustered. 'I only ever spoke to him the once. And he was very nice so he was. What's wrong with getting on? Aren't you always wanting me to look for an office job?'

'There's not a thing wrong with getting on if you've done it honestly and don't forget yourself.'

Chrissie shrugged and tried to look nonchalant. 'It's nothing to do with me. Only once I ever spoke to him. I've never had anything to do with him. And in any case, he can't help his mother or his grandfather. I don't suppose I'll ever see him again.' All the while she was talking she was remembering the ride on the bicycle, the smell of soap and peppermint, the feel of his body next to hers and her hair blowing against his cheek.

'Then there's no harm done and nothing to worry about. I wouldn't want Lizzie Fagan trying to make little of my flesh and blood. And that's what she'd do. A civil servant, no less – that's what she'll be looking for for him. Not the likes of you, not a reminder of who she was.'

Chrissie wanted to say, 'Oh, Gran, you know nothing. I love him. I know what he's like. He's lovely and kind. Art's not like his mother. He wouldn't belittle me. You'd like him. And he'd be mad about you. You'd make him laugh. I don't want to fight with you. I love you. And I'm sorry about your bunion. But I can't go for the coal. I couldn't let him see me carrying coal.'

To say any of it would make her cry. To say some of it would make a liar of her. So she remained silent. Then her grannie reminded her about the appointment with Ellie and that they had better make tea. Her brother and sister came home from school and asked where she was going because she was dressed up. She told the lie about Ellie to them and was glad that it got dark early so they'd be in bed before eight o'clock, not in the street playing games as they did in the light nights.

After the tea the children took out their exercise books and began their homework. The grandmother sat back to the fire and Chrissie cleared the table and washed the delf. Her grannie appeared to be dozing but as earlier when she was supposed to be reading now and then through half-closed lids she watched Chrissie rubbing vanishing cream into her cheeks, biting her lips to make them rosy and carefully combing the sugar and water curls round her face.

He was waiting for her under the lamp at the corner of Stamer Street. 'I've left the bike with Paddy. I wouldn't take you on the crossbar in the dark. We'll go for a walk.'

'That'll be grand,' she said. There was much more she could have said, like how thrilled she was that he had asked to see her. That now they were walking along like two sweethearts. Well, nearly like two sweethearts. Everytime they passed under a lamp she looked sideways at his face. He had a gorgeous face. He was the loveliest, the nicest boy she had ever known in her whole life. Her grannie was mad saying those things about his people. And even if they were true, if his grandfather had been a robber and his mother a bit of a consequence, that had nothing to do with him. You might as well say because her grannie cursed and snuffed that she would do the same. And she never would. Never.

'Me ma thinks I'm in Paddy's house – we're supposed to be swotting something.'

'I let on to me grannie I was going to see Ellie. I used to,' she stopped herself before saying 'I used to work with Ellie.' He knew nothing about the habit factory. One day she would tell him when she knew him better. 'I used to be in school with Ellie,' she said. 'Would your mother mind if she found out you weren't in Paddy's?'

'She might. Paddy's the dab hand at biology and I'm useless. He's helping me for the exams coming up. The mother's a great believer in exams. She wants me to be a doctor.'

'Is that so?' She could think of nothing else to say. Exams and biology were foreign to her as were people who wanted to be doctors.

'She has her heart set on it and I'd hate to disappoint her though I probably will.'

'Would you like that, to be a doctor?'

Art shrugged. 'I'm not sure. I suppose it would be all right. Don't let's talk about it any more.' He took hold of her hand and they walked on towards the bridge.

The suspicion had begun to form in her mind that her grannie might be right, that his mother was stuck-up and wanted big things for her son, but it vanished at the touch of his hand and she gave herself up to the sensation of his nearness. They crossed the bridge and turned to walk along the canal. A chill breeze came off the water.

'Are you cold?' Art asked.

'A bit,' she admitted. He let go of her hand and put his arm round her, drawing her close. She felt as if she was in Heaven. Along the banks they passed other couples strolling with arms about each other and now and then a man walking a dog.

After walking for a while in silence she wanted to say something, something that might impress him. Several incidents came into her mind – anecdotes about her grannie, for instance, but like pretending to be dead in the habit factory they were things that not everyone might find funny. You had to know someone really well to guess what they would laugh at or be offended by. There wasn't a moon nor a single star that she could comment on. Then she remembered how frightened she had been when he was away from school that he might have had diphtheria and she told him that.

'You were really worried about me?'

'I was,' she said.

'But why? You hardly knew me then.'

'I don't know but I was.'

He held her closer. 'Was it because you had a bit of a shine for me?' He laughed and she was glad of the dark night so that he couldn't see her blushing. 'I missed you when I was sick,' he said. 'I thought about you every day.'

'Honest to God?'

'Honest to God.' They were nearing the next bridge. Soon there would be bright lights and people, lots of people. 'Let's stop here for a minute,' Art said. 'Here by the tree.' They stood beneath it. 'Will you come out with me again, Chrissie?'

'Yes,' she said, and her voice was very low. 'I'll come out with you again.'

'It'll have to be only now and then because of the exams.'

'That's all right,' said Chrissie. 'Whenever you like.'

'I never asked a girl out before.'

'I've never been out with a boy before.'

'Can I kiss you?'

'I don't know how to kiss but you can.'

He moved her closer toward the tree, put his two arms round her and kissed her lips. It was, she thought, the most beautiful thing that had ever happened to her. He kissed her again and this time his lips lay on hers for longer and strange, wonderful, inexplicable sensations coursed through her. And she knew for sure that this was being in love. He laid his cheek against hers. 'I think I love you,' he whispered. 'Will you be my girl?'

'Yes, I'll be your girl. I think I love you, too.' And then the sound of a clock striking broke the spell. 'It's quarter after eight. We'll have to hurry.'

'I'll race you,' he said and gave her another quick kiss. Then they began to walk back, his hand in hers until they were near the house. And when they reached it, he said, 'We've a few minutes yet.' He sat on the stone wall that fronted the house and she, after looking up at her grannie's window, did the same. It was safe. Her brother and sister would be asleep this long time and her grannie dozing by the fire. In the summertime she'd have the window up and with a cushion supporting her arms on the cill, be looking out into the street. All the women in the street did the same thing. She was glad of the dark night.

'What about Wednesday at the same time?'

'I think,' she began to say when there was the sound of a sash window being pushed up. Without looking Chrissie knew it was her grannie. I'm in serious trouble now, she thought, rising from the wall. What'll I tell her? Let on I met him walking back from Ellie's.

She had scarcely formed the excuse when her grannie's voice shouted, 'Fire, fire!'

Art jumped off the wall and looking up earnestly shouted back, 'Where, ma'am? Where's the fire?'

'In every shaggin' grate in the house except mine,' she called back, then slammed down the window.

Oh, my God. Oh, Jesus Mary and Joseph. The ejaculations went through Chrissie's mind and at the same time she was making a great effort not to laugh out loud. But Art wasn't laughing as he asked, 'Who's that oul wan?'

'She lives up in the house.'

'Is she mad or what?'

'Mad, I think.'

'It's disgraceful, so it is. Roaring and cursing like that. Do you know her?'

She was already in the hall, running up the stairs, tears pouring down her face. Furious, broken-hearted and guilt-ridden for the denial. Her grannie was by a brightly burning fire. 'I was trying him out,' said her grannie. 'Seeing if he was his mother's son. Did he laugh?'

'I hate you. You've spoiled everything. I hate you. It was a terrible thing to do.'

'Did he laugh?' her grandmother asked again.

105

'Mind your own business. I hate you. I hate you. I'm going to bed and I hope I never wake up.'

She cried herself to sleep. She woke when her grannie was taking off her shoes, loosening her skirt and covering her with a blanket but she kept her eyes shut pretending sleep. And all the while vowing never to speak to her again. Never, ever to utter another word to her and never, not in a million years give her the satisfaction of knowing he was his mother's son.

The Vigil

Everywhere in the street through which I was walking were signs of Christmas; trees in the windows with twinkling fairy-lights, frosty reindeers, bells and snowmen stencilled on glass panes. Women with last-minute shopping hurried to and fro, their parcels brightly wrapped, calling the Season's Greetings to each other.

I thought of another Christmas a long time ago, when Michael O'Neil first came to Wales and got lodgings in our house and what a strange, sad coincidence it was that on this Christma Eve I was going to see him for the last time. As I walked on toward the house where his body lay waking my mind slipped back over the years, back to the night when I was a small girl and Mike and my father had sidled in through the scullery door, Mike with his cap in his hand squeezing its brim, foolish and awkward-looking, my father grinning all over his face, his voice full of plamas.

'I knew you wouldn't mind, Kate. He's just arrived and has nowhere to stay. Someone suggested Maggie McGurk's, someone who doesn't know her. He was at sea till today when he left his ship – never took to it, did you, Mike?'

'That's right, ma'am. I never took to it,' Mike said, swaying slightly. My mother said nothing for she was in bad humour. The boil had gone from under the bit of ham and she'd been expecting my father home earlier.

'Go in there you to the fire and sit down,' my father urged Mike and when he'd gone, turned to my mother and put an arm round her waist which she shrugged off impatiently. 'As I was saying, 'twas in the pub I met him.'

'Where else did you ever meet anyone except myself?' said my mother, pushing another bit of stick under the pot with the ham in it. 'May the divil fire you and him, walking in at this time of the night and me expecting you this hour or more.'

'I was thinking,' my father said, ignoring her scolding for he was well used to it and knew it went as quickly as it came, 'you might find room for him.'

'Where?' asked my mother, pausing from blowing with her breath at the fire.

107

'The room above that's been empty since your father died, Lord have mercy on him. The few shillings might be handy. And don't I know well a woman like yourself wouldn't wish Maggie McGurk on anyone, much less on a decent young fellow from out beyond Skibbereen.'

My mother had risen from before the fire. My father put his arm round her waist again and this time she let it stay. 'Maggie McGurk! Hunger's Mother! Indeed, I would not then. But all the same I wasn't looking for a lodger.'

'No Kate, sure don't I know you weren't.' His voice was still full of plamas. 'But aren't you the big-hearted woman. And all I'm asking is a few nights' shelter for him till he finds his feet.'

'Well, as it's Christmas Eve when I wouldn't turn a dog from the door I'll let him stay – but only for the time being. Now remember what I'm telling you – for the time being only.'

'The time being will be grand,' said my father as he went to call Mike and tell him the news.

And so Mike became our lodger. My father got him a start in the Tin Works, labouring, my mother relented about 'the time being', and before you knew it he was like one of the family. He was younger than my father and taller, too. So tall that when he forgot to duck he often banged his black curly head on the door between the scullery and the kitchen. Ruefully he'd rub his scalp and promise one day to rise the frame.

'Mike's the great promiser,' my mother said.

On Saturday nights when he, my father and a few of the neighbours returned from the pub with an armful of stout he'd make more promises, saying that when the weather or the work improved he'd go over to see his mother. Or maybe when the hay was being cut, at harvest-time, or Christmas, he'd surely go.

He had a good voice and after a few bottles of stout needed little encouragement to sing sad lamenting songs. Songs about Ireland, leaving it, mothers and sweethearts. I thought they were beautiful and said so. My mother thought otherwise, though she liked them well enough except on Saturday nights.

' 'Tis the drink talking. It would answer him better if he wrote or better still stirred himself and went across to see that unfortunate creature of a mother and she old and on her own. Talk is cheap and so is them songs,' she would say in an aside to me.

Not writing to his mother and, worse still, never going back once since he had left Ireland, which was a while before he came to Wales, were the only faults she could find in him. And frequently she told him so. 'Ashamed of yourself you should be. Oh, I know well you send the few shillings, for amn't I the one who posts it and scribbles the few lines to go with it.'

'You do, Kate, you do. And you're right, too. It's long ago I should have gone,' he would agree and promise, 'from next week now I'll give you a bit extra to put by for the fare. And tomorrow I'll write. First thing in the morning before I do another thing I'll get out the pen and paper.'

'Well, I hope you do, or one of these days when it's too late you'll be sorry,' my mother would say but she might as well have been talking to the wall. The letter was never written nor the visit made until his mother died and he went over for her funeral.

For a long time after he came back he did nothing of an evening but talk about her, the place where he had been reared, his father and the rest of his family. My mother and father encouraged him to talk, knowing he had not only grief but guilt to contend with. Being a child I knew nothing of either, but thought the stories were grand and an excuse for me not to go to bed.

I listened so often I felt as if I knew every stick and stone of the place in which he had been reared. I could picture the little whitewashed cottage, its flagged floor and tiny windows. The boreen that led to it with fuchsia hedges on each side and sweet-smelling honeysuckle entwined in the green branches and red-petalled, purple-centred bells. In the summer time warm winds from the sea blew the smell of the flowers into the house and the air round about was heavy with it. And at other times when the same winds turned into gales, you could hear the waves crashing below on the shore, imagine a voice on the wind, a voice that keened and moaned through the trees frightening Mike and his brothers and sisters above in their beds in the loft.

'It was easy enough then,' he would say, 'to believe in the banshee.'

Above the mantelpiece in a special niche his father kept a fiddle which on nights when the neighbours gathered in the kitchen he played: fast jigs and reels to which they danced, sometimes sweet plaintive airs. His father, he said, was a grand man, a great worker who when he wasn't attending to his small plot of land did a bit in the boatyard besides.

But it was mostly of his mother he talked on those nights long ago sitting by our fire. Telling us what a fine figure of a woman she was. How no one in the parish could wear the West Cork cloak like her. The grand light hand she had with the soda bread – big cakes of it, like cartwheels propped up to cool on the press. And how the same light hand could give him a clatter for picking it.

'Many and many's the time she did. And afterwards would be sorry, though she wouldn't let on, but would pile on the yellow butter and make the cuts thicker so I'd know,' he said, a smile spreading over his face. 'She was the grand woman, Lord have mercy on her, the heart of the house.'

When they grew up, one after the other his brothers and sisters went away. The fiddle was rarely brought down now. His mother devoted herself to Mike and his father, and watching for the letters from Australia and America. Then his father got sick and died. Mike said he did what he could round the place for a while after he left school. He had no great liking for the land and there wasn't much doing in the boatyard. There weren't all that many young people either about the place. Like his brothers and sisters they had taken the boat, and after a lot of thought he decided to do the same himself.

On the night he told his mother she cried in the silent way she had of crying. Rocking herself backwards and forwards, a hand over her face so he could not see the tears filling her eyes. She sat like that for a long time, he said. Just rocking to and fro the way he had seen women do with a child who needed comforting. Then with the corner of her apron she wiped her eyes, gave a big sigh and said to Mike, 'Sure, what else is there here for you? Don't you have to go. And wasn't I the foolish old woman to be hoping it could be different.'

When he left she went to the end of the boreen with him. It was winter time, the branches were bare and the sweet smell gone. She reached up to her tall son, took his face in her hands and kissed him. 'Go now, and may God go with you. I'll pray to Him and His Holy Mother to bless and protect you. I'll pray for you every day of my life and if God gives me the power I'll always watch over you.'

He would stop talking when he came to that part of the story and sit staring into the fire, seeing, perhaps, his mother's face and all the things he had left behind.

As time went on the stories became less frequent. 'Thank God, he's beginning to get over it,' my mother said. And when he met a girl she was delighted. Just before the Second War they married and moved to the house I was now approaching. It was all so long ago – forty years since the night he had arrived and my mother had said he could could stay for 'the time being'. All the grand times we'd had since then, all the changes, too. Me older than my mother was before the War, with a grown up family and grandchildren. Herself and my father dead these many years. Now Mike was gone, too, I thought sadly as I came to the house with no Christmas tree in the window and the curtains drawn.

In the back room I sympathised with the family. We talked of how sad and how sudden it was. Remembered times past, cried and laughed and cried again.

'Daddy's in the parlour. Will you come in?' Mike's daughter said.

'I will,' I replied, and my husband who had come in the meantime to collect me followed the two of us out of the room. Someone knocked on the hall door and she went to answer it, leaving us by the parlour. My husband who had been there earlier in the day did not follow me into the room, but stood waiting in the passage by the parlour door.

The room was small and square and in the centre of it Mike's coffin rested on trestles. White sheets were pinned to the wall and against it leant the coffin lid. I went in, moving round the woman already kneeling in front of the coffin. There was no mark of disease or suffering on the face at which I looked. Mike had died in his sleep and that was how he looked now, as if he was asleep. He was soft-faced and younger-looking than he had been for many years. One black hair escaped from an eyebrow and curled defiantly upwards the way it always had, and I remembered how as a child with spit on my finger I used to smooth it down.

After kissing him I moved back and knelt to say a prayer. The woman in front had her head bowed, a scarf or shawl covering it and her shoulders. A neighbour, I thought, a friend of Mike's wife. Someone fond of him and very devout, for she was still there when I rose from praying and joined my husband who had waited by the door. And I saw her again, still kneeling in the same position when after saying goodbye to the family we once more passed the open parlour door.

We didn't talk much on the way home and it wasn't until the car was slowing down to turn into our street that my husband said, 'Mike would have been pleased with what you did.'

'What did I do?' I didn't know what he was talking about.

'You know, kneeling down and praying.'

'Oh, that,' I said dismissively. 'Everybody does that when they go to see someone dead. You should know that. You've been married to me long enough and been to plenty of Catholic funerals and wakes. Please God that'll be the last for a long time.' I thought no more about it until we were back in the house, then I remembered the old woman and reminded him of her.

'What old woman?' He looked puzzled.

'I don't know who she was. Probably one of Mike's neighbours, someone from their street. I'd never seen her before, but she was praying for ages. Everybody does it when they go to see someone dead.'

'There wasn't anyone else in the room, only you.'

'But there was. You must have seen her – in front of me, a bit to the side with a scarf or a shawl over her head.'

'Listen,' he said good-humouredly, 'I may not be a Catholic, but there's

111

nothing wrong with my eyesight. I stood by the door all the time you were in the room. You were the only one there.'

You . . .' I was about to protest, tell him he must be going blind or had fallen asleep standing up when I remembered the shape of the parlour, the door opening flush against the wall. He would have seen every inch of the room. Anyway, the coffin was in the centre and the woman in front of it – not two yards from where he stood. He *couldn't* have missed her – yet he hadn't seen her. But I had: I'd been as close to her as I was now to him. I could have reached out and touched her. I never saw her face, but I could still see the shape of her, her bowed head and the soles of her shoes, the heels worn down. They were flat black shoes, an old woman's shoes. An old woman watching by the coffin and praying. And then I knew who she was . . .

But I'd say nothing. Who would believe me? Certainly not my husband. He'd laugh or tell me it was my imagination. That I was upset. That Mike's death had taken more of an effect on me than I knew.

'Well, have you sorted it out? There wasn't anyone else there, was there?'

'No, there wasn't. You're right, now that I come to think about it. I was getting mixed up with something else,' I said.

You're right, I thought as he switched on the television, you didn't see her. But I'm right, too. For I saw her. Saw the old woman – Mike's mother – who had been granted her wish and the power to watch over her son. And I was grateful I'd been granted the privilege of seeing her keep her vigil.

Survival

The little girl stood by the window and arranged the long lace curtain around her and began to twirl. Slowly at first then faster and faster, enjoying the slightly painful sensation as the hanging tightened its hold on her hair. The shabby room rotated, familiar objects blurred and took on strange and wonderful shapes. Above her head the bamboo pole strained under the unaccustomed weight.

She continued spinning until her hair became so entangled in the lace that the sensation of aching sweetness in her scalp was replaced by a smarting soreness, a stinging pain which made her begin to untwirl slowly. Little by little the curtain relinquished its hold on her hair. Gradually the room came back into focus. Behind the door the double bed ceased to pitch and heave on the cracked red linoleum. Her single bed settled in its corner. The tables and chairs came to rest in the centre of the floor, and the small, black-framed picture of a young woman in white flowing drapes with flower garlands in her hair lay flat against the wall. The picture was called *Spring* and the little girl believed it was a likeness of her mother when she was young.

Deliciously dizzy, she shrugged the curtain free, staggered away from the window and walked about the room with hands outstretched to steady herself. A sound of footsteps and clanking metal warned her that her mother was coming. Climbing the stairs, stopping now and then to rest the buckets, letting the handles strike the side of the pails. The child moved quickly back to the window and tidied the curtain before her mother entered the room.

A smell of boiling clothes filled the air. Grey soapy bubbles crept up and slithered over the rim of a huge pan on the stove, hovered for a moment, burst then cascaded on to the jet of gas. With a hiss and a splutter the flame died. The woman put down the buckets, ran to the cooker and turned off the gas. Then, glancing towards the window she noticed the carelessly arranged folds of the lace hanging. 'You've been at the curtains again, haven't you?' Not waiting for an answer she continued, 'I can't go to the yard for five minutes but you're pulling the place about.' She grabbed hold of the child and shook her roughly. 'Haven't I told you time and time again not to touch the hangings. Do you hear what I'm saying?'

The little girl didn't answer. Her eyes stared up at her mother. 'I'll take that look of derision off your face,' said the mother and slapped her across the cheek. 'What are you crying for?' she screamed. 'I'll kill you so I will if you don't stop that whinging.' The child knew crying infuriated her mother. She tried to swallow her sobs.

'Stop it this minute. Stop that crying! Stop that crying for nothing. You'll kill yourself one of these days, bring the pole down on top of your skull and split it. For the last time *will you stop it*! I can't stand it,' and in her fury the woman lashed out again and hit the child. 'Now,' she said, 'you've got something to cry for,' and pushed her away. The sobs slowly subsided though now and then one still hiccupped through the small body.

As she moved about the room making preparations to wash clothes, the woman kept an eye on the little girl and once her back was turned the expression on her face became contrite. She pushed two chairs together so that their seats faced each other, placed a tin bath on them then lifted and tipped in the pot of clothes from on top of the stove. She added cold water from a bucket, testing the temperature with her fingers until the water in the bath was right and then she started to rub and scrub. She began to sing, choosing songs she knew the child liked. The anger and harassment left her face and the room was filled with the sweet clear sound of her singing.

The child stood by the window looking out into the street, thinking that when her mother sang she looked like the woman in the picture. She fingered the dusty sunbeams and sang along in her mind with the songs. Her mother soaped and rinsed. Now and then with her soda-reddened hands which cracked in cold weather she picked an item out of the water to wring. Grimacing as if to crush the life out of the towel or sheet she wound the piece around her arm where it lay like a damp grey snake. Suddenly she stopped singing and glanced at the clock. 'Look at the time,' she exclaimed. 'Your father will be in any minute. Run down to the shop and get two ounces of tinned beef and a Spanish onion.' She dried her hands on her apron. 'Come on, now. Stop foostering.' The child gave up her attempt to catch a sunbeam and came to her mother, who counted out some coppers and as the child left the room shouted after her, 'And don't pick the meat.'

She ran down the stairs, stopping on the landing to work her fingers round the hole in the red raddled wall. Pieces of black horse hair bonded the mortar. She pulled at a hair, dislodging the crumbling plaster, enlarging the hole. She licked the chalky taste from her fingers and ran on

114

down the stairs and passed the place in the hall where something lurked in the dark. At night when she passed the place she sang.

She was afraid of a lot of things. Of what lurked in the dark place. Of the cows which came through the narrow street on a Thursday, running this way and that, sometimes even into the hall. They were going to the slaughter-house. She was afraid of the nun who had a long black hair growing out of a mole on her chin. Her eyes were as black as her habit. Her hands were long and her fingers bony. One day she would find out that the child didn't sleep with her hands folded on her breast in case she should die during the night. Every night she said her prayers, Hail Marys and the Our Father, then 'God Bless Mammy and Daddy, make me a good girl and don't let me wet the bed,' then folded her arms across her breast and tried to sleep but always the position was so uncomfortable that guiltily she would uncross her arms, put her thumb in her mouth, turn on her side and go to sleep.

She ran on to the shop, bought the meat and onion and once outside undid the packet and picked at the corned beef in such a way that she hoped her mother wouldn't notice. Returning to the room she found the table laid for tea. Her mother moved about tidying the place and herself, now and then addressing a remark to the child: 'I hope he's in good humour. I won't be at all surprised if he has something on for tonight.' She looked in the mirror and patted her hair. 'Off out he'll be as soon as he's had his tea.' The child, listening for her father's whistling, knew no answer was required.

She heard the whistling. 'There he is! There he is! Can I go and meet him? Can I, Mammy?' Without waiting for permission she opened the door and started down the stairs. She jumped the last few steps into his waiting arms, wound her two small ones round his neck and laid her cheek next to his. She breathed in the smell of him – a mixture of tobacco, horses and his own lovely smell. She rubbed her face against the stubble of his cheek. 'What did you bring me, Daddy? What did you bring me?'

'Is that all you have to say?'

'I love you. I love you the best in the whole world.' She kissed his face and hugged him. Every night they followed the same ritual, the kisses and hugs and protestations of love while he carried her upstairs. But tonight as they reached the first landing, he said, 'I'll have to put you down. I'm bunched. You're getting too heavy for me.'

'Ah, no. Don't please,' she protested but reluctantly allowed herself to be put down. She held his hand as they climbed the last flight of stairs asking again as they entered the room, 'What did you bring me, Daddy?'

The man and woman exchanged greetings. Then the child repeated her question. 'You have her ruined,' said the woman.

'She's only a child,' the man said.

The woman's voice was bitter as she replied, 'A spoiled child who knows how to wind you round her finger.'

The man ignored her and reached into his pocket and said to the little girl, 'Shut your eyes, put out your hand and see what God will send you.'

She closed her eyes and stretched out her hands. 'Oh,' she said, her voice filled with delight, 'Oh, they are beautiful. White satin and lace.'

'You can make clothes for your doll.'

She held the scraps of satin to her face. 'It's lovely, lovely and silky.'

Every night he brought her a gift. Pencils, a bag of beads to thread, a packet of Japanese paper flowers which, when placed in water, opened and blossomed before your eyes. Usually he brought her scraps of lace and satin or small blocks of polished oak which came from the coffin shop where he worked. She had been in the shop many times. On Sundays she went with him for walks in the Green and then on to the undertaker's yard. She had seen the rolls of satin and cards of lace, and seen the finished coffins lined with satin and their pillows trimmed with lace. She liked to touch the coffins, run her hands over the polished oak which was smooth and warm to her touch. She liked its smell. Coffins were nice when they were empty. She didn't like them when she went with her mother to see people lying in them. People were always dying and being put in coffins. Once she saw a dead woman in a coffin with a dead baby at her feet. And once her friend charged a ha'penny for people to go and look at her sister in her coffin.

'Put those things away and come to the table for your tea,' her mother said. She sat to the table and began her meal. Her mother cut and buttered bread while her father pushed the meat and onion about his plate eating only a little.

'What's the matter with it? Why aren't you eating it? I thought you liked tinned beef.'

'I'm not hungry,' he said, and rubbed a fist in his chest. 'I've had that pain again. It caught me coming up the stairs.'

The woman's lips tightened as she sawed through the loaf. 'I'd have a pain in my chest too if I stayed out half the night and filled my belly with porter. Wind, that's what ails you.'

The child ate her bread and jam and prayed, 'Please God don't let Mammy fight with Daddy.' She hated her mother for fighting with her father.

'Have you any Andrews?' asked the man.

'Where would I get money for Andrews?' said the woman. Her voice was quieter now and she looked alarmed for the man had changed colour and beads of perspiration were on his face.

'A bit of bread soda will do. That'll shift it,' said the man and kneaded his chest with his fist. 'It's as if something's stuck there.'

'Go quick,' said the woman to the child, 'and get a tin of health salts.' She gave her the money and her father reached and gave her two pennies. 'Buy yourself some taffee!'

'Leave the door open, Mammy, until I'm in the hall. And won't you come down and get me when I come back, Daddy?'

'I'll come down and carry you up the whole way.' He touched her face. 'Now be a good girl and hurry up.'

From the open door the light shone down the stairs and going past the dark place she sang loudly. Once in the street everywhere was brightly lit by the gas lamps. She ran and skipped along to the little shop that stayed open until late. Once it had been a front parlour, but now it sold sweets, loaves of bread, coal blocks, paraffin oil, babies' soothers, headache powders, health salts, snow-cake, needles and thread and bottles of minerals.

She stopped to look in the window, debating how she would spend her money. A bluebottle trudged through the icing on the snow-cake. On a dish next to the cake were pieces of pink and white coconut ice. She pressed her nose close to the glass, making up her mind and decided on the pink and white sweets.

The shop was full. She pushed and wormed her way to the counter and waited impatiently while a woman bought needles and white thread then remembered several other things she wanted. It was her turn but another woman pushed in front of her and kept the shopkeeper talking for ages. At last she was served. After leaving the shop she ate a piece of the coconut ice and ran all the way home. Her cheeks tingled from the cold night air and she felt like running for ever and ever.

There were people around her hallway, people she knew going in – neighbours – and everyone was talking. A group of people had gathered on the path and she couldn't get past them. She pushed and shoved. Then a woman reached and took hold of her, and she heard the talking. Heard someone say, 'Don't let her go up.' She struggled to free herself. Another voice said, 'A young man in the whole of his health. Lord have mercy on him and comfort his family.'

She kicked out at the woman's shins and broke free. She reached the hall and screamed up the stairs, 'Daddy, Daddy, I'm back! Daddy, come down and bring me up. You promised, Daddy. *Daddy*.'

From upstairs she heard the voice of her mother crying, 'Ah no, Sweet Jesus, ah no.'

A woman she knew brought her out of the hall. 'Stop screaming,' she said. 'Your Daddy's very sick. He has to go to the hospital. Whisht now. There's a good child.' She screamed and kicked and struggled but the hands held her tightly and eventually led her away and put her to bed in a strange room. And hands covered her and told her to go to sleep and that soon her Mammy would come.

In the dim light that came from the burning Sacred Heart lamp she lay and thought and knew that her father was dead. She wouldn't see him any more. Tears flowed down her face and she thought how there would be no one now to catch her when she jumped the last two steps or bring her gifts every night. No one to take her to the zoo ever again.

She lay on her back, blessed herself and said her prayers. 'God Bless Mammy and please don't let me wet this bed and Lord have mercy on my Daddy.' She crossed her arms on her breast and tried hard to keep them there but not even tonight could she manage it. She turned on her side, reached under her pillow and brought out the three-cornered bag of coconut ice. She put a piece in her mouth, chewed and let the sweetness trickle down her throat. Then she slept.

The Little Black Dress

'You won't forget my little black dress, will you, Ede?' said Mrs Deeping.

'No, Mum, I won't forget your little black dress,' replied Edith without looking up from the suitcase she was packing. Her mother stood in front of the dressing table unwinding metal Dinky curlers from her hair which was the colour and texture of coconut matting. One by one she unwound the curlers, wincing when they tangled in her hair, and laid them on the green glass tray of her dressing table set. Her hair fell in bends. She combed it carefully, arranging it to fall forward on to each cheek, then smiled approvingly at her reflection and talked again.

'You can go anywhere in a little black dress, that's what I always say. Except to a wedding, of course. Black's unlucky to wear to a wedding. But anywhere else – to a party, to an afternoon tea-dance at the Cadena, with beads and pearl stud earrings or flowers, you can wear it anywhere, even to a summer funeral. Then you'd want a hat, a big black straw or one of them close-fitting sailors. I can't remember what the sailors is called, but you know what I mean don't you, Ede?'

'Yes, Mother,' Edith agreed when Mrs Deeping's pause indicated she expected comment from her. 'I know what you mean but I can't remember either.'

Satisfied with the response Edith's mother continued to talk. 'Your Dad always liked me in black. Sexy he said it was.' She combed a half-fringe on to her forehead. 'It'll be funny going on holidays without him. We had good times in Margate, me and your Dad. He knew how to give a girl a good time, I'll say that for him. Funny him not coming this time.' Mrs Deeping stopped talking and began powdering her face.

Edith looked up from the suitcase and saw three faces, two in profile, and three hands applying three powder puffs in the triple dressing table mirrors. 'Mum!' Her mother, startled by the shout, looked round. 'That's the talc, Mum! You look like a clown.' She left the packing and went to her, removed the puff and put it in its green glass bowl, ramming down the lid before the puff had settled so that the powder flew up in the air then fell like a fine shower of snow on the walnut veneer of the dressing table. 'Here's your Max Factor, the Sun Kissed, and go easy with it – only a touch, mind.'

I shouldn't let her, Edith thought, returning to the packing. I shouldn't let her look such a sight. I shouldn't have agreed to rinse her hair. It's shocking – the colour of that fibre mattresses used to be stuffed with. I did warn her. Told her it wouldn't take on the new perm but she wouldn't listen, would she. 'I can't go on my holidays with my hair not right,' that's what she said and kept on and on about it. So what could I do? Anything for a bit of peace.

Every time Edith looked up she saw the triple reflections of her mother's face and hands. It was weird. It made her jumpy. She went again to the mirror and folded the side ones back. 'You all right now, Mum?' she asked, returning to the case.

'All right, love,' said her mother, opening and rolling up a bright orange lipstick. 'You did my hair nice. You should have gone in for hairdressing. I wanted you to be a hairdresser, didn't I Ede?'

'You did, Mum.'

'But you were always stubborn. Had ideas, you had. You wanted to be a teacher. Do you remember?'

'I remember.'

'Only you met Stan and couldn't wait to get married. A Breton sailor, that's what it was.'

'What what was?'

'The little black straw sailor. The hat.'

'Oh, yes,' said Edith absentmindedly.

'Your Dad loved my hair. A woman with red hair, he said, was very passionate. The things your Dad used to say!' Mrs Deeping laughed and began putting on the lipstick, outlining lips that had long ago lost their shape, drawing from memory, from habit, pressing one lip on to the other, smoothing it in with the tip of her little finger. She smiled at her reflection.

'We had lovely rooms in Margate. A smashing hotel. Lovely rooms and food. None of your dried egg and spam fritters. Oh no, your Dad wouldn't have stood for that. Real meat we had, steak and chips and chops and fried eggs. Real ones like before the war. Your Dad knew how to get what he wanted. He had the money. You could get anything if you had the money. And the stockings he gave me. Nylons. Remember the nylons, Ede? They were that fine you had to store them in jamjars so they didn't snag. Remember the way the seams and heels stood out on them?'

Edith bent over the case rolling one fluffy blue bedsock into another, pushing the ball on top of the matching blue bri-nylon nightdress, pushing down harder than was necessary for the case wasn't nearly full. She said nothing.

'I always had good legs. Looked beautiful in nylons they did. You last as

120

long as your legs, that's what they say.' Mrs Deeping raised a leg and held it out for inspection. 'Look at that, Edie. Not bad, eh?'

Edith looked at the extended leg, the swollen ankle spilling over the bedroom slipper, the crêpy flesh, the flaccid calf, the purple twisted varicose veins, the surface veins near the ankle red and black and puce. 'Not bad, Mum,' she said. 'Not bad at all,' and she thought, the last time Dad took you to Margate I was ten – the year the War broke out. You wore lisle stockings and we stayed in a boarding house. We had kippers every morning for breakfast and the floor was crunchy under my plimsoles from the sand that was walked in. We never stayed in a hotel. But I remember the nylons and your long legs and red curly hair and the Yanks that took you to Margate. 'Honey', they called me and brought me bags of doughnuts from the Doughnut Dugout and Hershey Bars and chewing gum. 'For you, Honey,' they said smiling, all teeth.

Her mother continued for a while to admire her legs then turned back to the mirror and talked as she fiddled with her hair. 'The war made no difference. Me and your Dad always had smashing times. We went to Brighton and Hastings, too. The best hotels and the best food. I don't suppose this holiday will be the same without him – still, I'm looking forward to it.'

No, it won't be the same, Edith said to herself. It was never the same. Not the way you remember it. You never stayed in hotels in Margate or Brighton or Hastings with Dad. You did with Elmer and Butch and Red and Rusty. I hated you then. All the years with Dad away at the war – all the nights on my own. Sick from eating chocolate bars and full of wind from chewing gum. Waiting for you to come home. Listening for the footsteps on the stairs, the sound of laughter and then you'd come in with one of the Yanks – I could never tell one from the other – smelling of drink and calling me 'Honey'. And your lovely red hair done up in sweeps, your face brown with the Sun Kissed make-up and your teeth, your gorgeous teeth. I hated it when you sat on the Yank's lap and your frock slipped up your nylon-covered legs. I hated the Yanks and I hated you when you got off their laps. I hated the smell of you, the scent of powder and gin all mixed up and you'd kiss me and hug me and say, 'And who's my best girl then?' and tip up my chin and kiss me again. I knew what was coming next. 'It's very late, pet, you'll be that tired in the morning.'

In bed I could hear the laughing and the wireless or gramophone with Vera Lynn or Anne Shelton singing and I'd think of Dad. Then the other noises would begin and I'd cover my head with the bedclothes and write a letter to Dad in my mind. And think that tomorrow before you came home from work I'd post it, I'd really write and post it. I'd tell Dad about the

Yanks and how you didn't want me to stay on in school, though the teacher said I'd pass the Eleven-plus flying. And Dad would come home the minute he got the letter and everything would be like it was before the war.

Mrs Deeping was applying rouge on top of the powder, spreading it in streaks and still reminiscing about her holidays in Margate. Edith wasn't listening. Her thoughts and memories were far back in the past. Mechanically she checked her mother's packing list: spare teeth, Sennacot, Vaseline, Preparation H, comb, brush. As each item was placed in the toilet bag she ticked it off the list and from a night long ago heard her mother's voice.

'Honey,' she said, for now she called her Honey all the time, 'Honey – be a good girl for Aunty Rene. No fighting with Marge. I'll be back on Sunday night and bring you a present.'

Aunty Rene who wasn't her aunt nor Marge her cousin. She slept head to tail with Marge in a single bed, the other girl's dirty feet close to her face. And Marge said, 'You know what your Mum does with the Yanks, well that's what she's doing now in that hotel. I heard my mum telling Aunty Jean.' Edith had let on to be asleep. She knew what 'doing it' was. Marge had told her a long time ago. She didn't believe her then. People wouldn't do that. The King and Queen wouldn't do that. Nor her Mum and Dad. But now she knew it was true about her Mum and the Yanks anyway.

'Did you hear what I said?' Marge poked at her with a foot. Edith could smell wee. Marge slept in her knickers.

She pretended to waken up. 'Stop kicking me,' she said 'I was asleep and you woke me.'

'She does it with a different one every night. My mum says it's a crying shame and your Dad out fighting. He'd kill her if he knew. And my mum says someone should tell him.'

'You smell! You smell of wee,' Edith said, and turned quickly so that Marge's vicious kick would miss her face.

She hated Marge and Aunty Rene but they were right, someone *should* tell her Dad. Before she went to sleep she promised herself that first thing tomorrow she would be the one to do it. He'd come straight home then. Mum wouldn't work any more nor meet the Yanks. Everything would be like it was before the war: her dinner ready when she came home from school, Dad back from work, still wearing his mechanic's overalls smelling of oil and Mum saying, 'Don't you dare, George Deeping, touch a thing until you've washed and changed.' But not crossly, with a laugh in her voice. Her Mum and Dad were always laughing and winking at one another. After supper they'd sit round the fire and listen to the wireless.

And in the summer go for the day to Southend. Dad would roll up the legs of his trousers and take her paddling while Mum read magazines in the deckchair. In the fair Dad would buy her candyfloss – 'cheat your guts' he called it – and she'd ride on the Hobby Horses and all the time the music would play with everyone singing and being happy. Going home on the train she'd fall asleep and not waken until next morning, tucked up in her bed.

Edith pushed the clothes down in her mother's case, making room for the blue quilted dressing gown, and wondered what would have happened if she *had* written the letter to Dad. Would the Army have let him come home? If they had, he wouldn't have been killed.

The telegram arrived just after her mother had come in from work. She screamed and screamed and the neighbours came running to her. 'Poor George,' they kept saying. 'Poor brave George. A hero, that's what he was.' Aunty Rene lent clothing coupons, to buy stuff for a black coat, and a woman living round the corner made an edge-to-edge style for her mother who dyed a cream straw hat black to complete her mourning outfit. Everyone, Edith remembered, told her mother how lovely she looked and she said it was because of her red hair. The Yanks stayed away and she had slept in her mother's bed until they came back.

Her teacher, Edith recalled, told her she was a very brave little girl and could be proud of her father who had died to save the world. And she had said, 'But Miss, I was proud of him already.'

'I know, dear,' the teacher said and gave her a sweet.

Mrs Deeping finished making-up, perched a little hat with a spotted veil on the crown of her head, sat down and asked, 'Have you got a fag, love?'

'I gave them up Mum,' Edith lied. 'Anyway, you shouldn't smoke. You know what the doctor says.'

Her mother made a contemptuous face. 'Doctors, what do they know? Keep away from them, that's what I say.'

Edith zipped up the toilet bag, placed it in the case, closed that too, and said to her mother, 'I'll just take this into the hall, then we'll have a nice cup of tea. You'd like a cup of tea, wouldn't you?' Her mother had fallen asleep, her head drooping on her chest, the little hat tipped on to her forehead.

Poor old Mum, thought Edith looking at the slumped figure of her mother. Who'd have thought you'd have finished up like this? It's just as well we don't know what's in front of us. That's what I said to Stan when you first got bad and he started on about you going into a Home: 'For all you know we could be like her when we're old.'

'All the more reason,' said he, 'why we should enjoy what's left to us before we go ga-ga.'

It's not that Stan's unkind, he's not. He didn't complain when Mum came to live with us. Of course, she was all right then, she only had angina, but some husbands wouldn't have been so willing to have their mother-in-law move in. It was setting fire to the bed that made him mad. It was awful wakening in the middle of the night, smoke everywhere. We could have roasted alive. I tried keeping the cigarettes and matches away from her but she could still get to the corner shop then and even though I'd told them they still sold them to her. I did stop that in the end, told them I'd report them to the police. I don't suppose the police could have done anything though. After all, Mum was over sixteen and didn't look funny or anything.

That was the end of the smoking or so I thought, forgetting how crafty Mum is. She'd pinch my fags or Stan's and light them from the cooker. The bed went on fire again and the draught blew out the gas. Stan said we could have been blown to smithereens. After that we took our cigarettes up to bed with us and I turned the gas off at the main. That kept Stan quiet for a while, until the doctor prescribed the new tablets. Of course *he* says it wasn't the tablets, just the progression of Mum's complaint but it's a funny thing she never saw black dogs under the table until he gave her those tablets. Oh, the screams of her. The dogs were coming for her. 'Look at them, Stan,' she'd scream, 'look at their eyes, green and shining like that clock you can see in the dark.' And nothing would satisfy her but that he'd hunt them out.

I don't think the doctor believed me. He changed the tablets but the damage was done. The screams were terrible. The neighbours must have thought we were knocking Mum about. She'd waken in the night calling for me or Stan, telling us the dogs were on the bed, under the dressing table. It was after one of those nights that Stan put his foot down. 'She's got to go – it's her or me. I can't stand it. I'll go to lodgings. At least there I'll get a night's sleep.'

'Poor Mum, poor old Mum,' I said, and that really started him. We had such a row. Never before in our life had we rowed like that.

'What's poor about her?' he yelled, standing there shivering in his pants and vest and Mum, satisfied that the dogs were gone, sleeping like a baby. 'What did she ever do for you or anyone?'

'She had me for one thing,' I shouted back.

'And would have left you if the Yank had married her.'

'Well he didn't, did he?'

'Too much bloody sense. How can you have any feelings for her? How can you forget all the things she did to you?'

124

I told him, 'I don't forget. I remember all the things.'

'Well then?'

I tried explaining. 'Stan,' I said, 'I only remember them the way you remember things like dates, things you learned in school, pictures you went to. You remember names and dates and places but not the feelings, not sadness or anger, nothing like that, the feelings have left, only the memories stay. I love Mum. I've known her longer than anyone else. I like her smell.'

'You won't when she starts having accidents,' shouted Stan. I broke down then, I was so upset. About Mum, about me and Stan. We had never rowed like this before. He's kind. He's a good husband. I love him, too. I couldn't stop crying. 'Oh, Ede,' he said. He's never been demonstrative, he's awkward about showing his affection. 'I'm sorry, love, don't cry. And I'm sorry about your Mum, too. I wish she was all right. I don't want it to be like this.'

He looked old. I do forget he's old, we're both old. He sat beside me and put an arm round me. 'Ede,' he said, 'it's not just for me, not just for my sake. She'll kill you. It's not as if we had a family, someone to give you a hand. It's not like years ago when you knew everyone in the street, when there'd be a neighbour to sit with her while you went to the shops. They're all young kids here, they're all out working. When was the last time you left your Mum alone while you nipped out. Well, come on, when was it?'

I had to admit it was a long time ago. That nowadays I waited for him to come home before going to the late-night shop.

'She'll kill you, Ede. She'll take to her bed. You won't be able to lift her – the two of us wouldn't be able. And supposing something happened to me, how would you manage then? It's for the best, love. Honest it is.'

The doorbell rang, waking Mrs Deeping and recalling Edith to the present. 'It's the taxi, Mum,' said Edith. 'I'll just tell him we'll only be a minute.' Her mother stared vacantly into space. 'Time to go now, Mum,' Edith said when she came back from the door, her voice full of forced cheerfulness. 'Let me fix your hat. There now, that looks nice. And your coat. We must put on your coat. Take my arm. Slowly now, there's no hurry.'

Mrs Deeping allowed herself to be led and guided through the hall and out into the cold bright sunshine. She stopped by the gate and looked up and down the road. 'It's a lovely day for going on your holidays, isn't it?'

'A lovely day, Mum. And you're going to a lovely hotel. We'll get into the car now. Mind the step.'

Her mother waved at the passing houses as the car moved off. Please God, prayed Edith, don't let it change into one of her good days. Don't let

125

her know it isn't a hotel in Margate. She dabbed at her eyes and stifled her tears.

'You've got a chill coming on,' said her mother, 'I can always tell. I said so yesterday when you went out to play without your cardigan. Straight to bed for you, my girl. We're not having a cold spoiling the holiday.'

'No, Mum, we don't want that.'

'I wonder if your Dad will come down later on?'

'I expect so, Mum.'

'You didn't forget my little black dress, Ede?'

'No, Mum, I didn't forget your little black dress.'

The Leaving

It wasn't fair nor right. It only happened in Ireland. It had *always* happened in Ireland. And what was anyone doing about it? Nothing. Talk, that was all. And as for the Government – the Ministers and TDs on television – all some of them did was justify it. Delighted to get the unemployment figures down.

Rosie Donnelly thought her angry bitter thoughts as she pulled the line up as far as it would go, looped the rope around the pulley and went back into the house. It was a grand day for drying she thought, looking out through the window at the clothes dancing in the breeze. Three pairs of jeans, six pairs of socks, six pairs of underpants and half a dozen shirts. Tears blinded her eyes as she watched the dancing clothes and she wished back a time when small trousers and little jerseys festooned the line. The clothes continued their dance, white clouds raced before the wind like sheep before a collie and tears ran down Rosie's face.

The years, she pondered, where did they go? Blown away like the clouds, like her hopes. And such hopes she'd had. Oh God, it wasn't fair. It really wasn't fair. For a while she continued to think of her grievance and to cry. Then angrily she wiped her eyes and talked aloud to herself: 'A lot of good crying will do. Not all your tears will alter what's in front of Sean or bring back the past. Like a good woman dry your eyes now and make yourself a cup of tea.'

But dismissing the past was easier said than done and as she made and poured the tea memories crowded her mind. Memories of the children – Sean, Thomas and Niamh when they were small, when they lived in London, when they came back to Dublin. When she cherished high hopes for them. And memories of the time before that. The night she met Jack. It seemed like only yesterday that night so long ago in the Olympic Ballroom. Every Saturday night when she was single she went to the Olympic all done up and full of hopes. Hopes that she'd get a good rec, that tonight she might meet a smashing fella – the fella. That was why you went – why everyone went, though you might let on it was the band and the dancing drew you.

On some nights you had a great time, up for every dance, jitterbugging

127

if the bloke could do it until the manager saw you and said, 'There's no jitterbugging allowed.' Under her breath Rosie hummed *In the Mood* and smiled wryly remembering her agility; some people thought jitterbugging was indecent, mostly them that couldn't do it, but it caught on and the management had to allow it, although only in a corner of the ballroom. Imagine that happening nowadays! The kids would have a riot. The poor kids – they thought they had it all their own way. Able to dress how they liked, dance how they liked. Yet when it came down to it they had as little say over the important things as she had had in the Forties and Fifties. Without work, without money you had nothing.

Her mind returned to the Olympic and how years ago you could be asked to leave for refusing to dance with a fella. Even if he was stocious. And the half of them were – only coming in after the pubs shut. Then one would stagger over in your direction and you'd be praying, 'Sacred Heart of Jesus don't let him ask me up.' And he would. Not able to put a foot under him and squeezing you so tight you could feel every bit of him. Poisoning you with the fumes of porter and grabbing hold of your bum. Letting on to do fancy steps so he could push his knee in. Rosie smiled remembering the jitterbugging, the drunks, the eejits of girls, herself included, standing like cows at a fair waiting to be chosen. And how often on the way home she'd vow, 'Never again. Never again will I set foot in it, it's like a cattle market.'

But you were there again the next Saturday, and had spent the week planning how you'd do your hair and what you'd wear. All the girls she knew were the same: Saturday night at the Olympic was the highlight of their lives. The excitement inside you as you queued to pay the entrance. The rush for the cloakroom, crowding round the mirror. Dabbing on a bit more Pancake, fiddling with your hair, pulling a bit this way, a bit that way. Eyeing through the mirror what the others were wearing – pitying some, envying the style of others.

A final dab of the powder puff, a smoothing of your frock, a tug at the skirt and then the big moment. The magic of entering the ballroom. The smell of it, perfume and powder, dust and sweat and French chalk. You felt drunk on it; your heart raced and you laughed and talked loudly. It was like being at the Pictures only different, for now you felt *you* were in the Picture. And if a reasonable fella asked you up you were the Star. It was magic and marvellous, glamorous and romantic.

Rosie let her tea go cold recalling the night she met Jack. *The Tennessee Waltz* was all the rage. The band-leader announced the last dance and struck up. Jack asked her for it. She liked him immediately. He wasn't too tall nor too goodlooking but he had a nice face and was a good dancer and didn't paste himself to her. The other couples dancing were singing with the music, softly singing, 'I was dancing with my sweetheart to the Tennessee Waltz when an old friend I happened to see . . .' It was beautiful. She glided round the floor in Jack's arms. The lights went down, in the ceiling the coloured glass ball revolved. She felt weightless, like a floating feather and wanted to dance for ever and ever. The ball in the ceiling spun slowly, spangling the dancers with all the colours of the rainbow. And she was praying Jack would ask to walk her home. And he did. 'Where do you live?' he asked when the music stopped.

'Kimmage,' she told him. 'Where do you?'

'The North Side.'

Her hopes were dashed. He'd have to be very keen to face that journey back from Kimmage. 'It's terrible far – you'd miss the last bus.'

And he said as they left the floor, 'I like walking. I'll see you when you've got your coat.' They walked home the miles and that was how it all started.

Rosie made more tea, sat down with another cup and suddenly had an overwhelming longing for a cigarette but cigarettes, too, were a thing of the past. Even so she could remember the taste of tobacco, smell the smoke, feel the lift of the first drag, see the dying match curl and wither in the ashtray. God, she had loved a fag until the Health warnings took the edge off her pleasure. Still, it hadn't stopped her smoking though often as she lit up she would think. 'That's another nail in my coffin.' She'd still be smoking if it wasn't for the Novena and promise she'd made when Sean was studying for his Leaving. 'Please God,' she had prayed, 'I'll make the Novena and give up cigarettes only let Sean do well in his exams.' When she told Jack he had that grin on his face, half a laugh, the one he always wore when he codded her. 'Do you know what, Rosie,' he had said, 'you're a grand Catholic. No doubt about it. A grand Catholic. "Do this for me God, and I'll do that for you".' He was codding her, she knew that. He always did when she talked about Novenas and Indulgences. Her insurance policies, he called them, but she never failed to rise to the codding with excuses and explanations as she had that night.

'Ah, Jack, you know well what I mean about the smoking. It's the sacrifice, the self-denial, you know.'

'Oh, indeed I know well and so will God. "Listen," He'll say to whoever is in charge of exams up there, "see to it that young fella does well in the Leaving, Honours in everything. His mother's giving up the fags, she'll put the money in the SVP box".'

'I promised no such thing – won't I need every penny if Sean goes to college?'

And Jack still grinning said, 'A grand Catholic, that's what you are.' And she threw a ball of wool at him; it hit him in the eye and wiped the grin off his face.

Poor Jack, Rosie thought. Poor Jack putting on the brave front but as broken-hearted as she was about what was happening. Here they were going on sixty. Some people had grandchildren before they were sixty. With the way things were going herself and Jack would be lucky to see the face of one. It wasn't their fault they had married late. That wasn't how they had planned it. But no more than the generation today what say had they had in their future?

She held out her hand and looked at her engagement ring – a little cluster of diamonds – and remembered vividly the night Jack had given it to her. She had been expecting it, for the previous Christmas he had given her a gold watch and everyone knew the engagement ring came after the gold watch. She let on to be surprised when Jack gave her the little blue box with the jeweller's name in gold lettering on the lid. She still had it in a drawer upstairs and back into it the ring went if she was washing by hand or doing heavy work. For all that she had guessed what was in the box when she opened it and saw the ring she was so overcome that she couldn't say a word.

'Do you like it?' Jack asked anxiously.

And all she could say was, 'Oh Jack!'

'Take it out, then, and put it on.'

'You're supposed to do that,' she told him, giving him the box. He was all fingers and thumbs and she had said, 'You're an awful eejit, let me do it myself. How did you know it would fit me?' as she slid the ring on to her finger.

'I'm not that much of an eejit. Do you remember one night when we were tricking and I took off your Claddagh ring?'

'I do.'

'Well, before I gave it back – you were in the kitchen – I ran a pencil round the inside of the ring on a bit of paper.'

'The cleverality of you,' she had said and then cried with joy and excitement and kissed him and told him she loved him. Afterwards calling her mother into the parlour to see the ring. Her mother had a bottle of Sandeman's Port put by for Christmas and she opened it and they drank a toast.

After the engagement they made their plans: they'd get married the following year. Only then, thought Rosie, I got ambitions. People like us were starting to buy their own houses, so why couldn't we? Jack was a plasterer earning good money and I was on piecework knocking out a fair wage. A couple of years saving and we'd have a deposit.

130

'Are you mad or what?' her mother had said when she told her. 'A purchase house and me with an empty room above.'

'We want our own place.'

'You'll be putting a rope round your neck for the rest of your life.'

'I don't care, I'm not living in rooms. Start off like that and you're in them until you've a streel of children to satisfy the corporation.'

'Supposing Jack gets sick?'

'Please God he won't.'

'What'll happen when you're expecting?'

'Ma, I'm at the sewing not in the Civil Service. I don't have to stop work because I'm pregnant or married.'

'Have it your own way then, but don't say I didn't warn you. A purchase house indeed.'

My poor mother, thought Rosie. Over the moon at the idea of her daughter owning her own house and yet frightened at the enormity of what we were undertaking. The Lord have mercy on her and her kind heart. From that week she gave me back five shillings every Friday out of my wages. 'Put that towards your deposit,' she'd say, 'and I hope it keeps fine for you.'

Glancing out through the window Rosie saw that the white clouds had darkened and no longer raced before the wind. It might rain. She'd have to keep an eye on the clothes. She returned her mind to thinking about the past. The plans she and Jack had made. Their saving for the deposit. Jack taking every hour of overtime he could get. And she racing frocks through the machine until her eyes blurred and her shoulders ached. Telling herself the pains and aches were worth it as bundle after bundle of dresses was finished and the forewoman entered them in her notebook from which her wages were made up.

The sacrifices they had made: Jack giving up smoking and she shutting her eyes to the shop windows with their new clothes. When the weather was fine they walked for miles, when it wasn't sat in her mother's parlour. Their only treat was Sunday night at the Pictures, the seats for the Adelphi or Savoy booked during the week. They'd meet at the Pillar and Jack always brought her a bag of sweets. And every so often they'd take out the bank book, see the savings growing and congratulate themselves.

God help our senses, said Rosie to herself. Thinking we had control over our lives – that with hard work and thrift we could move mountains. How did we know slackness was coming to the building work and that the sewing factories wouldn't be long before feeling the same pinch. Before we knew it we were both on the Labour and when the stamps were used up dipping into the savings. And still there was no sign of constant work.

131

'There's nothing for it,' Jack said one night. 'We'll have to go to England.'

Not being keen on leaving home she had said, 'Something's bound to turn up.'

'When?' asked Jack. 'Listen, I know fellas who've already gone. They've jobs, they could get me a start.'

And so she had agreed to emigrate. Though in those days it wasn't called emigration – not by ordinary people, anyway. It wasn't called anything. Only going to England, London, Birmingham or Coventry for the work you couldn't get at home. They were going over in their thousands – whole families, single men and women, young boys and girls. Every night the Mail Boat was packed with them. Some had degrees, but the majority had nothing but the Primary Certificate. Every single one of them desperate to earn a living.

Rosie remembered her mother's reaction on the night she told her they were going, the expression on her face and her shocked voice. 'Not without a ring on your finger, you're not. Going to England with a man – your name would be on the Market Cross.'

'Ah, for God's sake, Mother,' she'd said, 'I'm not a child.'

'What's that got to do with it? Now like a good little girl get yourself and him up to the chapel and make the arrangements for your wedding.'

And we did, thought Rosie. We had a quiet wedding and went to London, to Finsbury Park where Jack's friend had a start for him and a room for us. It was a basement like a dungeon with fixtures and fittings consisting of a greasy cooker, curtains in flitters, a cardtable to eat off and a bed that had a sag in the middle like a cow about to drop a calf. Once I'd stopped my crying they were all heaved out. I nearly went demented: you had to keep the light on all day; when it rained the pavement flooded and water poured into the room and all you could see were the legs of people passing. But I soon put a shape on it and made a vow that one day, no matter how long it took, I'd go back home. Not one of my children when God blessed me with them would be reared in England. And not one of them would ever have to take the boat.

When she did venture out she couldn't understand a word the Londoners said. They talked so quick but she got used to it. Paddy, the barrow boys called her. 'Eh, Paddy,' they'd say, 'are you getting used to the shoes?' Or, 'What do think of the electric light and the buses?' But she saw the laugh in their eyes and knew they were only codding her. She soon learned to give as good as she got but all the same, wished it was in Henry Street or

Moore Street she was buying her messages and not on the Holloway Road.

Jack seemed to settle down well enough – anyway, he never complained. He was glad of the constant work and good money, full of praise for the National Health Service. One night when she was giving out the pay about England he said, 'Well at least you can go to the doctor without worrying what he'll charge you.'

And she in bad humour snapped back, 'We never go to the doctor!'

'I'm only pointing out the difference between here and at home. And there's free education and the children's allowance.'

'They're a lot of good to us,' she told him.

'Ah, you know what I mean,' he said.

And she did. He was trying to console and comfort her but she wouldn't let him. He was content in London. If she hadn't pushed him they'd be there still. She wondered if he ever regretted giving in to her. 'I wonder does he think if it hadn't been for my insistence on coming home we wouldn't be losing Sean? He never says. He's not a complainer, not like me. But it's easier for a man. They have their work. They're out all day – have company all day. They don't have the time to think and ponder about things. I'd have gone mad in London if I hadn't gone out to work. Especially when month after month passed and no sign of a baby. I liked the job in Great Margaret Street in the sewing factory. It was like being at home again: the same smells of new materials and machine oil. The same noises, the clattering clanging button-hole and bartacking machines, girls singing as they sewed and a shouting foreman chasing through an order. The same time-clock to punch. I liked it. It was all right even if the voices *were* different.

'But the getting there and going back on the tube put the heart crossways in me. Stepping on to the escalators was like jumping off a cliff and stepping off was worse again. And there was a rush of warm wind when you got down onto the platform like a wind you'd never smelt or felt before. I wonder if any of it has changed. I wonder what Sean will think of it. I wonder if the people on the tubes have changed. Do they look at you nowadays, or still sit like statues? That was terrible. Not a smile nor a word. I used to think you could drop dead and they wouldn't turn a hair.'

Rosie looked out through the window. The rain was holding off, she'd leave the clothes for another few minutes. Her thoughts returned again to her years in London. She had finally got the knack of the escalators and become used to the London voices, used to everything except the idea that she would spend the rest of her life out of Ireland. She had given up crying and complaining to Jack about her homesickness. He didn't

133

deserve that and it solved nothing. But she had a plan – a goal. She would start saving her wages. Jack's money was good, they could live on that. Every penny of hers after her tube fares and a few shillings for the collections and raffles in the factory would go into the bank. It would take time but one day there would be the money for a deposit on a house in Dublin. She was determined that this time they would succeed. She said nothing to Jack about the plan: the savings, she told him, were for a rainy day. For months it all went well and she would look at the bank book and calculate that in another two years or so the end of their stay in England would be in sight.

Then she got pregnant and her feelings were all mixed up. For so long she had wanted a baby, prayed for one. Now she was having one and should have been down on her knees thanking God and instead she was thinking that although she could carry on working once the child was born, please God, she'd have to finish saving and that would be an end to her dream of returning home. But she found consolation quickly: the child was more important than anything else and she thanked God for the blessing of her pregnancy. And it didn't have to be the end of her hopes, only the postponing of them. You could never plan your life. Always there were disappointments and always consolations.

And such a consolation Sean was – a beautiful, big, placid baby that she fell in love with the minute she saw his face, though she cried too in her ward in the Whittington Hospital where he was born. She wasn't alone in her crying, surrounded by other Irishwomen grieving for the parents and relations not able to see their new babies.

In a little over three years she had three babies – Sean, Niamh and Tom. They kept her mind occupied and her body exhausted, leaving her neither the energy nor time to feel homesick. And so the years passed until a spring day in the year Sean was due to start school. She had taken the children to play in the park and while they played she talked to the other mothers, women from Cork, Donegal and Leitrim, Kildare and Mayo, Dublin and Derry, each one with her distinctive accent. At the same time she heard the voices of the children playing on the swings and roundabouts and she was struck by something odd. For a moment she pondered and then it came to her – not one of the children spoke with their mother's accents. They were all little Londoners, Sean as well.

'What difference does that make?' asked Jack when she told him that evening.

'All the difference in the world. They'll grow up talking like that: they won't be Irish. I'm not rearing them here.'

'You mean you want to go home?'

134

'Of course I want to go home. I've always wanted to go home. We've always said that we were only here until we got on our feet.'

'Ah,' said Jack, 'that's what we all say, but it's not that easy. We're settled now. We have a grand flat. I'm never short of work.'

'Things have changed at home. There's plenty of work. Ireland's booming – you saw that when we were over last year.'

'I know,' he said, 'but what about the children? Here if they have the brains they'll get an education for nothing. You take them home and in ten, fifteen years like us and millions before us they'll be on the boat.'

'That's where you're wrong. The education is easier to get in Ireland now and if God has blessed them with the intelligence mine will be educated. How many Irish with education have had to leave home? Those that went did it from choice. Doctors and nurses, priests. It wasn't stay and starve or get out. Not like for us or the thousands like us with nothing but the Primary Certificate, if that. Ours will have the education and be able to stay at home.'

'Maybe you're right but where will we live?'

'We'll buy a house. Everyone at home owns their own house. I'll go back to work.'

'What about the children?'

'Not to the sewing. I'll do office cleaning after you come home. We can do it, I know we can. Say you'll come. You want to, I know in your heart you do.'

Two years of cleaning offices it took. Acres of floors I hoovered: millions of toilet rolls I put into lavatories. Half out of my mind with fright every time I heard a noise in the big empty building. I got used to it. You get used to everything. And she smiled, remembering the first night she had started the job and noticed all the little bits of coloured paper round the desks and thought someone had left to be married and that the tiny circles of paper were confetti – until she learned about the punching machine. Jack laughed when she told him.

Two years of hard saving and they were back in Ireland in this house which they were buying. God was good to them. They prospered and settled in as if they had never left Ireland. The joy it was wakening in the morning and thinking, I'm home. Out there is Dublin. Up the road is my mother. In five minutes on the bus I can be in Henry Street, Grafton Street or down in Moore Street for my messages. And the children were bright and though you had to pay if you called the doctor they were seldom sick and the chemist was as good as any doctor if it wasn't a serious complaint.

It was all happening as I knew it would. Sean top of the class. No bother with Irish. The master telling me he was university material. And me that proud – never thinking as my mother used to say, 'Pride goes before a fall.' Lord have mercy on her. She didn't live to hear the best news that Sean was in Trinity. She'd have been so proud, but then she was saved the bad news as well.

How I didn't see it coming I'll never know. Of course I heard the talk: too many teachers, too many doctors, but I'd shut my mind to it. Telling myself a country like Ireland couldn't have too many engineers and thanking God that Sean would be an engineer. I'll never forget the day of the Conferring. My son in a cap and gown. My son an engineer. Thinking employers would be queuing up to collar him. My head in the clouds. Ignoring all that was going on round me. The voices of friends and relatives, them on the TV'. 'There's nothing here for them. They have to go.' And still I wouldn't accept it. Sean was bound to get a job – didn't he have dozens of applications in? No, I was still hoping until the night he told me.

'It's not what I wanted, Ma, but I'll have to go. There's nothing here and there won't be for a long time so don't bank on keeping Tom and Niamh.'

I went cold from the inside out. I thought I'd drop. 'But you're an engineer, you've an education behind you,' I said.

'I know, Ma, but so have thousands of others. It's not the end of the world. It's only England. Some of the fellas come home every weekend – they fly over. They do, honest to God.'

What could I say? God knows he was disappointed and angry. Me tearing my hair out wasn't going to help things.

The rattle of rain against the windows reminded Rosie about the clothes. She ran out and brought them in. The ironing board wouldn't erect first time and she kicked it and swore at it and swore again when it pinched her fingers. While the iron heated she hung the socks on the radiator then sorted the rest for ironing. She pressed the jeans, banging the iron harder than was necessary on the cloth. Tears fell from her eyes on to the blue material and she talked aloud. 'It's not fair. No one should be forced to leave home because they can't get a job. No mothers and fathers should have their hearts broken when their sons and daughters are forced to go. Life is too short to be parted from those you love.'

Gradually as she worked other thoughts came into her mind, the means of consoling herself. Sean was only going to England, not America or Australia like some. He'd come home. They'd go and see him. They wouldn't lose him. And maybe things would improve. Maybe in a couple of years he could come back. She had, and plenty of others. What she and all the other parents were going through their mothers and fathers had gone through before them. It wasn't the end of the world. You had to find a consolation. All your life you were looking for consolation for one thing or another. And at least Sean and the others were going better prepared than those who had gone before. He'd be all right. They'd be all right. But all the same it was a crying shame that the young of the country were forced to go. The young of some countries, anyway. Not the English – if they went, it was from choice. Nor the Americans. Only the poor countries, Italians and Turks, the unfortunate black people. She was only one of millions of grieving mothers all over the world. And grieve she would, always. But life would go on. She'd laugh again and so would Jack. And they'd have the letters and the phone calls. Life went on and you made the best of it and hoped and prayed that one day it might be better still.

Redundant

Daylight filtered through the thin faded curtains and fell on the face of the sleeping man. He woke, sat up in bed startled and bewildered-looking. 'Damn!' he said. 'I've slept late. It's that bloody clock, it didn't go off.' He reached for the offending clock, his fingers almost touching it before he remembered. Remembered that he didn't have to go to work – that he never had to go to work again for six months ago, Wilf Jones had been one of the first to volunteer for redundancy. Saying to his mates once he understood 'the scheme': 'Catch me working till I'm sixty-five when if I go now I'll get the lump-sum and two years' make-up pay besides. Working for nothing I'd be if I stayed.'

Once his mind was made up and the forms filled and sent in he became impatient to start his new life. Fuming as he waited for union and management to complete the formalities. 'Typical, isn't it,' he grumbled. 'Always on about overmanning and look what happens. It's weeks now since I put in to go and not a word. I ask you – where's the sense in it? Couldn't organise a piss-up in a brewery, that lot couldn't.'

Eventually his redundancy came through. Wilf was presented with a transistor radio from his mates, some retirement cards from the office typists and a handshake and short speech from a member of management thanking him for his forty-five years of loyal service. The lump-sum was forwarded by cheque.

The first two weeks were great – like being on his holidays, Wilf felt. He thought a lot about Margaret, wishing she could see his present and the cards. Poor Mag, she was a good old stick. Kept the place beautiful and always gave him a tidy box. He remembered how she loved flowers. Roses and godetias were her favourites – she had the garden full of godetias. He used to pull her leg about them, telling her they were like them paper flowers gypsy women used to sell and make. And she'd pick one and stick it under his nose. 'Now then, clever Dick,' she'd say, 'have a smell of that – no tissue paper there.'

He'd buy a bunch for her grave and go on Palm Sunday, only you never saw godetias in flower shops. You had to grow them from seeds. Nothing would grow in the garden now – hell of a mess on it. Have a fit, Mag would, if she could see it. Even if he planted the seeds now and they grew they wouldn't be ready for Palm Sunday. In any case, he hated cemeteries. You didn't have to go to remember someone and he thought about Margaret every day. Hell of a girl she was. Maybe they would have got on better now that he wasn't working shifts. She'd hated the shifts – he supposed that was with her being English. Oh, the rows they used to have: the rows they would have had now over the lump-sum. Terrible girl Margaret was for money – spend it like there was no tomorrow. All the same he missed her.

After two weeks Wilf lost the holiday feeling. The days were hard to fill and every morning he woke with the fear that he had overslept and would miss the Works' bus. Then like this morning would come the realisation that he never had to hurry anywhere again. Dejectedly he leant against the pillows, closed his eyes and tried to coax sleep back. From the bus-stop outside his downstairs flat he could hear the sounds made by the men waiting for the bus. He listened, recognising a voice, a laugh, even a cough and could picture their early-morning faces, pale with sleep still clinging to them, their bodies hunched inside their working clothes. He heard the bus whine to a stop, the doors open, the noise of them closing and then the stillness after the bus pulled away.

He burrowed deeper into the bed searching for the warm place, wanting sleep but it eluded him, so he opened his eyes and thought about the day that stretched ahead of him. It was Wednesday and Wednesday was a cow of a day. A dead day. He had found ways of killing the others. Mondays he went to the Job Centre to sign on for the make-up and show willing that he was prepared to take a job. That was a laugh, that was. Employers were queuing to grab men over sixty with coke oven experience. But if you didn't sign on your pay was docked. So he went, and met men he used to work with and heard about their Spanish holidays, new extensions, greenhouses and new cars. Now and then he joined them for a pint. He wasn't a drinker but it put in an hour. And after dinner there was his coupon to study.

On Tuesdays he changed the bed and took the sheets and towels to the launderette. His shirts and underthings he washed himself – and would have washed the other stuff if it wasn't for her next door. A widow – always offering to do the sheets and pillowcases for him. Wanting her foot in the door, more likely. Never offered to do his washing before he finished. He knew all about widows and redundancy money. On Tuesdays he also cleaned the house and had another look at his coupon.

Thurdays he went to the Co-op. Mag had always bought the goods on Thursday, said they were fresher then. After dinner he got the rubbish ready for the next day, flattening the tin cans so they didn't tear the plastic bags. Where all the rubbish came from always surprised him. He remembered his Mam's bin with nothing in it only ashes. When the bags were filled he secured the tops with elastic bands. Then a last study of form before completing his coupon and posting it.

On Fridays the rentman came. He was a bit of an old apple woman – knew everyone's business: who was bad, who had died, who was living tally. He sat himself down and gossiped. Still, it was a human voice and an hour put in. Later on the Society man came. You had to keep your policy in benefit, had to have a decent burial. Nothing flashy, mind, but a tidy send-off. Nowadays the price of a funeral was beyond, but he had seen to that. Put a bit of the lump-sum in a High Interest account. That was another queer thing, the way building societies had sprung up like mushrooms all down Station Road once the redundancy came in. Between the rent collector and the insurance man the morning flew. He didn't mind the afternoons, you could put them in with another look at the paper or a doze. And at night there was the telly – not that there was much on it.

His chance of more sleep was now gone completely and so reluctantly he got up, sat on the side of the bed and lit a cigarette. He inhaled deeply and began to cough. He coughed until his face went purple and a vein swelled and throbbed at his temple. Between bouts of coughing he continued to smoke until the cigarette was reduced to a wet stub. His finger and thumb held the butt at which he greedily sucked.

Afterwards he dressed, washed his face under the cold tap in the kitchen then made tea and porridge. When he had eaten his breakfast he tidied up and made the bed. There was nothing else to do now until the paper shop opened. The post office was part of the paper shop and Wilf thought that no matter how early he got there the place was always full of women and kids. Kids swarming round the counter where he bought his paper and fags, pushing and shoving, taking ages to decide whether they wanted chews or chocolate, crisps or bubble gum. It was the same at the post office section: gangs of women with plastic-wrapped packages to be sent back to the Catalogue, taking all day about it. And her behind the counter – supposed to be the post-mistress – every bit as bad. Rabbiting on about the dresses never looking like they did in the Catalogue when they arrived. About wrong sizes and wrong colours. And all he wanted was a stamp.

He sat back at the table drumming his fingers on it and wondering how he could put a bit of life into the day. He could go to the surgery – he hadn't been there for a while. *She* was there on a Wednesday morning –

the chopsy one. Cheeky little piece. He smiled recalling the first time he had met her. That was a Wednesday, too: a couple of months after finishing. Before he'd left the Works he could truthfully boast that only once in all his working life had he ever been on the Sick. But now he often felt bad – nothing you could put a name to, just out of sorts. And one day when he was feeling that way he decided to go and see Myers, even if it meant an hour's wait in the small parlour that was the waiting room and where winter and summer a gasfire hissed that could roast you alive if it was a warm day.

When he arrived at the house the place was boarded up and a notice informed him that the surgery had been moved to the new Health Centre. Cursing himself for a fool, for now he remembered having read of the move in the local paper, he made his way to the new clinic. He climbed the outside flight of concrete steps and arrived at the reception desk out of breath and temper complaining loudly to the young woman in the hatch beneath Dr Myers' name: 'There's a daft place to have a flight of steps! Sick we're supposed to be, not mountaineering.'

Wilf smiled remembering what had followed. Fit she was but not fit enough for him. Little crot of a thing, chopsy as hell. 'There's no need to climb the steps,' she said. 'There's a ramp and a lift.'

'Lift be damned,' he'd shot back at her. He wasn't letting her know he was afraid of lifts, even had he known where to find it.

'Suit youself then,' she said before asking, 'have you got an appoint-ment?'

'No,' he replied belligerently, 'I haven't no appointment.'

'You're supposed to have one. It saves waiting and Doctor knows whether he's coming or going.'

'How the hell am I supposed to know yesterday that I'm going to be bad tomorrow? I haven't got a crystal ball.'

That, Wilf remembered, shut her up all right. She took his name and told him to wait. All the same she had the last word, saying as he left the hatch, 'There's no call for bad language.'

After the encounter he felt better. The vague pains and aches which had brought him to the surgery had gone but as he was here he decided he might as well wait to see Myers and get something for his cough. While he waited for his turn he kept thinking what a little tartar the receptionist was, and how he had enjoyed having a go at her.

He had been back a few times since then and never made an appointment. Each time they had a run in but much as he enjoyed the scraps he couldn't go every Wednesday. He'd finish up being sent to a psychiatrist, that way. But he *would* go this morning: his back was giving him gip. Aching low down. 'A chill I've got,' he said aloud. 'A chill on my kidneys.' He massaged his back while still talking. 'I'll go and get something for it. Can't be too careful of your kidneys.'

His spirits rose and there was a spring in his step as he went and shaved then got his clean changes from the airing cupboard. On his way to the Health Centre he planned what he would say to the receptionist if she gave him any lip. Once she had threatened to report him to the doctor. 'Struck off Doctor's list you could be. Coming in here and swearing and never making an appointment. That's what'll happen if I report you.'

'Do it, then,' he said. 'Flaming well report me.' That had taken the wind out of her sails, Wilf thought as he walked down the street. Take more than her to frighten me. Any of her nonsense this morning and he'd put her in her place: ask her did wearing a white coat make her think she was a doctor. Cheeky monkey. He felt excited, elated at the prospect of doing battle. He quickened his pace and his heart beat faster.

When he reached the clinic he decided against the steps and chose the ramp instead. He walked up it slowly, breathless from hurrying and the anticipation of a fight. Halfway up he stopped, leant over the rail and looked in the direction of the new town centre – a grey prison-like structure, and at the raw concrete supporting the tangle of bridges and flyovers. 'A tidy little town, this used to be,' he murmured to himself. 'All the little houses and pubs that went to make way for this lot and they call it progress. Bridges and flyovers and bloody town-planners. Couldn't plan a street party that lot couldn't.' Then he took a deep breath and continued up the ramp.

He opened the clinic door. The noise was deafening: telephones ringing, the rattle of typing, filing cabinets being dragged open and slammed shut and a baby screaming. He went to the hatch – there was no one there. She was rabbiting on somewhere, he thought, drinking tea, having a quick drag on a fag. Never mind about the patients. Should be sacked, the whole lot of them – a waste of tax-payers' money. Surgeries managed for years without them. And then he saw her coming; she was backing out of another office on the far side of the reception area, yakking away. She turned and it wasn't her: like her, but not her and she was coming to Myers' hatch. 'Yes?' she said and smiled.

Wilf felt as if he had been poleaxed. He couldn't think, nor hear nor speak.

'Have you an appointment?' asked the new receptionist.

For a moment his heart rose. It might still be all right. He might manage to get a spark out of this one. 'No,' he said and his tone was abrupt.

142

She smiled and said in a pleasant manner, 'In that case you'll probably have a long wait. Take a seat please.'

He mumbled something and walked away from the hatch, hesitated and stood looking round the room reading the posters plastered on every wall. He read of the dangers of smoking, over-eating, lack of exercise and the times of the Well Woman Clinic, standing and reading in an effort to calm himself, to get over his disappointment and trying to decide if he'd sit and wait for the doctor. Then, realising he was drawing attention to himself by standing in the middle of the floor and making it neccessary for people to walk round him, he sat on one of the chairs arranged in front of the hatch windows. All round him other people sat and also waited their turn, some talking in whispers, some reading the magazines and others just staring into space.

After he'd been there a few minutes the woman sitting next to him spoke up. 'She got the poke – good job, too. Chopsy piece she was. Got the sack she did. Someone reported her. Mrs Bevan is ever so nice. A lady, she is.' Wilf said nothing. The woman nudged him. 'Did you hear what I said?' He ignored her. 'Some people!' she exclaimed, and picked up a magazine.

Twice the receptionist called his name before he heard her say, 'Will you go round now, please, Mr Jones.' He rose and began to walk down the long corridor then changed his mind. All Myers would do was give him a lecture about the fags, his weight and taking more exercise. It wasn't Myers he'd come to see. He turned and walked back the way he'd come, passing the reception desk where Mrs Bevan looked enquiringly at him. He hurried past, pushed open the swing doors and headed for the ramp thinking as he went that Wednesday was really done for now.

He began to walk home. From the other side of the street a voice called, 'How's it going, Wilf? Still enjoying your redundancy?'

He recognised the man, one he used to work with, one who was still working. He straightened his back and held his head high as he shouted back, 'Great, bloody great. The best thing I ever did.'

The Legacy

The train from Galway was late arriving in Dublin. Passengers spilled from it, hurrying towards bus-stops, waiting cars and the taxi rank. Maura Begley joined the throng going towards the cab rank. She stood in the queue and counted those in front of her: there were fifteen. She hoped that some were couples or families. A hand touched her shoulder. Instinctively she tightened the hold on her handbag and thought, surely to God not here. Not with so many people about. Then a man spoke. 'Maura, Maura Begley? It *is* you. I wasn't mistaken!' The voice which she immediately recognised made her heart race faster than the imagined mugger. She turned round.

'Danny, Danny O'Rourke! I can't believe it. Is it really you?'

'It's me all right,' said Danny and moved to stand beside her. 'I got off just after you. We must have been in adjoining coaches. For a minute I wasn't sure if it was you. Then you turned your head and I knew.'

'You shaved off the beard.'

'It had started to go grey. It's been a long time – nine, ten years.'

'Ten,' she said and could have told him the month, the day, the time it was when they parted. Her heart was still excited and her legs shaky, but outwardly she seemed no more than genuinely pleased and surprised at meeting an old friend.

'Were you down home for the weekend?' Danny enquired.

'There's no one there any more – my mother died two years ago. I was in Galway for the funeral of a great-aunt.'

'I hope she left you a fortune.'

Maura laughed deprecatingly. 'Indeed she did not. Only a ring,' she said, substituting a piece of jewellery for the sizable legacy her relation had indeed left her. As she spoke she wondered why she lied: once she would have told Danny everything, but ten years was a long time. You learned certain things. She hoped so, anyway.

'Tell me,' she went on, 'it's something I've often wondered about. Have you got your consultancy yet?'

'No,' he said, 'and won't until some hoor's melt drops dead and with my luck it'll be down the country. This queue isn't shifting – let's go and have a jar.'

'I'm waiting for a taxi – a lot will come together in a minute.'

'There's a pub across the road. We'll have a drink and by that time the queue will have gone.'

'So will the taxis. And anyway, I'm jaded. It was a big wake and I didn't get to bed until all hours.' She was dying to ask him if he was married.

The taxis began to arrive in a steady stream. The queue was diminishing. Danny tried again. 'Just a quick one, to warm you up.'

'Honestly, I'd rather go home.' Now only three people remained in front of them. Two more cabs pulled into the kerb. A couple took the first one and the remaining man the next.

'It might be ages before the next comes – let's have a drink.' Again Maura refused. Another car was coming, pulling up. 'All right so,' said Danny and opened the cab door. 'Where do you hang out?' She gave her address and he half-manoeuvred, half-pushed her in and on to the seat. Then he joined her and told the driver the address. 'Only stop at Cheers on the way.'

Maura began to protest. 'I want to go straight home. I'm . . .'

'Listen,' he said and took hold of her hand. 'Let's have just one drink for old times' sake. I've given your address. Five minutes is all it'll take: you don't think I'd keep a taxi waiting longer than that?'

Her hand fitted so well into his. It was a wonderful sensation to feel the touch of his flesh again. 'Well, just the one,' she conceded.

The taxi drove down O'Connell Street. 'They've destroyed the shaggin' city,' Danny said, looking out through the window.

'Yes,' Maura agreed, watching the derelict buildings, the garish shop-fronts, the parking lots. 'They've done terrible things to the city.'

'No one in Dublin eats at home any more.'

'No?'

'Well – ask yourself. There's McDonald's, pizza parlours, up-market fish and chippers . . . Look at them all chawing away as if their life depended on the next mouthful.'

'It's still a beautiful city, though sometimes when I remember what it was like I feel sad.'

'What?' asked Danny. And she recalled this infuriating way he had of starting a conversation, making a challenging statement and by the time you were ready to comment the issue was gone from his mind.

'I'm talking about the city – the changes here. How I feel about them. Sometimes I see all the dereliction as if for the first time and I'm upset, but normally it's like being with someone you know or have known for a long time: occasionally you do notice that they've changed or are ageing but it's only for a few minutes, because their smile is still the same, their eyes have the same expression, and the bones are still there beneath the changes.'

'Unless they've had a stroke,' said Danny, and she laughed. He could always make her laugh even when his humour was sick. He had made her laugh the first time they met. 'Are you sure it's not me you're alluding to – beautiful old bones, a bit run down but the eyes and the smile still the same?'

'You,' she said and leant against him for a moment. She felt as if she was drunk, delirious with delight at being with him again. He continued to talk, about what had happened to this one and that one from their past. She half-listened while her mind skipped back . . . to the first time they met. Someone in the office knew someone who was throwing a party. She was invited, asked to bring a bottle. She had only ever tasted wine at Christmas. She felt a sense of guilt going into the off-licence and at the same time daring and sophisticated. She remembered that it was May. How from the partygiver's flat high up in a Georgian house she looked out into the trees that grew in a small park opposite. There was a chestnut tree, its branches laden with candles and she had thought how wonderful it would be to live in such a flat and watch the candles day by day until they blossomed.

Staring at the trees gave her an excuse to appear occupied, for so far, although the room was packed with people talking, laughing and screaming greetings to new arrivals, no one paid her the slightest attention. Her friend and the partygiver were mingling, everyone was mingling except her. So she was glad of the tree. Maybe in a minute when the sour-tasting wine she was forcing herself to drink had an effect she would find the courage to mingle, also.

Then from behind her she heard a voice reciting, 'I think that I shall never see A poem lovely as a tree.' She turned to look and saw a young man. Danny. He raised his glass. 'Hello,' he said. 'That used to be my party piece. Recitation with actions.' She laughed because she didn't know what else to do. And he kept making her laugh even after she found the courage to say a few words now and again. He talked about himself. He was a medical student in his last year. Like herself he was from the country. His hair was thick, black and curly and he had a beard to match. Through the beard she could see his very full mouth with lips like a girl and very white teeth. She heard very little of what he said for most of her attention was given up to admiring him. Thinking how never in all her life had she seen anyone so handsome.

He asked her questions. She told him she was a civil servant, and shared a flat on the southside. One of her flatmates had brought her to the

146

party. She felt she had known him always. He kept plying her with wine. It didn't taste sour any more.

There was the memory of music, a song she had never heard before – a beautiful, haunting song. And Danny had said, 'Come on, let's give it a twirl.' It was music to smooch to. He held her close. She leaned into him, her two arms round his neck, her face against his chest. He stroked her back and his hand slid down her dress until it rested on her bottom. And she was bewitched.

The taxi crossed Baggot Street Bridge and stopped outside a public house. Maura returned to the present. Danny was talking, telling her she would like Cheers. 'Downstairs they've a great pianist.' As he talked he was manoeuvring her out of the cab.

'D'ye want me to wait?' asked the driver.

'No,' said Danny, paying him.

'But,' protested Maura, 'you said he would. One drink, you said, five minutes. I really don't want a drink.'

The cab drove away. 'You must have changed, so,' said Danny, taking hold of her and propelling her towards the public house.

'I have. Lots of things change in ten years.'

'What you want is a couple of Jamesons. On you go, down the stairs. Sit on the sofa while I get them.'

There were sofas, chintzy ones and soft lights and a pianist playing Gershwin. And on the walls tastefully erotic prints. Looking at one facing her Maura wondered what you called the opposite of a full frontal. No wonder Danny used this pub – he had a thing about a woman with a fine arse. She was back in the past again remembering the first time he paid her the compliment. And she thought, oh God, why did I have to meet him again after all these years? I love him. I don't think I ever stopped loving him but I don't want to be involved again. He's probably married – I hope he is.

He returned with the drinks. 'Say when.' He poured water into her tumbler. Jasus, you'll drown it.' He sat down and looked hard at her. He had gorgeous eyes. She loved his eyes. 'Yes,' he said, 'you have changed. But you look great. A bit – no, not older, not a day – but different. More sure of yourself. I like your hair. It's darker. You used to have blonde hair.'

'Age,' she said. 'Blonde hair darkens with age.' She wanted to look away from his scrutiny but she couldn't. His eyes compelled her.

'Your long blonde hair and brown eyes. That's what I first noticed about you. I told myself it was dyed but you proved me wrong.'

'Are you married, Danny?'

'Me! Married! Sure who'd have me. You threw me over.'

147

You never asked me, she thought. 'No, I'm not married. From time to time I live in sin but married, no. And yourself? I noticed no ring. But nowadays that means nothing.'

'I never married either.' She wouldn't give him the satisfaction of saying, 'I never met anyone who came near you. I measured them all against you.'

The pianist finished the Gershwin medley. Danny asked if she wanted another drink. She refused and watched him walking to the bar. She saw that his hair was thinning at the back. His body had thickened. She was glad to see the flaws in him. She was mad with herself for having allowed him to coerce her into coming for the drink. The trouble, as it had always been, was that she could refuse him nothing. After ten years it should have been different, but it wasn't. Her mind was clear about the sort of man he was, but what chance did your mind have when your body yearned for him, when your heart and soul cried out to let it be? To let it all begin again . . . But she wasn't eighteen any more. She was a woman going on for thirty. It was ridiculous to act the starry-eyed young girl again. She was going home. She began gathering her things together and was about to stand up when Danny was back with his drink. 'Eh,' he said, 'What's this? Where d'ye think you're going?'

'I've a headache. I have to go home.'

'You're hungry – they do food upstairs.'

Steeling her resolve she refused. If she allowed herself to stay all she'd remember were the good times – the carefree summer nights, the lovemaking. He was getting fat and going bald but what did any of that matter? His eyes were the same. His mouth would taste the same. His body would smell the same. Oh God, she mustn't let it happen again. *She mustn't.*

'OK,' said Danny, 'if you're that tired we'll go.' But he continued to sip his drink slowly. And then the pianist began to play again, the very song they had danced to the night they met.

'You've gone far far away from me, Maura Begley. What are you thinking about?'

'Lots of things. The night we met. The first time I ever got drunk.'

'And were sick all over me,' said Danny.

'I'd forgotten that. You're right, I was. I felt terrible about that.'

'So did I. They were my best, my only jeans.'

'You took me to the bathroom and cleaned us up. And when we came back that song was playing and I'd splashed someone's aftershave over me to cover the sick smell. Listen, it's the same song,' she nodded towards the pianist.

'And we danced,' he reminded her.

'You remember?'

'I remember and you said . . .'

'What? What did I say?'

'That you'd pay to have my clothes washed.'

'I didn't!'

'Honest to God you did.'

She didn't remember that bit, but it was probably true. With the thrown-up wine would have gone her newly acquired sophistication, leaving the naive country girl she was – embarrassed at what had happened. He had probably laughed at her up his sleeve, sizing her up for what she was: a country thick. An easy mark. The whiskey turned sour in her stomach. Her face became sullen.

Danny tossed back the remains of his drink. 'Come on, then, I'll take you home.'

'Don't be silly. I'll get a taxi or an eighteen bus.'

'And be mugged or raped. This is now, not ten years ago.' On the way up the stairs he put an arm round her. 'Ah, Maura,' he said. 'I was a fool. I never should have let you go. We've wasted so much of our lives.' She wanted the world to stop. The clock to go back. His arms round her forever and ever. They climbed the stairs and went out into the street.

His arm was still about her and she felt the beginning of an urge to say, 'Come home with me. Let's make up for the lost time. Let's never part again.' She knew it was what he planned on, hoped for. It would be so easy. So easy to start all over again, to slip back into the way it was. She took a deep breath to clear from her mind her confused thoughts. She mustn't give way to this whim. Not yet, anyway. Not until she had time to think, to ask herself lots of questions. And so without making a fuss, she withdrew herself from his hold and said, forcing her voice to be calm and steady, 'Look Danny, it was fantastic meeting you again. But I do really want to go home and on my own. I'll take a taxi – I'll be all right. I'll wait for one on the bridge. It's very well lit. I'll be all right. You go on.'

'I'm seeing you home safe and sound and I'm not taking no for an answer.' A prostitute passed and crossed the road to Wilton Place. She was a young girl, her midi-coat swinging open, her mini-skirt riding high with each stride so that her knickers showed. 'Thirty quid,' Danny said, looking at her.

'Danny, I don't want you taking me home.'

'OK. Fine.'

Despite herself she was fascinated by what he had said about the prostitute. 'Were you serious about the thirty quid?'

'That's the going rate, so I'm told.'

'Thirty quid!' she repeated incredulously, then added, 'Wouldn't you think they'd be afraid of AIDS?'

'No more than their grannies were of syphilis,' he quipped and stepped into the road to flag a passing taxi.

'I'm going on my own, remember,' said Maura.

Danny opened the door, she got in and before she knew it Danny was in beside her and giving the driver her address. 'A cup of coffee, just one,' he said in the mock-childish voice she remembered him using when other means failed to get him his way. 'Only the one, as true as God.'

'No,' she said, 'not even a drink of water, not tonight.' With a mixture of relief and disappointment she heard him accept her refusal. The taxi turned into the square. She began fumbling in her purse for the fare.

'Forget it,' Danny said, 'I'll take it on home.' His voice was sulky. The driver asked the house number, she told him and the car pulled up outside it. Danny got out and held the door for her. 'Will I see you again?' he asked.

'The number's in the book, give me a buzz.' And she ran up the steps, half-hoping to hear him following her. Taking the decision out her hands. As she closed the door she saw the cab pull away. The week-end bag with only a change of clothes in it felt leaden and her legs like ton weights but heaviest of all was the weight of her heart.

Her lovely flat looked cold, lonely and uninviting. She switched on a fire and lights, drew the curtains, plugged in the kettle, put her bag in the bedroom, wet tea and brought it to the living room where she sat and thought about Danny and their meeting. And how for years after they had parted she had imagined such a happening. In a city as small as Dublin it had seemed inevitable and yet in all of ten years it had never come about.

A car stopped outside. Her heart raced – he had come back. He hadn't taken no for an answer. But she wouldn't let him in, definitely not. She was trembling. The car started up, drove away. The bell didn't ring.

She went to bed but couldn't sleep and thought about Danny, regretting not giving him her telephone number, which was ex-directory. He might be able to get it: Irish operators often fell for a plausible story. She became angry and frustrated with herself. 'Make up your mind one way or the other,' she told herself angrily. 'Do you want to see him again or don't you? If you don't, forget him and go to sleep and if you do, the rest is easy. He'll find your telephone number somehow. In any case, he knows where you live.'

Making the decision wasn't easy. If she hadn't met him again tonight her life would have gone on as before: quite a pleasant life, with friends, lovers now and then, a good job – even a pension for her old age and now the money her aunt had left her. Things, she thought, fell into your lap when you were least expecting them and in most cases could have done without them. But once – ten years ago – the difference an inheritance would have made to her life was crucial. She wouldn't have been lying here alone agonising about whether she should see Danny again.

It was a long time since she had thought in detail about what had happened between them, and never objectively. She had never considered it from his point of view. Her mind had always swung between condemnation of him and a yearning for the way things were then, back in the early seventies when they had become lovers. When she had moved in to live with him, telling her mother she was sharing with a new friend, finding excuses any time she suggested visiting Dublin. What a time it was! What a time to be young and in love.

It had lasted a whole summer, during which she learned how to drink the vinegary wine, swallowing it down as if it was sweet milk. She was proud of herself when Danny said she had a liver like an ox. There were parties night after night in basement flats, sessions in the popular pubs. She was known as Danny's bird, feeling that at last she really belonged in Dublin. Walking home in the middle of the night, sometimes almost morning, walking along the canal with the sky full of stars and sometimes a moon, sometimes the dawn sun, with Danny's arms and hers entwined about each other. And the lovemaking . . . early in the mornings, in the daytime, any time, any place where it was possible. Her Halcyon Days on which she thrived and blossomed. People told her she was beautiful, that her hair, her skin was gorgeous. And she felt beautiful and gorgeous and delighted in her body. And every day throughout that summer was magical.

And then one morning when the first hint of autumn was in the air she woke and didn't feel well. 'Maybe your liver's not what it was,' said Danny as he gathered his books together. 'You drink a hell of a lot these days.'

She took Alka Seltzers, a vitamin C tablet, a cup of tea and for good measure a piece of chocolate. The girls at work said she didn't look well. By lunchtime she felt better but the feeling of being unwell became a regular part of her early mornings. The girls at work said she might be run down. Her hair wasn't as glossy as it used to be and her skin was blotchy. One told the tale of a friend who felt like that: there was no terrible pain or anything – it was a grumbling appendix. She woke up one night screaming and only got to the hospital in the nick of time.

That evening Maura told Danny about the girl with a grumbling appendix. 'There's no such thing,' he said dismissively. He was always dismissive when she spoke about anything medical.

'This girl nearly died. It burst and she got peritonitis. I think you should examine me.'

'I've told you before, if you're sick you have to see somone else.'

'That's stupid and you living with me. I don't have a doctor.'

'Go to Casualty, then.' His manner, she thought for the first time, could be too brusque, brutal even. She told him so. 'It's nothing to do with my manner. It's bad medical practice to diagnose for someone close to you.'

'Are you telling me that if I get tonsilitis you wouldn't look at my throat?'

'Shag off, will you, I'm trying to read.'

'My stomach is very bad and you're nearly a doctor. If I wake up in the night with a burst appendix and die, you'll be responsible. Are you going to look at me!'

He threw down the textbook he was studying. 'Get up on the bed, pull down your knickers and lift up your dress. You haven't actually vomited, have you?' He palpated her belly, asking, 'Does that hurt?' repeating the palpating and questions as his hands moved over her abdomen. She was ticklish and laughed once or twice. 'There's nothing wrong with you – it's all in your mind,' he said when the examination was finished but his hands didn't leave her belly, only the motion of them changed from palpating to stroking and he lay beside her and kissed her and said, 'This is another reason why doctors shouldn't examine women they are extra close to.'

Maura looked at the radio alarm on her bedside table: it was a quarter past three. She wouldn't be able to get up in the morning, but neither would she be able to sleep for she was now totally back in what had occurred after Danny's examination.

The sick feeling continued in the mornings. She thought of pregnancy but almost as quickly dismissed the thought, for in the beginning of their affair when fear of pregnancy had outweighed her sense of sin, Danny assured her he would take care of that. She had implicit faith in him. He was almost a doctor, after all. And in any case she hadn't missed a period. She definitely wasn't pregnant, thank God.

After another couple of weeks she woke one morning and felt marvellous. Whatever it was that had ailed her was gone. She told Danny and he grinned. 'I'll be the best consultant Ireland's ever known and prove that there's no such thing as a grumbling appendix.'

At work the girls told her she looked her old self again. Her hair and skin were gorgeous – everything in the world was gorgeous, she used to think. And soon, once he had qualified, Danny would mention marriage. She had told her mother about him in a long letter. She wrote long letters regularly to stall her mother's visits to Dublin. Her mother was very soft, not a pusher. You could blind her up to the two eyes. She

152

loved her mother and longed to bring Danny to meet her. Longed to marry him.

Her sense of wellbeing lasted for several more weeks and then her breasts began to ache. They became so tender that she found lovemaking painful and bit her lips when Danny caressed them, but she didn't complain or he really would think she was off her head. Not long after the painful breasts she noticed that she needed to pee oftener than ever before. And snatches of conversation overheard in the office came to her mind: young married women describing the symptoms of their pregnancies. How could she find out? Who could she talk to? Then she told herself that this was something that just existed in her mind. Everyone knew that the very first symptom of pregnancy was a missed period and she had never missed one in her life. Her aching breasts and need to pee were because of the sudden change in the weather: it was very cold and as usual she was, as her mother used to say, going round half-naked. She would dress in warmer clothes. She did but the tenderness, the frequency and a niggle in her mind persisted.

One day at lunchtime she went to the library and in the reference section asked for a book about pregnancy. She found a table away from other readers and read the book, about symptoms and signs of pregnancy. And her heart almost stopped at the paragraph which described how in rare cases some women continued to menstruate – some for a few months, some throughout the term. The flow was usually scant.

She reread the section. Her breasts were tender and she had noticed the veining there but had thought nothing of it, and when her nipples seemed to be turning brown she had put it down to imagination. She had veined breasts, had experienced morning sickness without the vomiting, and now had frequency. Whether her flow was scant or copious she couldn't remember, never having paid it much attention. But of one thing she was now certain: *she was pregnant*. Maura wanted to scream. She wanted to cry. In the library she could do neither, so she sat for a while pretending to read and thinking how her belly would grow. It would grow and grow until it was enormous, dragging up the front of her skirt. She'd get varicose veins and would walk like a duck. And Danny – what would he say? He wouldn't be over the moon. She didn't want this thing growing inside her. She didn't, she didn't! She looked up and saw the library clock – she'd be late back for work. She stood up and thought she was going to faint. Slowly she made her way to the counter.

'You don't look well,' the librarian said. 'Can I get you a drink of water?' Maura shook her head. 'Well, sit down for minute, you're like a ghost.'

'I'll be all right. I've had a touch of food-poisoning. I'll be grand in the fresh air.' The librarian said there was a lot of it about.

This time Danny examined her without any protest. 'I'm not that well up in obstetrics but I'd say you're definitely pregnant and months, at that – three, maybe four. Why on earth didn't you say when you missed?'

'I never missed.'

'Trust you to be a freak! What are you going to do about it?'

She shrugged and on her face was an expression of hopelessness and helplessness. 'I don't know. I thought – I thought that maybe . . .'

'Maybe what?'

She hated his voice when it was like that. 'Maybe we could get married.' She began to cry.

'On what?'

'You'll be qualified soon and I can work still and go back afterwards and I have a hundred pounds in the post office. Other people get married and manage.'

'Not other people. Knackers.'

It isn't only tinkers. Ordinary young people marry and have babies – even some students – you see them round town.' She felt angry and stopped crying. 'And,' she said, 'it's your fault. You were supposed to be looking after the contraception. So what happened?'

'How the hell do I know? By the time they're smuggled in anything could have happened to them. You'll have to get rid of it.'

'Get rid of it – what do you mean, get rid of it?'

'Have an abortion a D and C, a scrape.'

A scrape. The thing now became a baby in her mind. Scraping anything sounded painful. You scraped paint off a chair and there was a protesting noise. You scraped a pot and the pot and scourer squeaked. Paper being scraped from a wall, anything that was scraped, fell in bits and flakes. You couldn't do that to a baby: it would break it in bits, kill it. You couldn't kill a baby. Inarticulately she tried to explain this to Danny.

'For Christ's sake it's got nothing to do with pots, paint or plaster. Women have D and Cs every day of the week. It's a minor operation.'

'The baby is killed – that's a sin.'

'It's not a baby. It's nothing – a group of cells, nothing. If you saw it on a plate you wouldn't know what it was.'

'I am not having a scrape or whatever you like to call it.'

'What'll you do, then?'

'Why can't we get married?'

'I'm not going to marry you. I don't want to marry, not for ages. Not until I have my career on the road.'

154

'Then I'll go home. I'll have the baby and keep it. I'll go home to my mother.'

'You must be joking. How can you? You couldn't even let you mother come to Dublin in case she found out we were living together.'

'This is different. You don't know my mother. She's kind and good. She'd have me.'

'And face the village and the priest, the back-biting? You're not thinking straight.'

'She would so. She'd rather all that than I committed a mortal sin by doing what you want – so too would the priest.' Now her voice wasn't as certain as at first. She was remembering other girls in the village who had got pregnant. Girls who suddenly got jobs in London and Dublin. A few who stayed on for a while before going to a Home run by the nuns for unmarried mothers. She didn't know of one illegitimate child in the village. And her mother . . . She *would* take her in, would stand by her. But it wasn't fair to inflict that on her – the back-biting, the gossip, the pitying or scornful looks. It wasn't fair on her mother, who had sacrificed so much that she could stay on at school. Who was so proud of her . . .

As if he had been reading her thoughts, Danny said in a kinder voice, 'It's not so easy, is it?'

'I don't want to talk about it any more. Leave me. I want to go to sleep. Put the light out and go in the kitchen. I don't want to talk any more.'

And Maura ten years on lay in her bed in Dublin and saw the pale light of dawn coming through the curtains she had not properly closed and remembered what had happened later on that evening when she had fallen asleep so adamant that she wouldn't have an abortion.

Danny woke her with a cup of tea and thin bread and butter the way she liked it. He sat on the bed and put a cardigan round her.

'How are you feeling?' he asked solicitously.

'I don't know – mixed-up, frightened. I don't know. I don't know.'

'I'm sorry,' he said. 'Honest to God I don't know how it happened. I never touched you without using something.'

'I believe you. I don't know what to do. You're right, I can't go home. I couldn't do that to my mother. Before I fell asleep I was thinking why couldn't I keep the baby. You know – without us getting married. Just have it and live here.'

'Oh Jesus, Maura, that wouldn't work. We've one room, a bit of a kitchen and share the bog and bath with eight others. You couldn't bring a child up in here.'

'Then maybe I could get a place of my own and someone to mind the baby during the day.'

'Who'd give a room to you? You're only eighteen – who's going to take in a girl like you who'll have a child screaming all night. You'd never be able to go across the door. You'd be shagged out in the mornings and before you knew it you'd be sacked. There's only the one answer.'

'It's a sin. I can't do that. It's killing a child. That's murder. I could stay here until it was born and have it adopted.'

'You couldn't. I wouldn't want that. And as for having it adopted, everyone would find out, including your mother. There's only one way out: you *have* to have the operation. It's best for you and for the baby.'

'Hardly for the baby – but it's the easiest way out for *you*.' She was lost and she knew it. If he wouldn't even let her live in the flat any more unless she got rid of the child she was lost. 'Will it have a soul and what'll happen after they've . . . after they've finished with it?'

'I don't know,' he lied. 'There certainly won't be a funeral. It's nothing, just like a heavy period that's all, so how can it have a soul?'

'Where will I have it done?'

'I know a fellow in London who works in a clinic. How much money have you?'

'A hundred pounds. I saved it for a rainy day.'

'That'll do. When I'm in funds. I'll pay you back.' He sat beside her and put an arm round her. 'Honest to God there's no other way.'

'How long will I be over?' she asked.

'Two days travelling and two there. I'll fix it so you get done on a Monday and travel on the Sunday. Then you'll only be off work for three days.'

'Ring in and say I have the 'flu. I only hope to God I meet no one I know.'

'It's unlikely at this time of the year.'

There were birds singing outside and Maura could hear the first milk-float driving round the square. She might as well get up, have a cup of tea. While she made the tea she thought about the night she had gone over for the abortion. The force nine gale that pitched the ship from side to side and sent crockery crashing. And how, while she retched into a sick bag, she kept praying that the child would come away naturally for she was terrified of dying under the operation without having confessed. And she recalled how empty the streets of London had been, rain-lashed, dirty and dreary, and how the clinic, with its cream painted walls peeling and damp patches round the front door, smelled revoltingly of disinfectant and chips.

She was wracked with shame and guilt. The clinic staff seemed falsely friendly while the doctor was breezy, assuring her there was nothing to it – it was just a minor op. And then he asked about Danny and the money.

She expected to wake from the anaesthetic feeling a murderess, but instead felt nothing but a soreness and an overwhelming tiredness and thirst. It seemed as if with its removal from her womb, the fact that the baby had existed had also been removed from her mind. It wasn't until the boat was almost in Dun Laoghaire that the impact of what she had done hit her. She supposed the after-effects of the anaesthetic had dulled her mind.

Danny was there to meet her, hugging and kissing her. Hurrying her back to the flat. Her mother had rung the pay phone in the hall and he had told her that Maura had had to go to London suddenly, to accompany a workmate whose mother had died there. She listened and watched him talking, moving about the flat making coffee for her. For him it seemed as if there never had been a baby or an abortion. She had gone to London for a funeral, that was all. The body was buried – that was an end to the matter.

For her it was different. Though every minute of her day wasn't consumed with thoughts or guilt about the baby, she did think about the child and what she done to it. She attributed all the blame to Danny. He had forced her. By refusing to marry her or let her stay in the flat until the child was born, he had forced her hand. By pointing out every disadvantage against keeping it he had left her no alternative.

She stayed with him for another fortnight but the sight of him was a constant reminder of her grievous sin. She told him of her decision to leave, explaining that she didn't want to see him for a while. She needed time to think things out. He wanted her to stay – he said he loved her. Nevertheless she went and had never seen him again until tonight.

Last night, she corrected herself, and went to run a bath. She had spent all night thinking about him, about herself and the abortion and whether she wanted to have him back – assuming he wanted to come. She knew he could be a bastard. At times there was a streak of brutality in him and he could be ruthless. But he hadn't *made* her have the abortion. He hadn't dragged her screaming to the boat or to the clinic. He had presented her with the options. *She* had made the choice: even paid for the operation.

Looking back to that time she realised he must have been desperate, terrified; he was a few months off his finals and confronted with being a father. With no money, no decent place to live, no guarantee even that he would qualify, he was suddenly responsible for a wife and child.

It was true that he had been neither sympathetic nor helpful. He had thought only of himself. But so had she, if she was admitting the truth. Her mother would have stood by her: it was herself who couldn't face returning to the village. And had she believed deeply enough in the sin she was about to commit, the child could have been allowed to live and put up for adoption.

Maura had confessed her sin and been given Absolution, and confessed it many times since as a past sin. She often looked at children whom she judged to be about ten years old and wondered about the one she had never had.

She dressed and made breakfast and took it to a small table near the window. It was a fine summer's morning, the beginning of May, her favourite month when the chestnut trees were heavy with candles. Surely Danny would ring or call soon . . . before the end of the month. She wanted him to come in May. It would be a good omen to the start of their affair.

She heard nothing for a fortnight and then one evening the phone rang. As she had every night since meeting Danny, she ran to answer it with her heart full of hope.

'You bloody bitch,' his voice said. 'Every night for two weeks I've tried getting put through to you. I've been your father and your mother, your doctor, your long-lost cousin from America. I don't know – Ireland has changed. Not one of the bastards would buy the story and put me through until tonight.'

'You knew where I lived,' Maura replied with a rapturous expression on her face.

'I wasn't coming on a fool's errand. Will I be welcome?'

As the flowers in May, she thought but only said, 'I'll be here – what more do you want?'

'That'll do. See you in half an hour.'

She hugged herself and stroked her bare arms and looked in the mirror. Then she became practical. Checked on food and drink, and in the bedroom that the toiletry bag with her diaphragm and spermicide cream was in a certain drawer. It was.

It was such a good feeling to have him here. It was what she had wanted through all the years. He admired the flat. She was nervous and wondered if despite his laid-back manner he might be, too. He wandered round the living room looking at a picture, picking up an ornament, a book. He hadn't kissed her or even touched her yet. She had expected that when she opened the door to him he would have grabbed hold of her. Perhaps he *was* nervous.

'Will you have a drink?' she asked.

'Let's go out for one.' Like most of the men she knew he preferred drinking out. In a pub they could drink as much as they liked or could pay for. She had come to dislike pubs, the smoke, the noise, the speed with which the whiskeys were knocked back. So she said, 'I'd rather stay in.'

'OK, let's drink here.'

'Sit down, make yourself comfortable. What'll you have?'

'The same as usual.'

She poured two Jamesons and brought them to the small table in front of the couch where he sat. She sat beside him. He lifted one of her hands and looked at it. 'You've beautiful hands. I missed you so much. You shouldn't have run out on me.' He kissed her hand and gave it back and drank half of his whiskey at one swallow. Putting down his tumbler he asked, 'Why did you never marry?'

'Why didn't you?' was her riposte.

'I asked you first.'

'I never met anyone I liked enough. The older you get the more difficult it becomes.'

'I know,' he said.

She refilled his glass and poured more whiskey into hers. Nowadays she seldom drank, but tonight was a very special occasion.

'I kept making comparisons,' said Danny.

'I did too,' admitted Maura.

She had poured his fourth whiskey before he made an advance, and then he went at it like lightning. His hands were on her face, neck, his lips on her mouth and then her blouse was off and with expertise he undid her brassière. 'I love you,' he murmured, with his face against her breasts. Her hands pressed his head to her and she kissed his hair where it was thinning. He turned her so that she was lying on the couch.

'Wait,' she said, sitting up and taking the cushions from the settee and arranging them on the floor. They lay down again. He worked her skirt off and she helped him with her tights and she pushed his trousers down over his hips. And with her foot in the crotch she pushed them to his ankles.

'Hang on,' he said and reached for them.

'It's all right – you don't need anything. I've taken care of that.'

She lost count of the number of times they made love, the different positions. She was conscious of nothing except exquisite pleasure. She was drunk with it. She wanted it never to end. She wanted to be forever in his arms. She could have died and not minded.

But eventually they lay apart holding hands and she waited for him to sleep as he always did after making love. She waited for his soft snoring to begin but instead he began to talk. 'I didn't expect you to be prepared.'

'Why not?'

'I don't know, I just didn't. Somehow it doesn't seem you.'

'It is me – but a different me. It's the nineteen-eighties, don't forget.' Briefly the thought of what had happened when she was 'the other me' flashed through her mind, but it wasn't the time to remind him. With luck it would never be the right time. He had his little boy look on his face and because she loved him and because loving him again was so wonderful she said, 'I don't throw it around. You'd be surprised at how few other men there have been.' Further than that she felt no need to explain.

Then he slept and she showered and dressed and made supper. He arranged to come the following night, and thereafter he came several times a week. They ate and drank and made love. Sometimes he took her out – to a theatre, the cinema, to see an exhibition, to pubs – but wherever they went they came back to the flat afterwards and made love.

After some time he suggested moving in. 'I hate leaving you. I want to sleep with you again. Waken in the mornings with you in my arms.'

'And have me wash and cook for you.'

'And make love to you when we waken.'

'That too,' she said, smiling at him, her face suffused with the love she felt for him, the joy he brought her.

They lived together for several months on a wave of tempestuous love and passion. Maura felt as if she were eighteen again. Nothing dampened her spirits, not even the fact that at no time did she and Danny talk about their future. And then a change came about in her. It came first as a fleeting thought one night after lovemaking when Danny lay snoring softly. Sex, she realised, was the predominant thing in their lives. It was good, she enjoyed it, but tonight for instance she had felt tired and instead of lovemaking would have preferred to lie for a while with Danny and talk and then sleep. Instinctively she had known that Danny would have been offended had she refused his advance. And so for the first time since their reunion she had pretended a desire she didn't feel. 'Your age is catching up with you,' she told herself. 'You may think you're eighteen but you're not. You and Danny had better have a talk before you start letting your imagination run away with you – begin thinking you made a mistake in taking him back . . .' She fell asleep.

They never had the talk. She knew of old he wasn't the sort of person you had talks with. And so she on the nights when her desire didn't match his, pretended. He never seemed to notice. She became irritable – not outwardly so, but always there was a niggle going on in her mind. For instance, how even on the nights he was home before her it wouldn't cross his mind to lay the table. Little niggles. Picking up after him. How few interests they had in common. He read the headlines and the sports page, she the editorials and articles – there could be no discussion. Petty

160

niggles. He'd plaster the last of the butter on his toast leaving her to go without.

When they weren't out on the town or in bed together they would sit in silence and she found nothing companionable about it. She came to the conclusion that she had made a mistake: she wasn't in love with him. For years she had deluded herself, fed her fantasy by remembering how it had been when Danny and she were scarcely more than children. When sex could be easily confused with love. When to drink and dance and walk home in the small hours and make love was all that mattered. It was no longer what she wanted from a relationship, but how was she going to tell this to Danny?

As the days passed she saw more clearly the truth of her conclusions. Although both of them had said they had always loved each other, during their separation neither of them had ever sought to find the other. And yet it would have been so easy. In a place like Dublin it would have been the easiest thing in the world: a question here, an enquiry there. So easy. The truth was, neither of them had really wanted to find the other. What was she to do about it? She became frightened. She was a coward – she could never tell all this to Danny. He might persuade her that it was all in her mind. They could drag on for years like this, maybe forever. He might ask her to marry him, and she mightn't be able to refuse. That could happen – she could *see* it happening. It probably happened in lots of cases. Two people deluding themselves that they loved each other then one discovers the truth, but habit, expectations and cowardice prevent them from speaking the truth. She began to pray that he would walk out on her.

He didn't and then she missed a period. She was thrown into a state of shock and disbelief. This couldn't be happening for the second time. It couldn't. She took responsibility for birth control and apart from removing the cap for cleaning, wore it morning, noon and night – well, once she was home from work. To Danny she said nothing about the missed period but all the time she thought about its implications and silently prayed to make the right decision.

After missing the second one she went to the Clinic and asked for a pregnancy test. 'It'll be back on Wednesday,' the receptionist told her as she handed over the specimen jar with her sample of urine.

That night Danny told her he had to go away for a few days. 'There's a seminar in Galway with an American guy who's the tops in osteoporosis.'

'Will you be away long?'

'A couple of days.'

There was nothing in the *Irish Times* about the seminar. She was surprised, as osteoporosis was constantly in the news, but there might be

161

something later in the week. On Wednesday she went for her result. This time she saw the doctor.

'The test is positive,' she told Maura.

'I thought it might be.'

'Do you want to keep the baby?'

'Yes,' she said. 'I do.'

'I'll just fill in these forms and then have a look at you.' The doctor asked questions, about her health, marital status, age and occupation. There were pages of questions. 'One other thing – was the baby planned?'

'No,' said Maura. 'I was using a diaphragm.'

'They usually have a good record. Where did you have it fitted?'

'Here,' replied Maura.

'How long ago?'

'Ages.'

'You didn't come for regular checks?'

'I didn't bother.'

'That's the reason, then. You put on a little weight, lose a little – even a fraction affects the fit. You're quite sure you want to have the child?'

'Quite sure,' said Maura.

Danny was in the flat when she came home. She could see he was in a great mood, although it hadn't stretched to making him lay the table. 'What have you done to yourself – you're looking gorgeous,' he greeted her.

'Amn't I always gorgeous?' she laughed. 'You're looking great yourself.'

He took hold of her and kissed her. 'I have fantastic news,' he said, letting go of her.

'You've won the lottery.'

'Better than that – I got the job.'

'What job?'

'All in good time. Here, sit down.' They sat on the couch. He put an arm round her. 'How would you like to be buried with my mother's people, as they're supposed to say in the country when they propose. Will you marry me?'

'Marry you?' she said, astounded.

'Don't sound like that – wasn't it always on the cards that we'd marry? What d'ye want – me down on one knee? I know it's a bit sudden but I got the job.'

'What job?'

'It was like this. You know about Galway and the seminar?'

'Yes,' she said.

'Well, there wasn't one. I went to London for an interview as a senior

162

registrar. And I got it – I bloody well got it! Will you marry me? I can fix up a flat. I know a fella with a house, another doctor.'

Maura wondered was it the same doctor, the one to whom she had handed over the one hundred pound notes. 'I can't make up my mind just like that.'

'What d'ye mean you can't make up your mind? I'm offering to marry you, for Christ's sake.'

'It's very nice of you.' She tried not to let the mock humility show in her voice. 'Thanks very much, but . . .'

'But what, in the name of God? What?'

And she was amazed at herself, she who had been afraid that she wouldn't have the courage to refuse. 'I'm not sure I want to get married.'

'Don't give me that. Every woman wants to get married.'

'Not any more they don't.'

'That's a lot of feminist balls.'

'Hardly balls,' and she laughed.

'You don't want to finish up a bloody oul maid. You want children, don't you?'

'Oh, yes,' she said. 'I want children.'

'Well then?'

'At least give me time to think about it.'

'There isn't time to think about it. I'm taking up the post at the end of the month. If we're to be married before then there's no time.'

'I couldn't decide like that.'

'What's got into you! Why are you talking like this? I came here bursting with the news – anyone would think I was trying to sell you insurance! We've known each other for years. We've been living together for six months: I thought you'd jump at the chance.'

She wanted to tell him crudely what to do with his proposal. She wanted to tell him a lot of things, things about men and women. And trust. And taking each other into your confidence. About men's presumptions and women's expectations. About sharing and companionship. Things that men like Danny would never understand. She saved her breath. Got up from the settee and poured him a whiskey and remembering the baby, a Ballygowan for herself. She sat on a chair opposite him.

'I can't marry you,' she said. 'I'm grateful that you asked me. We probably loved each other years ago but we don't now. It's as simple as that.'

'You're turning me down – that's final?'

'That's final.'

163

'You're a mad, stupid cow. You've never forgiven me for the last time – that's it, isn't it?'

'Nothing,' she said, 'could be further from the truth. I forgave you. We were only kids. I think you should pack your things and go now. I hope you'll . . .'

'Don't,' he said getting up, 'don't you wish or hope anything for me. I never want to lay eyes on you again. And don't think if you change your mind you can come running to me.'

He went into the bedroom and she heard him opening and crashing drawers shut. In the bathroom she heard the sound of breaking glass. She went into the kitchen and closed the door to avoid seeing him again. Then she heard him charging down the stairs and the front door slam after him. Whether he walked or stopped to look for a taxi she didn't know or care.

She tidied the bedroom and went into the bathroom. A broken tumbler lay in the bath. She picked up the pieces and let the tap run to wash away the minute splinters and when they were gone put in the plug and ran a bath. Lying in the water she felt a mixture of emotions. Sorrow, that something which had once been beautiful had ended, and ended with such bitterness for Danny, and enormous relief. She had found the courage to do the right thing, and this courage she must nurture. In the months and years ahead she would need it. Times had changed: a single woman with a baby was no longer treated as a pariah, nevertheless society was still geared to the two-parent family. But she was more fortunate than many in her position. She had a good job with all the social benefits, understanding friends and money. *And her legacy.*

I will be all right, she thought. *We'll* be all right, she smiled, and stroked her belly. You're in there, safe and sound. No one will touch a hair of your head. She spoke aloud. 'And please God in there you will stay until the time is right for you to be born.' She kissed her fingertips and placed them on her belly. 'That's for you,' she said. 'I love you. You're my precious angel. My little dote. My other most precious legacy.'